563
58
9392

My Man,
HER SON

J. Tremble

Bestselling Author of *Secrets of a Housewife*

Life Changing Books in conjunction with Power Play Media
Published by Life Changing Books
P.O. Box 423 Brandywine, MD 20613

Library of Congress Cataloging-in-Publication Data;

www.lifechangingbooks.net
13 Digit: 978-1934230688
10 Digit: 1-934230685

Acknowledgements

First, I would like to thank my family and friends. This book is only made possible because of the strength I receive from you all when times are tough. All that I am and will ever be is because of your love and support, so I'm truly grateful.

Next, I would like to thank my extended family at Life Changing Books. To my publisher Azarel. You've managed to create a company that's meaningful to so many people, and have surrounded yourself with amazing people like Leslie Allen aka Red Pen Bean, Nakea Murry, Tasha Simpson and others. Not to mention, you've collected a group of first time authors and made many dreams come true. I hope you know how special you are to me. Thanks for each and every opportunity.

To Leslie Allen, that little before mention was just a name drop and no way near enough for you. I hate to repeat another author, but you are a phenomenal woman. I know if you weren't in my corner, I'd truly be lost to travel in circles. Even though it may seem that I don't listen at times, trust me I do. I thank you again for all your hard work and dedication to each one of my projects.

To my other family, the Rough Rider Flag Football Team. You're not just friends, but blood brothers who I would go to the end of the earth to assist and support. So, thank you to Kurt, Jamal, Gerald, Snack, Derrick, Big Ray, Ray Lite, Marlin, Wayne, Charmin, Speedy, Rudy, Naughty, Moe, Darryl, Choo, Jerelle, Go-Go, Chris, Tony, Kevin, Damon, and all the past and future team mates. A special shout out goes to Dave and Team

Mom, Trina.

What up to my Benjamin Stoddert Middle School, and my P.G. County family from old Region 1, the Zone 5 and my new home over at Suitland Elementary. Thank you so much. To all the principals, teachers, support staff, building staff, cafeteria staff at the numerous schools that lend me their support as well. Thanks to Curry, Michelle, Gary, Gayle, and anyone else who gave me an ear to bounce ideas off when I hit a wall.

To my LCB authors: Thank you, Danette Majette, Tonya Ridley, Tiphani, Mike Warren, Ericka Williams, Capone, Chantel Jolie, Kendall B, Sasha Raye, C. Stecko, and all the other new authors on the growing roster at LCB. I wish the best for each one of you. Thank you, to all the test readers and editors who work so hard in helping me put out good quality products that are worth reading.

Lastly, I would like to thank all my fellow authors out there working hard and trying to make a decent living. I know I don't have to tell you all how tough it is to write a book and get it out there. Keep your heads up. Thank you to all the vendors, independent stores, and distributors who support and help promote my work. However, the biggest thank you must go out to all the readers/fans. If it weren't for your support, none of us would be where we are today. I hope you enjoy my latest erotic tale.

Visit me at:
www.facebook.com/jaytremble
www.twitter.com/jmakesutremble

Peace,

J. Tremble
King of Erotica

Also By J. Tremble

Secrets of a Housewife
More Secrets More Lies
Naughty Little Angel

Chapter One

"Fuck this. I thought I made myself absolutely clear the last time you chose the spot for girl's night out," Tootie said, slamming the car door. "Why are we always at these damn freak spots?"

"Bitch, don't start. Do I ever say anything when it's your turn?" Ko-Ko replied before adjusting her black studded Roberto Cavalli dress. She wanted to make sure the plunging neckline showed every inch of her 36D breasts. She'd paid good money for her saline implants and loved showing them off.

"That's because we do normal shit like clubs and restaurants. Whenever you pick a place, we get lesbian parties, fucking orgies or strippers," Melyssa added.

Even though they were all childhood friends, Melyssa and Ko-Ko never got along, so she knew her comment would probably start a heated argument.

Ko-Ko gave Melyssa an evil expression before taking one last pull from her Virginia Slims cigarette. "Did anybody ask you anything? Damn, we haven't even made it to the door, and y'all are fucking up my night already."

"Calm down ladies, you know the rules. We all take turns picking a spot for our night out, no questions asked. Tonight is Ko-Ko's turn to pick a place and I guess this is her choice," Lynn chimed in. She was always the peacemaker of the group.

"Yeah, calm down and loosen the fuck up, grandma," Ko-Ko said to Tootie. She pulled on her friend's white button down shirt. "Maybe if you unbutton this shit a little bit, you can stop being so uptight. Damn, how much starch did you put on this thing?" Ko-Ko was always picking on Tootie's choice of style. "Just because you're a school teacher doesn't mean you have to dress like a nun."

"Get the hell off me," Tootie demanded. "Don't hate on me 'cuz I got class. Besides, it's the beginning of January, and you're dressed like a hooker on the Las Vegas strip. Put some damn clothes on. That Lil' Kim shit went out in the 90's."

"Fuck you, Tootie. Was your New Year's resolution to dress like your grandmother? " Ko-Ko shot back.

Melyssa shook her head and knew right away that this was going to be another one of those nights. She then stared at the large single family home and wondered what the hell could've been awaiting them from behind the double oak wood front doors. Even though they appeared to be in a classy Rockville, MD neighborhood, something still didn't seem right. Suddenly, her thoughts were distracted when Ko-Ko popped the trunk to her new snow-white Range Rover and grabbed a brown paper bag.

"What's that?" Lynn asked.

"You'll see," Ko-Ko returned with a devious grin.

Tootie sucked her teeth as Ko-Ko sashayed past them swinging her full hips from side to side.

With complete apprehension, the ladies slowly followed their friend up the brick stairs to the front door. Melyssa and Tootie's faces frowned again when Ko-Ko did some type of code with the thick gold door knocker.

Tootie let out a huge sigh. "I am not in the mood for this shit."

"Well, what are you in the mood for then, Tootie? Huh? You want me to go get you a fucking chalk board or something?" Ko-Ko asked in an irritated tone.

Right before another arguing match could get started, the door opened slightly, even though they could barely see inside. Ko-Ko smiled as a women's voice whispered from inside.

"Are you sure you have the right place?" the mysterious voice asked.

Ko-Ko leaned in and whispered, "Fucking is my job and tonight…business is good."

Tootie glanced over at Melyssa. "See, this is some bull-shit."

Ko-Ko looked back and smiled. However, the frowns on Tootie and Melyssa faces said that they weren't feeling her choice at all or the puzzling greeting. Lynn on the other hand was at least staying open minded about the whole idea.

When the door opened fully, a beautiful Asian woman with long, straight black hair stood in the door frame. Her nipples were clamped with nipple rings connected to a silver chain that circled her body down to her naval. The sheer white robe she wore allowed her fish net stockings to be seen as well as her lace lingerie. Ko-Ko admired her six inch stilettos which had straps that crawled up her legs.

"Come on in, ladies. I'm so happy you decided to join us on this beautiful night," the Asian woman said.

Ko-Ko, Lynn, and Tootie stepped inside into the Italian marble foyer. Melyssa, however didn't move. She really didn't want to go inside.

"Are you coming inside?" the Asian woman asked. "There's no need to be scared."

Lynn looked back to see Melyssa still standing outside the door with her long arms folded like a three year old. Most of the time Melyssa only seemed satisfied when it was her time to select the venue. All the other times, she did her best to try and ruin it for everyone else.

"Come on, Melyssa. Don't act like that. We don't have to stay long," Lynn tried to convince her.

After standing there for a few more seconds, Melyssa finally decided to step inside the door shaking her head in disgust the whole time.

"Please step over there." The Asian woman pointed to a glass counter with a naked black woman standing behind it before disappearing behind a curtain. Inside the glass counter were several edible panties, whips, chains, dildos and lubricants.

Ko-Ko walked to the counter with confidence while the other three women walked as if they were going to a death sentence.

"Good evening, ladies that'll be forty dollars," the black woman stated.

The ladies began pulling out their money to cover the cost of admission. Everyone except Ko-Ko held out ten dollars, which made the woman behind the counter chuckle.

"I'm sorry, that's forty dollars for each of you," she replied.

"You've got to be joking. I'm not paying forty dollars to get into some freaky-ass house party. Ko-Ko, have you lost your damn mind!" Melyssa shouted.

"Shut up and just give me your ten dollars. I knew you would act this way, so I'll cover the difference," Ko-Ko responded.

"Well, you must got me too, because I'm not paying that shit either," Tootie added.

Ko-Ko was annoyed. "You know what…y'all bitches are really starting to blow me."

Trying to keep the peace once again, Lynn pulled out an extra thirty dollars and handed it to Ko-Ko. "Don't worry, I'll pay my portion."

Both Tootie and Melyssa gave her the look of death.

"Thanks, girl. You're the only *real* friend I got," Ko-Ko replied. At that point, she could care less if her comment struck a nerve with the other two haters in the group.

As Ko-Ko paid their fee, she noticed that the living room had been converted into a little boutique with lingerie and all sort of costumes since the last time she'd been there. One wall even had shelves filled with rubbers, dental dams and body paint.

"What the hell is this place anyway?" Melyssa asked before seeing a sign that read TABOO.

"It's a place where you can fulfill your wildest fantasy," Ko-Ko replied in a dramatic tone. She then flipped her thick dark brown hair off her shoulder. Besides the Beyonce like figure she'd been blessed with, Ko-Ko was extremely proud of her long natural hair. Weekly trips to her white homosexual hairdresser in an upscale salon was a must.

Lynn smiled showing off the one dimple in her left cheek. She wasn't sure if her fantasy would be fulfilled, but she had to admit…the place was exciting. Working double shifts as a registered nurse, she needed to let her hair down and have some fun.

"Ladies, you all can go ahead through the black curtains but remember, there are no rules here at Taboo. Anything goes," the black woman said with a slight laugh.

"Great," Tootie replied in a sarcastic tone.

They all stepped inside the main level of the house to find several people spread throughout. Some were kissing, some were bumping and grinding on the homemade dance floor, while others were standing around socializing at a long bar on the far east wall.

Ko-Ko waved at a few patrons as she led the group over to the bar then gave the bartender the mysterious brown bag that she'd retrieved from her trunk. "What's up, Sunny? Here's our poison for the night."

"Nothing much baby. You looking good as usual." The heavy-set bartender smiled before pulling out a bottle of Grey Goose and Remy VSOP, then placed numbers on each one. When she finished, she gave each of the four women the same number on a small piece of paper.

"What are the numbers for?" Lynn asked.

"The government is not in the habit of giving liquor licenses to underground clubs. Besides, Taboo doesn't want to be held responsible for anything that may happen when you leave here, especially if you drink past your limit. So, whenever you need a drink or a refill, just show the bartender your number and she will mix you up whatever you want using those two bottles of liquor of course," Ko-Ko answered.

"So, this place charges forty dollars a person, and it's BYOL. How fucking ghetto," Melyssa stated. She and Tootie both started laughing.

At that moment, a tall dark skinned guy slid up behind Melyssa and wrapped his arms around her small waist. At 5'9 and a hundred and thirty pounds, she could've easily been a model, especially since she wasn't the most shapely one out of the group. With a small ass and breasts to match, she easily put one in the mind of a white girl.

"Hello, pretty lady. Are you in the mood for a soft swap?" he asked.

Melyssa immediately jumped then quickly pushed the guy's hand away. She turned around and stared him down. "What the fuck is a soft swap and how dare you put your hands on me?"

"This must be your first time at a swinger's party," he said, smiling like an idiot. "A soft swap is oral only, you know me eating you or you giving me head."

"You've got to be joking. You don't even know my name and I'm just supposed to drop down and suck your dirty-ass dick!" Melyssa yelled. "Get the hell away from me."

"You need to take your ass home if you ain't down," the guy said, before walking off. He was up in another girl's face within seconds.

You could see steam coming from Melyssa's head as she turned toward Ko-Ko. "I can not believe you brought us here. I have a fucking fiancé you know."

"Yeah, I do know, and I was thinking you could learn a thing or two by being here. Like stepping your head game up," Ko-Ko replied. "I'm sure your man ain't happy in that department."

"You know what…fuck this. I'm not staying here another minute. You with me, Tootie?" Melyssa asked.

"Hell yeah!" Tootie quickly co-signed. "If someone from my school were to see me here, I would be fucking banned from teaching."

"If you can't suck it up and do this shit for me, then carry y'all stuck up asses home then!" Ko-Ko yelled.

"I'm not sucking a motherfucking thing in this place," Melyssa answered.

"You coming Lynn?" Tootie asked.

Lynn shook her head. "No, I'm not gonna leave Ko-Ko here by herself."

"Suit yourself," Melyssa responded, then walked away.

"Let's see how they get all the way back to Greenbelt at this time of night," Ko-Ko said, with a deceitful grin. "Those bitches will walk before I give 'em a ride."

Lynn watched as her two friends walked across the floor and through the black curtains. She was contemplating if she was making the right choice by staying there when a well-built bald headed man caught her attention. Her eyes outlined his entire six foot frame and muscular build.

Now, he might be able to get me into a soft swap, Lynn thought as she continued to admire his physic. His long powerful legs made her mouth moisten. She thanked the Lord for allowing him to walk around in only a pair of white boxers. The tiny beads of sweat running down his six pack stomach caused the juices to twirl inside her red thong. At that moment, she could care less about Melyssa and Tootie either. Her eyes followed the stranger all around the room, eyeing the bulge in his boxers, which told her he was hung like a horse. It had been over four months since she had sex, so it felt as if drool was about to come out of her mouth.

After asking the bartender to mix them up two Grey Goose and Cranberries, Ko-Ko turned around to see Lynn licking her lips. Glancing around the room, she realized what had Lynn so hypnotized, and began to stare at the handsome man herself.

Damn, I'm a sucker for a sexy man and a big dick too, Ko-Ko thought.

She continued to stare at the eye candy until the bartender placed two glasses in front of her and the guy disappeared. "Like what you see?" Ko-Ko finally asked.

Lynn began to rub her hands through her shoulder length chestnut colored bob. Something she did whenever she was a little embarrassed or nervous. "Girl, yes."

"Yeah, he is fine," Ko-Ko said, taking a sip of her drink. "You know I'm so glad you stayed 'cause I'm sure you could use a few tips about fucking your damn self. I'm starting to really worry about you. How long has it been since you had some dick? About two years now?"

"Real funny. Shit, you don't have to worry about my love life because I have all the toys I could ever use and an endless supply of batteries."

Ko-Ko laughed. "I'm serious. You work too damn much. Besides, you know how I feel about electrical devices. They just don't compare to the warmth of a nice hard dick pounding inside of you."

"Look, don't worry about me." Lynn tried to play it off, but knew Ko-Ko was telling the truth. The constant twelve hour shifts to pay her sons college tuition made it hard to find time for herself. "Besides, Rayshawn always acts funny when I bring men to the house."

Ko-Ko frowned. "Does Raysahwn pay the damn mortgage? Who cares what he thinks, he ain't your man. You know what…I'm gonna bring that fine-ass dude over here."

Lynn began to blush. "I mean he is fine, but I don't wanna meet a man in here. Look, you go and have some fun cause I'ma be ready to leave in a minute. And trust me bitch, you are taking me home."

At that moment, Lynn began to think about Melyssa and Tootie again. She made a mental note to call one of their cell phones once Ko-Ko was off doing her thing.

"It's nothing wrong with talking. I'ma go find him and bring his ass over here, so y'all can keep each other company. Be right back," Ko-Ko replied, before quickly walking away. It was obvious that she wasn't about to take no for an answer.

It only took a second for Ko-Ko to disappear in a small crowd of people. At that moment, Lynn downed her drink, held up her number and asked the bartender to make her another one. As she waited for the bartender to hook her up, a young black woman tapped her on the shoulder.

"Would you like to dance?"

Lynn was pleasantly surprised when she turned to find a woman standing there holding out her hand. Her eyes went immediately to the tiger paw tattoos on the inner portion of each breast. Looking like a broke version of the rapper Eve, the short blonde hair woman looked at Lynn with lustful eyes.

"I'm really flattered, but I'm strictly dickly boo," Lynn replied.

Even though it had been a while since she had sex, Lynn wasn't about to go that route. She left the lesbian thing up to wild-ass Ko-Ko, a woman known to be a tri-sexual and proud of it.

"Oh, so what about me? I would love to dance with you, too," a short guy with long dreads said stepping out of the shadows.

Just as Lynn was about to turn him down as well, he spoke up again. "Come on, pretty one. Please don't let me down. I just learned a few dance moves, and wanna try 'em out."

Lynn looked the Bob Marley looking dude up and down. With a t-shirt that read *I Love Jamaica* on it, he wasn't the most attractive person, and certainly didn't look like the bald-headed guy from earlier, but did appear nice. Not wanting to be a bitch all night, Lynn finally agreed.

"Excuse me, but I'ma take him up on his offer," Lynn said to the woman.

Moments later, she and the miniature Bob Marley were grooving to the sounds of Jamie Foxx's *Blame It On The Alcohol,* and having a blast.

Time seemed to be flying once Lynn danced through three more songs. She was enjoying herself so much it didn't even matter that her dancing partner had been changed with every song or the fact that the strange men were starting to grind up against her ass. It had even been awhile since she'd seen Ko-Ko, but that didn't matter. Lynn was having a really good time. All the different dance partners turned what she thought was going to be a terrible night into a really good one.

Tootie and Melyssa should've stayed. Can't wait to tell them what they missed out on. she thought.

After becoming a little overheated, Lynn excused herself from the latest dance partner, then made her way back over to the bar for another drink. Seeing that Lynn had finally loosened up, the bartender kept the drinks coming until Lynn felt extremely tipsy.

"You know what, Sunny, I don't know where the fuck my friend is. She went to go find me a nigga, and ain't been back since," Lynn said, with a shot of Vodka in her hand. "I mean how long does that shit take?"

Sunny shook her head. "Knowing Ko-Ko she probably found her some trouble to get into."

"Yeah, you're right. That's why I need to go look for her ass. Hell, maybe I'll find the dude myself."

Not waiting any longer, Lynn left the bar and made her way to a set of stairs that led down to the basement. Holding onto the railing, she slowly walked down the narrow steps hoping not to fall, especially since her head was starting to spin a little bit. Once Lynn reached the bottom, she realized that the basement had several private rooms with large glass windows for onlookers to gaze through.

"What is this shit? Some kind of peep show," Lynn said to herself, as she walked down the hallway and stopped at the first glass.

A human train with three men and two women made her giggle. They looked like a triple Oreo sandwich, with a black man on each end, one in the middle and two white chicks between them all. After watching the live orgy for a second, Lynn walked to the next window where there was a guy wearing a dog costume fucking a woman in the authentic doggy style position.

"What the hell? These people are crazy," she said, walking to the third window.

However, what she saw this time shocked her even more. This time, it was Ko-Ko dressed in an all black leather dominatrix-type outfit from the waist up riding the shit out of a guy, who was tied to a chair and wearing a blindfold. The sight of Ko-Ko fucking a guy wasn't the shocker because she'd seen her childhood friend act like a hoe on several occasions. But when Ko-Ko removed the blindfold and Lynn realized it was the bald headed guy she'd been looking for, her eyes budged. Tipsy or not, it didn't take much to know that what Ko-Ko had done was foul.

I can't believe that hoe. I always take up for that bitch and she fucks me over every time. She ain't shit when it comes to loyalty, Lynn thought before reflecting back.

Ever since their childhood days in the Berry Farms housing project, it was a known fact that Ko-Ko was off the hook. All throughout high school, Ko-Ko never dated the same guy for more than a week, and ran through the entire football team at least twice. Not to mention, every girls' man was never off limits. Even Lynn and Melyssa's. While getting caught sucking Melyssa's boyfriend's dick in a janitor's closet, she also got caught with a guy Lynn liked in the boy's locker room. However, despite Ko-Ko's devious ways, Lynn ended up forgiving her best friend once they both became pregnant during their sophomore year. Since both of their moms were neighborhood crackheads, and fathers were nonexistent, they figured they needed each other for support. Melyssa however, didn't come around so easily. From that point on, she thought Ko-Ko was shady, and didn't trust her. Tootie jumped on the hater bandwagon too, even though she couldn't keep a man.

As minutes passed by, Lynn stood and watched her friend like a peeping Tom. Ko-Ko then untied the guy before guiding him to the edge of a cheap looking air mattress. Once he sat down, she stood over top of his mouth, pulled his head up by his ears and ordered him to eat her pussy. The guy painfully did as he was instructed while Ko-Ko reached down and smacked his bald head. Her moans began to shake the basement walls as his thick tongue softly slid all around her inner walls flickering at her clit. Ko-Ko then grabbed the back of his head to force his tongue further into her dripping pussy. Smacking his head even harder, she wanted his eyes wide open to see how flexible she could be. At that point, Ko-Ko sat on his face then bent over backwards until her hands touched the floor displaying a crazy-ass cheerleader type of move. Next, she placed her mouth over his large dick, then began to suck it upside down.

Damn that shit looks like a 69 on crack, Lynn thought.

Seconds later, the door to the room opened and another man entered. His eyes almost popped out of his head when he gazed upon the human jigsaw puzzle in front of him. Walking over to Ko-Ko, he smiled.

"Now, it's my turn," he said.

Pulling her pussy away from the baldheaded guy, the second man held onto Ko-Ko's ankles until she'd completed a one hundred eighty degree turn. Even though she was being bent like an acrobat in the circus, Ko-Ko never allowed the first dick to leave her mouth.

With Ko-Ko's feet now planted on the floor, the second man removed the towel around his waist exposing his rock hard dick as well as a strap on. Ko-Ko's knees didn't even buckle as he jammed both dicks that were longer than nine inches into her dripping pussy and throbbing ass. The man began to make the air bed bounce banging inside her with tremendous force. It was almost as if he was looking for oil.

Tired of looking at the x-rated movie, Lynn had enough and began to bang on the glass. Before Ko-Ko and the guys could even look up, Lynn began to shout. "Can you get that dick out your mouth long enough to come out here?"

Once Ko-Ko cut her eye toward the window, she finally released the dick in her mouth and flashed a huge smile. She motioned for Lynn to come in and join them, but Lynn shook her head no. Ko-Ko instantly got an attitude. Telling the guy behind her to stop, Ko-Ko told her sex partners to hold up for a moment then stormed outside. Her manicured vagina fully exposed.

"I can't believe you just did that. You just fucked up my flow. I didn't even cum yet," Ko-Ko said.

"I don't give a damn. That shit you just did is foul. Do me a favor...don't sit up in my face and lie to me. If you had plans on fucking that dude all along, then you should've said something."

Ko-Ko was pissed. She couldn't believe Lynn was making a scene. "Look, I had every intention of hooking y'all up, but shit just didn't go as planned. I think he likes smaller women, anyway."

Ko-Ko's comment stung. Lynn looked toward the floor knowing she'd let herself go a little over the years. Her once perfect size eight figure was now more like a curvy sixteen.

"Besides, stop acting like that nigga is your husband or some shit. If you still want him, then take your clothes off and join us. There's enough dick to go around," Ko-Ko continued.

When Ko-Ko looked through the glass, the guys seemed to be getting impatient. She held up her finger, letting them know it wouldn't be much longer then blew each one a kiss. "Look, I gotta go. What are you gonna do? My dicks are getting cold."

Lynn ignored her friend's invitation. "I'm ready to go home."

"Damn Lynn, when are you gonna stop acting like you ain't down with shit like this? We used to be wild as hell back in the day."

"Bitch, all we did was go to clubs and smoke weed everyday and you call that wild? We've never done a threesome."

"Well, it's a first time for everything. Come on...why you in such a rush? Your ass ain't got nothing waiting for you at home, but a bunch of dildo's. Why not get the real thing right here?"

"See, you said the magic words. Back in the day. Ko-Ko, we're going on thirty-seven years old. I'm not trying to fuck random nigga's at this age. Besides, dildo's aren't the only things waiting for me at home. I always have Rayshawn."

Ko-Ko smiled. "I understand that, but you can't fuck your son, Lynn. I mean, I know y'all have always been close and everything, but you be up on him way too hard sometimes."

If Ko-Ko was joking, Lynn didn't find her comedy too funny. She didn't play around when it came to her son. "I'll find my own way home."

Lynn turned and walked back up the stairs, never turning around when Ko-Ko began calling her name. When she got to the top, Lynn reached inside her Gucci messenger bag, and pulled out her cell phone; a birthday gift she'd gotten from Ko-Ko two years prior. While all her other friends had I-phones and Blackberry's, Lynn still carried an old flip phone that was completely outdated. In her mind, she had better things to do with her money like supplying Rayshawn with textbooks and tennis shoes. Lynn stood by the bar and hit the speed dial for Melyssa's number, but after being sent straight to voicemail, she knew her friend was pissed. Tootie, of course, did the same thing a few seconds later. At that point, her only other option was to call Rayshawn. Lynn dialed his cell phone number as Sunny offered her another drink, which she quickly declined. The last thing she needed at the moment was more alcohol. When Rayshawn didn't answer, she called her house. She was taking a chance calling home, being that the only land line was located in her bedroom, which Rayshawn never answered. But it was worth a shot.

"Hello," a female voice answered after the second ring.

Lynn looked at her phone like a foreign object. "Hold up…who the hell is this and why the fuck are you answering my phone?" Lynn shouted. "Where's Rayshawn?"

The line immediately went dead.

Chapter Two

Lynn stood in front of her three-story townhouse in Largo, MD an hour later and stared up at her walnut-colored plantation shutters in the front window. She'd been calling her house and Rayshawn's cell phone non-stop since leaving Taboo, but never got an answer. Hoping the mysterious woman was still in her house, she power walked up the steps and to the door before placing her key into the lock. When Lynn walked inside, she found her son in the living room watching a rerun of *Flavor of Love* and eating a bowl of Fruity Pebbles. To make matters worse, he was sitting on her brand new ultra suede sofa with nothing but his Calvin Klein boxers on. Lynn went ballistic.

"I can't believe this shit!"

Rayshawn jumped, spilling some of the cereal on the carpet. "Ma, what are you doing here?" He placed the bowl on the floor and grabbed a pillow to cover himself up.

"I live here!" Lynn shouted. "Where is she?"

"Where's who?"

"Don't act dumb. The bitch who answered my phone!" Before Rayshawn could answer, Lynn ran upstairs at top speed to her room, then came back down a few seconds later with her Sony cordless phone. The ringer had been turned off. "Is she still here? If so, she better come out before I find her ass." Lynn had been catching girls in her house ever since Rayshawn was thirteen, so she was a pro when it came to finding their hiding spots.

Rayshawn looked shocked. He couldn't believe that his mother had already found out about the company he'd just entertained. "Umm…no. Not at all."

Lynn stared at her son's half naked body. "And you had the nerve to let that bitch in my room. Did you fuck her on my bed? You know, I'm not running a damn motel around here, Rayshawn!"

"No, Ma not at all. I wouldn't disrespect you like that. It was just my friend, Asia from high school. I ran into her yesterday, so she came by to say hello and catch up on old times, that's all."

Rayshawn knew his mother had a zero tolerance for lying, but he wasn't stupid enough to tell her the truth. Her bed was much more comfortable than his old twin down in the basement, so normally he always did his little escapades in her room. However, he still had no idea that his friend would pull a dumbass move and answer the phone. Rayshawn made a mental note to try and spray some Febreeze on Lynn's bed before she went back upstairs.

"Well, what the fuck was she doing in my room?" Lynn asked.

"She asked to use the bathroom, and since you're remodeling the one on this level and in the basement, she had to go upstairs. I swear, I had no idea that she would go in your room and use the phone." *I can't believe that stupid bitch*, Rayshawn thought to himself.

"Why the hell do I have to keep telling you about those nasty lil-bitches up in my house, especially when I'm not here? I'm tired of that shit. I mean, it's bad enough that you didn't answer your phone. I've been calling the house and your cell phone for over a damn hour!"

"I'm sorry, Ma. I didn't know you were calling. My cell phone is downstairs in the basement."

"I needed you to come pick me up from Rockville. Do you know I had to take a fucking cab home?" Lynn stood with her hands on her wide hips.

Rayshawn looked at the clock on the cable box. It was almost 1:00 a.m. He felt bad that his mother needed him and he wasn't there, especially since it was so late. He lowered his head. "My bad. I thought Ko-Ko was gonna bring you home. What happened?"

"That's not important. But what is important is that we're not even going to start this shit with all the girls again. So, don't even think about getting comfortable. You're taking your ass back to school. I don't slave all those hours in that hospital to have you drop out and waste my money. You were meant to be a doctor and that's what you're gonna be."

By Lynn keeping him on a short leash, Rayshawn had spent the majority of his life in the books. During high school, he wasn't allowed to go to a lot of parties, spend the night over friend's houses or watch television after eight o'clock during school months. Even his summers were spent in advance science and math classes at Prince George's Community College. Lynn was determined to give Rayshawn all the opportunities that she never had growing up. Even though Lynn was a nurse, it was hell trying to get her degree as a single mother. That's why when Rayshawn told her he needed a break from Xavier University after two successful years, she was crushed.

"Ma, I'm not sure that I want to be a doctor anymore."

Lynn's eyes almost popped out her head. The muscles tightened in her face as the anger continued to grow. "You're not sure. Well, I've got a damn news flash for you. It's not what you want to be. It's what you're gonna be. I'll give you one semester to come to your senses, then you're on the next plane back to New Orleans. Even if I have to strap your ass to a seat myself!" Lynn barked. "Dropping out in your Junior year was some stupid shit." She looked at her son with extreme disappointment. "And go put some fucking clothes on!"

When Rayshawn turned around to go downstairs, Lynn eyed his deep mocha coated skin and muscular build. As fine as he was, she couldn't blame all the girls, who wanted to be

around him. He was definitely easy on the eye. He even reminded her of a younger version of Idris Elba with his thick
eyebrows and almond shaped eyes.

Lynn bent down to pick up the bowl of cereal and clean
up the small mess; a ritual she did on the regular. Cleaning up
after Rayshawn was another part of her daily duties. However,
before she could even make it into the kitchen, Rayshawn was
back upstairs. Lynn hated the dingy grey sweatpants and black
wife beater he always wore to lounge around in.

"Ma, I've been thinking. It's my life. I don't want to be a
doctor. I want to be a photographer. I love taking pictures of
people," Rayshawn said, pulling out a brand new digital camera.
He quickly snapped Lynn's picture.

"Where the hell did you get that camera from?"

"I used the bank card to get it."

Lynn stared at her son. "Hold up. So, you went into *my*
bank account and used *my* money for your tuition to by a damn
camera. How much did it cost?"

"It was on sale for six hundred dollars." Rayshawn said,
admiring the high powered digital Nikon D60.

Lynn couldn't believe her ears. "Are you serious? You
took six hundred dollars from my account and bought that shit
without even asking me. You know what…you're taking it
back."

"Why? This was the cheapest Nikon I could find. The
one I really wanted was thirteen-hundred. Besides, I took it out
of my account." Rayshawn informed.

"You don't have an account. All the money in that bank
comes from my check and is for school or an emergency. I'm
not funding this little infatuation you're experiencing right now.
Open your wallet and give me that damn bank card."

"You're joking, right?"

"Does it look like I'm joking?" Lynn asked, holding out
her hand.

Rayshawn took a deep breath. He shook his head as he
pulled out his Wachovia check card and laid it softly into her

open hand. "I can't believe you're doing this."

"I can't believe you stole six-hundred dollars. You know I don't fuck with that crack head mentality. You want something from me, you need to get permission not steal shit." Lynn placed the card in the back pocket of her jeans. "Make sure you put the camera back in the box before you go to bed."

"So, what am I supposed to do tomorrow? You know I'm starting a new job."

"Actually Rayshawn, I don't give a shit what you do tomorrow. I don't even want you working at that place, so I could care less. Borrow someone else's camera."

Rayhawn had been offered a job working with Ko-Ko as an assist photographer at an adult magazine, a job that he was overly excited about. Seeing tits and ass all day was any man's dream.

"I can't believe this," Rayshawn said. "You playing me, Ma."

Lynn was pissed. "I'm not doing shit, but trying to help you be a better man. Hell, it's not like your sorry-ass father is around to give you some advice."

Growing up, Rayshawn knew better than to ask about his father. A man, who'd chosen not to be in his life. Lynn was obviously still bitter even though his father had broken her heart over twenty-one years ago.

"I'm going to bed," Lynn announced. Normally, she kissed her son on his cheek every night, but she was too pissed to show any affection at the moment. She didn't even wait for him to respond before dropping the cereal bowl in the kitchen sink, then walked upstairs.

Rayshawn wanted to ask his mother to keep the camera again, but decided to leave her alone. The last thing he wanted to do was piss her off even more. He sat on the couch and began playing with some of the camera's features one last time before Lynn yelled his name.

"Rayshawn! What the fuck is that smell? It smells like pussy in here!"

Chapter Three

The next morning, Lynn's bedroom door began to squeak as Rayshawn slowly slid it open. Lynn rolled over and removed her eye mask to find her son walking into the room carrying a tray of food and glass of orange juice.

"Hey, you. I want to make a truce. How about a little breakfast in bed?"

Lynn was still pissed from the night before. "I don't think so. Breakfast is not gonna make up for that shit you pulled last night. I mean, I can't believe you sat in my face and lied to me. Talking about you wouldn't disrespect me. Why would you fuck some girl on my bed, Rayshawn?"

He tried to lie his way out of it at first, but when Lynn found a pair of pink Victoria Secret underwear on the floor, it was a wrap. Rayshawn had been caught red-handed...again.

He felt horrible. "Ma, I'm sorry. I don't know what got into me. I admit it was very disrespectful."

"See, you messed up. I was gonna let you keep the camera, but you can cancel that shit now," Lynn said.

Rayshawn was disappointed, but had to take his punishment like a man. "I understand, Ma. Maybe once I start getting paid at my new job I can buy another one." He walked a few more steps toward her. "I still want you to have some breakfast. You need some energy when you start your shift today."

Although Lynn was mad, a smile managed to make it's way across her face. She sat up, and pulled her green night shirt down a little further to hide her self-conscious body. Then she took off her fake Chanel scarf and sat up to allow him to place the mahogany wood tray over her lap. Rayshawn had made her French toast, scrambled eggs with cheese, bacon and grits. Even the orange juice was freshly squeezed.

Why can't God send me a man like Rayshawn. I really need for my son to teach these guys how to treat a woman, she thought staring at the plate. "When in the hell did you learn to cook?" Lynn asked. "This is too much food though. I'm trying to watch my weight, so I'm only gonna eat a few bites."

Rayshawn chuckled. "Well, I've dated a few ladies back at school who could throw down, so I guess I learned a few things."

Lynn frowned. "What things? You know what Rayshawn, you better not have any babies running around back in New Orleans."

Rayshawn ran his fingers over his chin that had a slight dimple like John Travolta. "Yeah, I'm not even gonna lie. I do think I got one girl pregnant."

"What?" Lynn asked with her mouth wide open. She hoped like hell her son was joking. She began to play with her hair.

Rayshawn didn't answer. He just gave her a little smirk, glanced at his watch then turned around to leave the room. He had to get ready for work. Lynn picked up the fork and threw it, hitting him in the back of the head. Rayshawn turned around and gave her a look that said his joke had probably gone too far.

"Dag, Ma. I'm just joking."

"You better be. I will fuck you and the girl up if you ever brought some baby in this house talking about I'm a grand-mother," Lynn replied. "Besides, I'm not trying to share you anytime soon."

Rayshawn had no idea exactly what his mother meant by that, but decided to just let it go. He didn't want the butter knife to be the next thing she used.

Rayshawn's heart pounded with excitement as he entered the run-down four story office building on Rhode Island Avenue. After scanning the small directory in the lobby, he got on the elevator for a short ride up to the fourth floor. Apparently, his new employer, Fantasy Girlz Magazine occupied the entire top level, which was good due to the nature of the business. Although it had a Don Diva Magazine type of flavor, Fantasy Girlz was definitely a bootleg version of the popular men's magazine, Playboy. Specializing in tits and ass, the magazine described itself as frisky and playful and currently had over 10,000 readers.

Once the elevator came to a stop, Rayshawn got off and walked toward two thick wooden doors. When he pulled on one of the handles, he realized the door was locked. That's when he saw a white doorbell type buzzer on the wall. He pushed the button.

"Yes, can I help you?" a woman asked.

Rayshawn cleared his throat. "Yes. I'm the new assistant photographer, Rayshawn McMillian. I was supposed to report to work at nine o'clock."

"Oh, yes Mr. McMillian. We were expecting you," the woman replied before buzzing Rayshawn inside.

He walked in to find a heavy set girl sitting behind the front desk, who immediately reminded him of the comedian, Monique. She sported a thick bun on top of her head, long red fingernails and eyebrows that looked as if they'd been drawn on.

"Shit, how you doing?" the woman said, looking at Rayshawn up and down. It was obvious that her professional demeanor had completely disappeared. "You fine as hell. Mr. McMillian, right?"

Rayshawn smiled, showing a perfect set of teeth. "Yes, but just call me, Rayshawn."

"Hey, boo. My name is Nikki." She continued to stare. "My…my you got that good wavy hair and you tall, too. Just the way I like 'em. What, you about 6'1?"

"Close…6'2." *I can't believe we're having this type of conversation,* he thought.

"See, I know my measurements."

"I guess you…" Rayshawn stopped mid sentence and damn near had a heart attack when he saw several beautiful, thick women walking around in nothing but thongs.

Their breast looked like ripe grapefruits. His eyes continued to bulge like a little kid in a toy store when the women went on with their business, like being completely naked wasn't unusual.

"Damn," Rayshawn said out loud.

"Yeah, you might as well get used to that shit 'cuz them skinny bitches walk around like that all day. Now, back to us. What time you goin' to lunch today 'cuz I need us to get to know each other before all these other hoes try and holla," Nikki said. Her direct hood approach was amusing.

When three more half-naked women walked past, Rayshawn adjusted his erecting penis inside his baggy Sean Jean jeans. He tried to keep his cool, but couldn't take it any longer.

"Umm…where's the bathroom?" Rayshawn asked.

"It's down the hall. You need me to help you with anything?"

Rayshawn watched as Nikki fluffed up her double D breasts and licked her tongue across her large lips. "I really need to find that bathroom," he said.

Nikki pointed down the hall. "It's a unisex bathroom, so I can come help you if you want me too."

Rayshawn smiled again. "No, that's okay. I can handle it."

Hoping Nikki wouldn't offer again, Rayshawn quickly walked away and made his way toward the bathroom. After walking into the small space, which smelled like a cherry air freshener, his eyes bulged for the second time. The walls were completely covered with beautiful naked women from past editions of the magazine. Rayshawn was in heaven.

"Damn, I love this place already," he said, looking at one woman whose pussy had been shaved in the shape of a heart.

Knowing his dick wouldn't be going down anytime soon, Rayshawn felt the desire to release some of his creamy protein after staring at the abundant amount of ass before starting his day. Leaning up against the sink, Rayshawn pulled out his nine inch tool and began pulling it back and forth. He normally liked to use baby oil when he gave himself a treat, but in this case the sweat from his hand would have to do. Rayshawn worked his dick like a jack hammer for the next several minutes until the bathroom door opened. With his eyes closed, he didn't even notice when a thick, beautiful woman walked in.

"What the fuck are you doing?" the woman shouted.

Rayshawn quickly opened his eyes to see a tall woman standing with her hands on her slender hips.

"Oh, I'm so sorry. I thought I locked the door. I can't believe I just did that," Rayshawn said, trying to put his dick back into his pants.

"Who the fuck are you? Get out of here! I'm going to have your nasty-ass locked up for trespassing."

"No, please. It's my first day and I just… Please don't call the police," Rayshawn pleaded as he continued to fix his clothes. "I'm so embarrassed. I guess I just got a little carried away. I mean…I've never been in a place where so many women just walked around naked and I didn't have to give them dollar bills." Rayshawn hoped that his joke would lighten the mood.

"I need you to follow me out to the front desk. But make sure you wash your hands first," the woman ordered.

"Oh, sure…sure," Rayshawn replied. He quickly washed his hands then grabbed a paper towel before following the woman back to the front desk.

"So, Felice, I see you met our new assistant photographer. He's sure gonna make it a lot easier to come to work around here. I could sit and look at him all day," Nikki boldly said.

"Oh, so that's who you are. Well, I hope you can take pictures as well as you can do other things," Felice said to Rayshawn.

"Kourtney just arrived and asked about you, Rayshawn. I told her that you were in the bathroom. She went into the conference room," Nikki added.

"Nikki, can you please escort our new employee to the conference room. The meeting should've started by now," Felice announced. Just before turning around, she looked at Rayshawn again. "Oh, one more thing, don't stop by the bathroom on your way, Mr. Sticky Fingers."

Nikki walked around her desk. "It'll be my pleasure. Come on sexy, you can hold my hand so you won't get lost." The bathroom comment had gone completely over her head.

After walking to the other side of the office, Rayshawn stood in shock after Nikki smacked his ass. "This is the conference room. I'll see you at lunch time."

All he could do was shake his head as Nikki blew him a kiss and sashayed away. "I gotta stay away from that girl," Rayshawn said, then opened the door.

As soon as he entered, he felt every eye in the room starring at him. Even Ko-Ko gave him a weird look.

"Can we help you?" a man standing at a white dry erase board asked.

Ko-Ko quickly got up from the table and walked over to Rayshawn. "You're late," she whispered to him. "I'm sorry everyone, this is our new assistant photographer, Rayshawn McMillan."

At that moment, the beautiful woman he'd just had an encounter with stepped in from behind him. "Well, Mr. Rayshawn McMillan, I'm Felice Contour, CEO of the company," she mentioned. "You're a few minutes late for the meeting, but since I know the reason, I'll excuse it this time. But don't make it a habit. All Fantasy Girlz employees know that I'm a bitch when it comes to promptness. Take a seat in the corner and try to catch up. And please keep your hands where I can see them." Her jokes just wouldn't stop.

Ko-Ko wondered what Felice was talking about, but went back to her chair. Rayshawn could hear the faint sounds of snickering as he took a seat at the table. He then grabbed a notepad and a pen from the center of the table. Since he was late, he wanted to make sure he at least took good notes.

As the meeting continued, every now and then, he would catch Felice starring at him. As beads of sweat formed on his forehead, Rayshawn didn't know if it was the heat from the vents he sat directly under or Felice's pretty green eyes that were making him hot. With a smooth, honey coated complexion and a long, jet black weave, the woman was surely a dime. Even her makeup was flawless.

When the meeting finally ended several hours later, everyone including Ko-Ko rushed out of the room. Glancing at his watch, it was obvious that they'd worked half-way through lunch, which Rayshawn was happy about. The last thing he wanted was to be harassed by Nikki for an hour. After scanning his notes one last time, he stood up and made his way over to Felice.

"Umm…excuse me, Ms. Contour. I just want to apologize again. I know that was totally inappropriate."

"The girls you saw earlier, is typical around here. You're gonna need to control yourself a little better if you wanna keep this job. Besides, haven't you seen tits and ass before?" When Rayshawn didn't answer, Felice continued. "You need to have high expectations for yourself. I've gotten where I am today by having even higher expectations then my competitors. Let me ask you a question. Do you understand baseball?"

The question had Rayshawn puzzled. "Yes, of course."

"Well, I love baseball. I pride myself on the simple things. The biggest aspect that drives my life is the three strikes rule. You already have strike one. If you get to strike three, Mr.

McMillan you're out of here. Do you understand?"

"I do. But, in my defense, I must say that I never strike out."

Felice found amusement in his answer. She gave him a head to toe look-over before flashing her heart warming smile. She then collected her belongings and left.

As Rayshawn watched her strut away in a tight pencil skirt, a short older gentlemen, who looked to be in his late fifties entered the room. "Hello, Mr. McMillan, my name is Sam, but everybody around here calls me Sammy for some damn reason. I'm the lead photographer. From here on out you're gonna be my shadow, so pay close damn attention."

Rayshawn looked at the short statured man, and couldn't help but grin. He definitely put him in the mind of Sammy Davis Jr. or the Looney Tunes cartoon character, Yosemite Sam. With his thick glasses and receding hairline, Sammy wasn't the best looking man. Everyone at the magazine seemed no- non-sense, but Rayshawn didn't mind. He was used to that type of attitude from his mother.

"Did you bring your own equipment?" Sammy asked.

"Umm…no sir. I had a Nikon, but it was defective, so I had to return it," Rayshawn lied.

"Now, what kind of damn photographer shows up to work with no camera? Hell, you could've at least went to CVS and bought a disposable one."

Rayshawn couldn't help but laugh. He could already tell that Sammy was going to be a handful. However, he also knew that Sammy would probably teach him all about the business.

"Well, you'll just have to use one of mine for now. But if you break it, that's your ass."

Rayshawn smiled. He was about to respond when Felice walked back past the door. Wanting to get another look, he stuck his head out the doorway and watched her perfect ass switch from side to side.

"My first free bit of advice, don't even try for Ms. Contour. She's the one woman who will destroy everything you have," Sammy said, tapping Rayshawn on the shoulder.

Rayshawn ignored Sammy's words of advice and kept his eyes locked on Felice until she turned the corner.

"Come on, shadow. Let's get to work."

Sam escorted Rayshawn to another room, where the photo shoots obviously took place. The room was completely bare with the exception of several colored backdrops, a few props, an Apple computer and of course Sammy's high powered camera. Ko-Ko was busy putting three girls in sexy positions when the men walked inside.

"It's about damn time," Ko-Ko said to the two men.

Rayshawn's dick was almost at full attention when he saw the girls lying on a bed using huge dildos on one another. Not to mention their bodies were glistening in baby oil. Rayshawn became fully erect once Ko-Ko went over and adjusted one of the girl's legs so that her pink vagina could be seen.

"Are we going to stand there watching like little boys or are you going to go to the camera and make some magic happen?" Ko-Ko asked Sammy.

"Now, I've already told you about your nasty mouth," Sammy answered.

Ko-Ko gave Sammy a slight tab on his butt. "You know you love me."

"Yeah, me and a lot of other men," Sammy countered.

When Ko-Ko walked away to adjust the set one final time, Rayshawn leaned in Sammy's direction.

"What exactly does she do around here?"

"Ms. Kourtney Jackson's official title is Stylist, but as you can see she's a diva, too. She's the one who picks out all the clothing and designs all the sets. She also hires all the models and even does advertising sometimes."

"I heard that damn diva comment, old man. Now, can we start? This girl's pussy is about to dry up," Ko-Ko stated.

As Rayshawn watched Sammy pick up the camera and begin to shoot, he couldn't believe how he could be around so many beautiful women and not have a pitched tent. Then again, Sammy had probably been around pussy for so long, the shit probably didn't faze him anymore. Ever since his freshmen year in high school, Rayshawn always had a secret desire for photography and this opportunity had just culminated it for him. He couldn't believe his luck. The magazine was getting ready to pay him to take pictures of beautiful naked women. He fell in love with his new job instantly, and needed to thank Ko-Ko for giving him such a sweet assignment. Rayshawn watched Sammy snap picture after picture as his dick remained hard for nearly three straight hours.

When the girls were tired of bending over in awkward positions and their mascara was beginning to run down their faces, it was finally quitting time. Rayshawn realized that the day had come and gone without him even noticing.

"Okay, everyone, that's a wrap!" Sammy shouted before turning to Rayshawn. "So, what do you think?"

"I'm going to love this job," Rayshawn replied with a huge smile.

"Hey, some of us usually go over to this little hole in a wall down the street to have a drink after work. You wanna come?" Before Rayshawn could respond, Sammy continued. "Wait… is your ass even legal, yet?"

"Yes."

"Oh, okay. Well, in that case, Felice might be there."

Rayshawn was actually about to decline when Ko-Ko walked over and smacked him on his back. "I hope you learned something from Sammy today. Why don't you get your stuff together and join me for a drink, so we can talk about any concerns."

Rayshawn was contemplating on not going but something that Sammy said caught his attention. "Felice might be there," echoed in his ears. He knew he probably didn't have a shot in hell with her, but at least he could just look at her for now.

Rayshawn nodded. "Sure, I'll go."

"Good. I'ma head over there now. Follow Sammy to the spot," Ko-Ko replied.

Rayshawn waited for Sammy to pack his camera into his bag, then followed his mentor and a few other co-workers to a placed called, The Wet Bar. It was a small two story home that had been gutted and refurbished into a cozy lounge.

The laughter rolled out into the busy D.C. streets as they stepped inside. In a matter of seconds, Rayshawn quickly scanned the bar and dance floor looking for Felice. The feeling of disappointment began to take over when he couldn't find her. At that point, Rayshawn took position near the back of the bar and ordered a shot of Remy with a Heinekin chaser.

"Can I see your I.D.?" the bartender asked.

Rayshawn laughed as he pulled out his license from his wallet. He'd been twenty-one for two months, so he felt insulted that the bartender had even asked for it. *I'ma grown-ass man,* he thought.

"Thank you, sir," the bartender replied.

As Rayshawn waited for his drink, little did he know that Felice, the magazine's accountant, Gina and Ko-Ko were all at a table in a dark corner looking at him. Felice, however, was more so watching him like a hawk.

"Don't even fucking think about it," Ko-Ko said.

Felice put her glass on the small cocktail table. "What are you talking about?"

"I see the way you looking at him. But you might as well stop, because he is entirely too young for you."

"Damn, baby boy is fine," Gina added. "It's about time you brought in some eye candy, Felice. I'm tired of looking at old-ass men like Sammy with his linty dress socks and Hawaiian print shirts."

"Shit, don't forget about those awful Hush Puppies dress shoes," Felice added.

All the women started laughing.

"Oh, no her ass can't get the credit. I brought him in," Ko-Ko announced.

"So, what about you? Isn't he to young for you, too?" Felice asked.

Ko-Ko shook her head. "Are you crazy? He's like a son to me. How dare you say some silly shit like that?"

Ko-Ko took a sip of her Apple Martini, then looked away. She had no idea how Felice had peeped her game. Ko-Ko knew she'd been staring at Rayshawn ever since he walked into the conference room that morning, but she had no idea it was that obvious. Hell, she'd had her eye on him ever since he'd gotten the rock hard body a year ago. And just like always, Rayshawn was causing several little goose bumps to swim up and down her body.

Damn, even though my pussy throbs every time I look at that nigga, I gotta shake this shit. Besides, Lynn would kill me.

Chapter Four

Over the next two weeks, Rayshawn acted as an apprentice for Sammy. Following him around and watching his every move was something that he'd come to enjoy. He also enjoyed coming to the office everyday and seeing all the nude models walking around. However, what had him overjoyed was when he learned from Felice in a staff meeting that Sammy was leaving the company for an early retirement in Florida. Felice also told Rayshawn that he would be the lead photographer for all shoots, which had some people shifting in their seats. A few wanted to know why they weren't going to hire a more experienced photographer until Rayshawn learned more, but Felice wouldn't hear of it. She told everyone that Rayshawn was more than capable of handling the job, and if anyone had a problem with her decision they knew the way out the door. A comment that boosted Rayshawn's confidence even more. She even presented him with his own brand new camera equipment, which was another thing that had him walking on air.

After the meeting, Rayshawn went to organize a few of the cameras as Ko-Ko began to select the appropriate costumes for the sports themed shoot. So far, she'd pulled a cheerleading and a referee uniform. When Ko-Ko realized no one was around, she walked over to Rayshawn and planted a soft kiss on his cheek.

"Congratulations, on your promotion, handsome." She

placed her hand around his arm. "I can't believe I've never noticed your build before. Your arms are pretty buff."

Rayshawn felt a little awkward. "Umm. Thanks. Actually
I've been meaning to call you after work and thank you again
for the job anyway. Hell, I owe it all to you."

"Don't mention it." As Ko-Ko planted another kiss on
his cheek, Sammy walked from around the corner.

"You know you can get locked up for messing with
young boys," Sammy stated.

"Shut up. You just mad because I'm not kissing your old-
ass," Ko-Ko returned.

Sammy smiled. "Don't matter. I don't like my milk
spoiled anyway."

Ko-Ko went over to her old co-worker and playfully
punched him in the shoulder. She was definitely going to miss
them going back and forth with each other.

"Alright people, I don't have all day. Let's roll! I want to
get the hell out of here, so I can go home and screw my wife!"
Sammy shouted in his normal demanding tone.

"Oh, that's a nasty thought," Ko-Ko responded.

Once the action began, Sammy guided Rayshawn like
the perfect teacher. Although Rayshawn made a couple of mis-
takes and his first few pictures came out blurry due to the wrong
lighting, he quickly found his groove. He worked vigorously
throughout the shoot. So much that he didn't even notice Felice
standing off to the side watching him like a hawk. Ko-Ko however, did notice. She'd been at the magazine since it's first issue
and knew that Felice had never stood in on a shoot.

Felice waited until Sammy took a restroom break before
she decided to interrupt. "Mr. McMillan, you seemed to be running things as if you've done this all your life. I guess you have
other skills than pleasing yourself in a public bathroom."

Rayshawn kept his cool as he grabbed a bottle of water,
twisted the cap off and took a long gulp. "I told you that I
wouldn't strike out. Besides, I'm known for knocking it out the
park."

Felice grinned. "If I didn't know any better Mr. McMillan, I'd swear you were flirting with me. It doesn't sound like we're talking about pictures anymore."

Ko-Ko couldn't believe that Rayshawn actually seemed interested in Felice, which was surprising because she didn't seem like his type, especially since she was just as tall as he was. Ko-Ko had been around pretty women all her life, but they never worried her in the least, especially since she felt that God hadn't created a woman who could compete with her.

"I'm not trying to get a sexual harassment charge during my first few weeks to go along with my indecent exposure beef I caught on my first day," Rayshawn said.

"I must say that I've never met a guy before in that way. You win the award for the most memorable first impression," Felice replied.

Rayshawn laughed. "You got me there. I don't have a comeback for that one."

"Maybe if you last another inning, you'll get your chance to…" Felice didn't get a chance to continue before Ko-Ko interrupted them.

She swung a long black rubber dick between the two of them. "I need to make an adjustment to the budget. I need some better props if the sports themed pictures are going to turn out right. Stop being so damn tight with the money."

"Why don't you use some real dicks in the next shoot?" Felice stared right at Rayshawn. "I know for a fact that we have an employee who would look great on film."

Ko-Ko looked over at the dumb smile on Rayshawn's face and realized that she might as well been a man. Rayshawn wasn't paying her any attention. *What the fuck is going on here?* Ko-Ko wondered. She never played second fiddle to another woman and today wasn't going to be the first.

"Why don't you call your mother and tell her you'll be home late. We're gonna have to run through several frames because I haven't gotten my shot yet," Ko-Ko said trying to embarrass Rayshawn in front of Felice.

Felice seemed shocked. "You still live at home with your mother?"

Rayshawn looked over at Ko-Ko with a *thank you very much* look. "For now. I just left school in New Orleans and needed somewhere to stay until I can find a place that I could afford."

"Oh, really. What was your major in school?" Felice questioned.

"Pre-med," Rayshawn replied.

"Really? Well, I have some aches that I haven't been able to get rid of with over the counter remedies. What if you give me a private physical and see if you can diagnose me?"

Ko-Ko couldn't believe Felice was flirting with him right in front of her face. "Aches and pains my ass. Look, Rayshawn enough about that. Do you wanna make some extra money?"

Rayshawn shook his head. "Yeah."

"Well, I'm having a few girls over my house tonight to model for my new lingerie line, and I'll pay you to do the shoot. Plus, I need to load some mini-commercials on You Tube. You know anything about that stuff? I'm actually horrible with technology and shit."

"I didn't know you had a lingerie line," Felice chimed in.

"It's a lot of things about me that you don't know. Like I'm sure it's a lot of things about you that people around here don't know about." Ko-Ko stood with a devious grin, which seemed to make Felice heated.

Rayshawn decided to break up the mini cat fight. "What time should I come over?"

"Eight o'clock is fine. I'll write down the address because I don't live near Rock Creek Park anymore. I've moved since the last time you brought *your mother* over," Ko-Ko answered. Rayshawn gave her another crazy look.

"Well, I guess you have plans for this evening, maybe next time you can pencil me in. I need to get back to my office anyway," Felice said, before walking away. She then turned around. "Oh, Kourtney. Let me see if I can move some money around so you can get some better dicks to play with."

Rayshawn chuckled. His neck almost completed a three hundred and sixty degree turn as he spun around to watch Felice walk away in her tight fighting slacks. Ko-Ko couldn't believe that Felice had his young-ass nose wide open. She turned to stare at Felice walking down the hall, trying to figure out why Rayshawn was so intrigued.

"I know you've probably never really had a *real* job, but it's never a good idea to get involved with your damn boss. They hold your job in their hands and if the fling doesn't work out, they make your life a living hell or fire your ass all together."

"Thanks for the advice, but I think I can handle a twenty-five year old," Rayshawn replied.

"Is that what that bitch told you? Shit. Ms. Thunder Thighs is actually going on thirty nine." Ko-Ko could care less that she was being a hater at the moment.

"Oh no, she didn't tell me anything. I just figured that's how old she was. She looks really young. Besides, it really doesn't matter. I don't mind if my women are seasoned. It ain't fun for me if I can't learn a few things."

Oh my, there are so many things that I would love to teach a young stallion like you, Ko-Ko thought. At that moment, she felt a tingling sensation between her thighs and her pussy beginning to moisten just thinking all the things she wanted to do.

Ko-Ko laughed. "If you think she's old, I would hate to hear what's running around in your mind about me."

Before Rayshawn answered, he stepped around Ko-Ko almost knocking her down just so he could get another look at Felice's tight ass when she walked by to go into the copying room. *I'll bet my right nut that her pussy is off the hook,* Rayshawn thought. Once Felice was totally out of his vision, Rayshawn went back over to the naked models and started shooting again. He never did respond to Ko-Ko's question.

This young boy must not know a real woman when he's

standing next to one. Rayshawn really needs to redo the math he uses to figure if a woman is a zero or ten. I've never been overshadowed by another chick in my life, and the shit is not gonna start now. Lynn might not approve of me doing this, but at this point who cares. Fuck this…game on, Ko-Ko thought.

Chapter Five

Rayshawn stopped to get a bite before going over to Ko-Ko's to shoot her lingerie line. There was only one other car in the drive way when he pulled up to her new single family house near The Washington Harbor. Excited about seeing even more half-naked beautiful women, Rayshawn grabbed his camera bag and headed toward the front door with a cheesy grin. However, when he walked past the huge curtain less window in the living room, it didn't look like anyone was there. Even ESPN's show Sports Center was playing on the flat screen T.V. which was extremely odd. He knew a bunch of girly models wouldn't be sitting around watching highlights of their favorite football team.

"Maybe I'm the first one here," Rayshawn said to himself as he adjusted his scarf. It was a fairly chilly evening, and if it wasn't for the much needed money, he would've asked Ko-Ko for a rain check. With New Orleans always having pretty decent weather, he could no longer handle D.C.'s blistering winters.

He pushed the doorbell and waited patiently for Ko-Ko to answer.

"Umm…you did say that you wanted me to work tonight, right?" Rayshawn asked when the door opened a few seconds later.

With a black satin robe on, Ko-Ko stood in the doorway with a wine glass in one had and a cigarette in the other. After getting one last pull, she tossed the butt outside then signaled for

Rayshawn to enter. She never took her eyes off the way his firm ass filled his jeans as she closed the door behind him.

"Of course, but the girls just called to tell me that they had a scheduling issue, so they aren't gonna be able to make it. But we shouldn't let that stop us from working. Since you're here with all your stuff, you can take some pictures of me."

"You want me to take your picture to use for your own line? Don't you think that would be a little tacky?"

Ko-Ko removed her robe and let it drop to the floor. "Are you saying that I don't have the body for lingerie?" She twirled some of her locks with her index finger.

Rayshawn couldn't answer. He stood in one spot, stunned at how she looked in her hot pink lace bra and matching thong. His dick twitched as Ko-Ko began to slowly spin around for him to see her juicy ass jiggle. Entering the house, he hadn't noticed that she was wearing five inch pumps that made her calves bulge like tiny peaches.

"So, what do you think? Will it be a waste of time taking my picture in different numbers like this one?" Ko-Ko asked. She stood in a sexy stance.

"Naw, it won't be a waste. Can I get a glass of water? My throat is dry as hell from that burger I ate on my way over," Rayshawn said, taking off his coat and scarf.

"My bar in the basement is fully stocked with nothing but top shelf alcohol if you want something a little stronger."

He seemed mesmerized from her succulent breasts, but tried to snap out of it, constantly telling himself that she was his mother's best friend. "Yeah...I guess that's fine."

"Well, follow me downstairs. Oh, and bring your camera. We can start shooting down there."

Rayshawn watched as Ko-Ko elegantly strolled across the living room to the basement door. He followed behind her at a distance that allowed him to study every dimple and mole on her sensual body. She was gorgeous, but the fact that she smoked was a slight turn off. When they got downstairs, Ko-Ko had several racks of lace, silk, leather and cotton lingerie hanging on the back wall. It looked just like a miniature Fredrick's of Hollywood.

"Have a seat and get your stuff ready while I make you a special drink," she informed.

As Rayshawn bent down to take out his camera, he couldn't get his mind off her. He'd spent a lot of time around Ko-Ko growing up, but her body had never made him look twice before. He studied the muscles in her long legs as she took each step, along with the little bounce her ass did as her hips switched to an imaginary beat. Rayshawn wondered if Ko-Ko had always looked this beautiful or if he was just feeling a little horny.

When he felt his dick getting hard, Rayshawn forced himself to pull his eyes away. He then walked over to the black leather sofa and began taking out the rest of his equipment. When Ko-Ko went behind the bar and started to mix him up a drink, she constantly glanced over to see what Rayshawn was doing. After it seemed as if he was having a hard time finding something in his bag, Ko-Ko pulled out a small bottle that contained two crushed pills and dumped the white powder into his drink. She used her finger to swirl it around.

"Here you go."

"Thank you," Rayshawn said, taking the glass out her hand. He shook his head once he tasted it. "This is pretty good. What is it?"

"I made it up myself messing around with different liquors. I call it, Twenty-Four Hour Pleasure. Hurry up and knock it out so we can get started. You know time is money and I want to get every pennies worth of my money tonight." Little did Rayshawn know, she'd gotten the name from the fact that it would probably take twenty-four hours before his dick would go down. Ko-Ko had managed to slip two Viagra pills in his glass. Something she did to her men all the time.

After downing the drink until not even a drop remained, Rayshawn picked up his camera and wondered where they should start. Seconds later, Ko-Ko walked over to the bar stool

and lifted her leg so the lace could be seen hanging from between her thighs. She then grabbed a bottle of Moet and slid her
tongue around the top.

"Oh, that shit is hot. Don't move," Rayshawn said, snapping a couple of test shots.

Ko-Ko turned her back to the bar, spread her legs even
further then flung her long hair wildly into the air. She continued to bend in all sorts of positions until Rayshawn's memory
card was full. When he went to get a different card, it didn't take
long for him to notice Ko-Ko taking off the hot pink set.
Rayshawn immediately felt a warming sensation building in his
body. He watched closely as she walked her naked body over to
the rack and pulled out a sexy black diamond studded outfit. She
looked amazing after slipping it on.

Rayshawn rubbed his forehead. "Is it me or did it get really hot in here?"

"Baby-boy, I think it's just you," Ko-Ko said, pulling out
a dildo with pearl beads in the middle.

When Rayshawn began to sweat, he pulled off his v-neck
sweater, leaving him with just a white t-shirt and his True Reli-
gion jeans on. Rayshawn's dick was hard as a rock. The heat
continued to overcome his body like a tidal wave as he then removed his boots.

"I hope you don't mind, but I'm hot as hell."

But Ko-Ko didn't answer him. She sat on the sofa and
began to insert the dildo in and out of her pussy until her eyes
rolled back into her head. Not saying another word, Rayshawn
got down on the floor to shoot her from a different angle. He
licked his lips as her moans grew in volume. Not even aware,
Rayshawn grinded his dick onto the carpet in the same motion
as if the dildo entering Ko-Ko's moist pussy were him.

Ko-Ko glimpsed over at Rayshawn fucking the floor and
knew that her plan was working. She crawled off the sofa down
to the floor next to him. "You know these diamonds are really
edible candy. Would you like to try some?"

Rayshawn felt like he was in heaven. "Umm…I would

love to, but I can't. My mother would kill me if she found out. Hell, she doesn't even know I'm here with you now. She keeps calling me, but I won't answer."

"Stop acting like a damn baby. I hate a fucking momma's boy. Look, I won't tell if you won't."

Rayshawn looked around like someone was in the room. "What about your daughter? Where's she?"

"Don't worry about that either. Besides, she's not here right now. She'll be back tomorrow night." When Ko-Ko stuck her index finger in her mouth and began to suck on it in a seductive manner, Rayshawn could no longer control himself. Smoker or not, he no longer cared.

Without further hesitation, he took off his clothes, pushed Ko-Ko over onto her back and bit several pieces of the sweet treats. He then licked around the outside of her pussy. His tongue was an instant weapon.

"Oh shit," Ko-Ko said, as she quickly took off the lingerie. Her clit began to thump like a pulse.

Within seconds, she began to feel his long thick tongue twirling around inside her, banging against each wall. At that moment, she couldn't resist. Ko-Ko flipped Rayshawn over and straddled her thighs on top of his face. Little did she know, that move didn't even get Rayshawn off his game. He quickly went back to work, licking her pussy and ass simultaneously.

Ko-Ko reached over and grabbed a can of caramel flavor whipped cream from a bag that was on the floor. She popped the top off the can and squirted a large amount on his dick. Before Rayshawn could even contest, Ko-Ko switched her body into the sixty-nine position so they both could continue to suck and eat. They both used their tongues to twirl around each other until warm cum squirted into each others mouth.

Rayshawn pushed Ko-Ko off his face as her juices warmed his throat. Going into Ko-Ko's obvious toy kit on the floor, he tried on a pair of five finger massage gloves then rolled Ko-Ko onto her stomach. After finding the right setting, Rayshawn slowly began to rub his hands all over her body. The

vibrating fingers slid down her lower back and over the rose tattoos she had on her inner thighs.

Ko-Ko's body started to relax but it didn't last. She became startled for a second when she felt Rayshawn lock her
arms behind her back with a pair of furry cuffs. Ko-Ko then
watched as he stood up and pulled a black leather strap from off
the rack.

"Oh yeah motherfucka, whip me!" Ko-Ko screamed.

Ko-Ko's nipples became extremely hard. Her fingers and
toes curled tight as the strap continued to make contact with her
naked ass. All of a sudden, Ko-Ko's entire body tensed up when
Rayshawn slid a string of different sized Ben-Wa- Beads into
her unsuspecting ass. The escapade had her wanting him more
and more.

"What's your favorite position? You can put me in any
position you want. This pussy is ready," Ko-Ko said seductively.

Like most men…doggy style was his favorite position.
Rayshawn began to tickle her pussy lips with the tip of his dick.
When it seemed as if both of them were about to go crazy,
Rayshawn took off the cuffs and turned Ko-Ko over. After grabbing a condom from out the bag and quickly rolling it over his
shaft, he forcefully inserted his manhood deep inside her. It did-
n't take long for him to catch a steady groove and work her
juices into frenzy.

"Talk dirty to me. Tell me how bad you've wanted this
pussy from the very first time you saw me," Ko-Ko moaned.

What she wanted him to say wasn't really the case, but
he decided to say it anyway. "Oh baby, you know I wanted this
pussy. There is no pussy in the world that can compare to this.
Say it's my pussy. Call me, daddy," he replied.

"You've been watching too many porn videos. You gotta
fuck me harder than that if you want me to call you daddy."

At that point, Rayshawn reached up and grabbed a handful of her long hair. He couldn't believe that Ko-Ko had the
nerve to taunt him. Rayshawn pulled her head back, arched her
back more and rammed his dick inside. Little did he know, in-

stead of screaming out in pain, Ko-Ko reached back with both hands to spread open her butt cheeks even wider. She jiggled her hips and laughed because Rayshawn was trying his best.

Rayshawn could work his well built body, but although it was his favorite position, Ko-Ko was having a hard time reaching an orgasm. Becoming frustrated, she threw him off her then jumped on top. She began to ride his dick with no regards to his dangling nuts. Even though her plump ass was killing his testicles, he gritted his teeth and allowed her to continue. It didn't matter because Ko-Ko knew that no matter what his size was, she could always cum in this position.

Ko-Ko continued to ride even though she'd finally hit an orgasm a couple of times. One even made her legs shake uncontrollably. Moments later, Rashawn had reached his peak as well. After finally becoming a little winded, Ko-Ko paused for a moment, then fell onto his chest. She began to feel around Rayshawn's body. His skin felt like a baby's ass under her gliding fingers. She smiled, knowing Rayshawn's dick was the biggest she'd had in a while, and that he was going to be her new stallion. With her high sex drive, he was perfect for the job.

Once they got the normal small pillow talk out the way, Rayshawn and Ko-Ko went at it again…for hours this time. They even used every toy that was in the bag, including a dick extension, which Rayshawn really didn't need and a cordless Humm Dinger bullet. When things finally began to simmer down, the sun was coming up. However, even though they'd finally stopped, Rayshawn's erection still wouldn't go down.

I can't wait to get to work tomorrow. I wonder if that bitch Felice will be able to smell my pussy on him next time she's all up in his face, Ko-Ko wondered.

"I need to get home. I know my mother is going to freak the hell out that I didn't call," Rayshawn said rolling over.

That's when it hit her. She had just fucked the shit out of her girlfriend's son. Ko-Ko was so obsessed with fucking him before Felice to prove she hadn't lost anything, that Lynn's feelings never came to mind.

"You can never tell her about this," Ko-Ko warned.

"What do you think, I'm crazy. I'll never tell her." He kissed her hand. "It'll just be our secret."

Ko-Ko smiled like an immature schoolgirl. It was a secret she was damn sure willing to keep.

Chapter Six

After going into the dryer to get Rayshawn a washcloth and towel, Ko-Ko smacked him on the butt and told him to go freshen up.

"I just moved in this house, so there's only one bathroom with a shower curtain and that's upstairs."

"Cool. Are you gonna miss me while I'm gone?" Rayshawn joked.

Ko-Ko smiled. "I sure am, boo. Hurry back."

However, as soon as Rayshawn disappeared, her smile quickly faded. Although, she'd enjoyed the multiple orgasms, it still didn't hide the fact that she still felt bad. Ko-Ko sat on the leather sofa looking at all the toys and rubbers they'd used the night before. She couldn't believe that she allowed jealousy to control her like that. The past had come back full circle. She was now a predator like the many drunken men her mother brought home from bars and were allowed to fuck Ko-Ko after they finished with her mother. The thought of her past made her stomach crawl. It always did.

As Ko-Ko made a trip down memory lane, Rayshawn made his way upstairs to the bathroom. With the door slightly ajar, he pushed it open and walked his erect dick inside. However, he immediately dropped the towel and washcloth when Ko-Ko's daughter, Kiara screamed to the top of her lungs.

When she realized who Rayshawn was she stopped screaming, but was just extremely hype. "Oh my God! You scared the shit out of me. Why the hell are you standing naked in my bathroom? How did you get in my house?" Kiara asked.

Rayshawn stood frozen. He didn't know what to do except stare at Kiara's hour glass shape. The cute little Victoria Secret Pink underwear she wore and her perky B-cup breasts had his full and undivided attention. At 5'2, and a hundred and ten pounds, Kiara looked like Rudy from the Cosby Show. But not the cute little girl everybody used to love. The Rudy who'd blossomed into a beautiful woman.

"Answer me!" Kiara belted.

Under normal circumstances, she probably would've covered herself up, but she didn't see a point covering up for Rayshawn. Since they'd been having sex since high school, he'd seen her naked on more than enough occasions.

Rayshawn finally snapped from his trance, and quickly realized the tight situation he was in. *Damn, Ko-Ko said she wasn't here*, he thought. "Shhh. Calm down."

"No, I'm not going to calm down until you tell me what the hell is going on!" At first, Kiara thought that maybe her mother had accidentally left the front door open, and Rayshawn had come over to surprise her like he'd done a few times in the past at their old house. He was the master at early morning loving. Her mother was known to leave out without locking the front door sometimes, so her theory was possible.

Kiara let out a slight smile at the thought of the two of them always sneaking around. "Boy, my mother is going to kill you if she finds out you're here." She then paused for a second. "But we can still get a quickie in."

When Kiara moved toward Rayshawn, he quickly pushed her away when he heard Ko-Ko marching up the steps at top speed. By now, she'd put back on the black satin robe.

"What the hell is all that yelling about? What's going on?" she asked out of breath.

Kiara's eyes bulged when she noticed her mother's attire.

She knew Ko-Ko never wore that particular robe unless she was entertaining a man, which was quite often. Kiara turned her attention toward Rayshawn, then back to Ko-Ko. She held a look of disgust. "I know you didn't fuck my mother."

"And what if he did? What business is it of yours what we were doing?" Ko-Ko responded. "Rayshawn why the hell are you standing in front of my daughter like that anyway? Your dick looks like the Washington Monument. Pick up the damn towel. You too, Kiara. Grab your robe or something."

Before Rayshawn could follow her orders, Kiara had picked up a flat iron and began swinging widely. "You fucked my mother!" She continued to clobber Rayshawn's body with a few more major league swings. "Get the fuck out my house."

Ko-Ko couldn't help but laugh when she saw Rayshawn trying to block the ceramic weapon in Kiara's hand. "Kiara calm your ass down. Besides, this is my house, and Rayshawn is my guest. Like I said, what business is it of yours, and for the last time, cover yourself up!"

Kiara finally put the flat iron down then grabbed her terrycloth robe off the toilet and wrapped it around her petite frame. "For starters, because it's Rayshawn. How could you have sex with him? He's only a couple of months older than me. You used to babysit him growing up. And most important, he's the son of your best friend…that's why," Kiara said in a matter of fact tone. She was embarrassed and hurt at the same time.

Rayshawn covered his manhood with his right hand. "I know this may not be a good time, but I really need to get in here." He pointed to the toilet with his free hand.

Kiara glanced over at Rayshawn. She could tell that his dick was still hard even though he was trying to shield it with his hands. *No wonder she let him knock the dust off that stank coochie, who doesn't love a big dick* she thought. When Kiara stepped to the side, Rayshawn rushed over to the toilet and began pissing. Ko-Ko then grabbed Kiara's arm and pulled her out into the hallway, then shut the bathroom door.

"Don't you ever embarrass me like that again. I know

you're just mad because I got to him before you did."

Kiara chuckled. She wanted to tell her mother so badly that she was getting her sloppy seconds, but decided against it. Ko-Ko showing her competitive nature with every guy Kiara brought around was normal. However, if her mother wanted Rayshawn to be a competition, then she was game. In Kiara's mind, it was time to teach her mother a lesson.

"Do you let your vagina make all the decisions?" Kiara asked.

Ko-Ko frowned, showing that she didn't care for the question. "Don't get knocked the fuck out in this hallway, okay?"

"You're a real piece of work. I'll hate to be you when Lynn finds out you've fucked her son," Kiara said, walking off to her room.

"She's not going to find out. Is she?" When Kiara didn't respond, Ko-Ko turned around and tapped on the bathroom door. "Honey, I'll see you at work. I'm going to my room and get a couple more hours of sleep before I go in."

Rayshawn didn't care for his new label. To him, pet names were for married couples. "Alright," he said, cleaning up the piss that he'd sprayed all over the toilet seat. His shaft was still hard. Rayshawn began to get worried that his erection didn't even have a slight hint that it was going down anytime soon. He quickly washed off his dick in the sink with some vanilla scented soap then covered his body with the towel. Afterwards, he walked back down to the basement to get his clothes.

"How could you fuck my mother after all the good times we've had?" Kiara asked, stepping up behind him.

Her voice startled him. "Do we really have to talk about this right now?" Rayshawn asked. "I need to get out of here."

"Yes we do. I mean do you even care that you've fucked both of us now?" Rayshawn looked at her, but continued to get dressed. "Do you remember the night before you went away to college? The night I was in your room expressing my feelings for you. I mean damn Rayshawn you were my first."

"Can you turn around so I can put my pants back on?" Rayshawn asked.

"Are you serious? What's up with you? I just seen your ass naked upstairs. Now you trying to act all shy."

Rayshawn turned his back. He wasn't being shy. He just didn't want Kiara to know that he couldn't make his erection go down. Rayshawn quickly put the rest of his clothes on, then headed for the steps with Kiara not too far behind.

"Why continue to have sex with me if you were interested in screwing other women, and of all people my mother? Why ask me to come over your house the other night and fuck you on your mother's bed if things were gonna come to this?"

Rayshawn had completely forgotten about the other night when Kiara was over and accidentally answered his mother's phone. "You got me into a lot of trouble with my mother over that dumb shit you pulled. I can't believe you did that."

Kiara folded her nutmeg colored arms. "Oh, so everything is my fault now, huh?" When Rayshawn didn't respond, she continued like a nagging wife. "I can't believe you're treating me this way. I can't believe you have nothing to say to me. Well, let's just see what your mother thinks about all of this. I bet this will make one hell of a birthday present."

At that moment, it was almost as if lighting struck him. It was his mother's birthday, and he'd totally forgot. Rayshawn ran up the steps and out to his car without looking back even once. To say that he didn't have time to deal with the drama between Kiara and Ko-Ko was an understatement. He started up his car, then peeled out of the subdivision imitating an old Dukes of Hazard move before moving onto Highway 210. Trying his best to get home before his mother got up, Rayshawn ran through several lights then exceeded the speed limit on the beltway all the way to Largo.

When he made it home, fifteen minutes later, Rayshawn quickly parked his car then headed inside. Cursing at himself that he didn't stop and get a card first, he took off his Nike boots with hopes of not making too much noise when he walked across the hardwood floors. Rayshawn was relieved when he finally made it downstairs to his room and fell across his bed.

"Did you think you were just gonna stroll your ass up in here and not have me to answer too?" Lynn questioned. She was sitting in an old recliner that sat across the room with an evil scowl.

Shit, he thought. In a way, he hated that fact that she treated him like a little boy all the time. "Ma, let me ask you something first. Are you down here because I didn't come home last night or are you down here to say that I can't stay out all night?"

"I'm saying that while you're still under my damn roof, you'll at least call me, leave a message on the voicemail or some kind of note on the fucking refrigerator to let me know that you're alright."

"Okay, that's not a problem. While I'm under *your* roof that won't be an issue."

"So, who were you with?"

"Ma, does that even matter?"

Lynn twirled her hair around her fingers. "Yes, it does. I need to know who you're with at all times. I'm still responsible for you, Rayshawn. I mean who and what would keep you out all night?" Before he could answer, Lynn began to shake her head. "Never mind. I already know the answer. I hope she was worth it."

Lynn stood up and smoothed the wrinkles out of her shirt. "Now get your ass up. I need you to follow me to drop my car off at the auto shop," Lynn said, walking toward the basement steps.

Rayshawn rolled over and pulled his pillow over his head. The sound of his mother's voice banged against his brain like a sledge hammer. All he wanted to do at the moment was rest.

"Get up, Rayshawn. I want to be one of the first persons at the service door when they open." Lynn could tell that his night out was getting the best of him. "Nobody told your ass to stay out all night, fucking some girl. Get your ass up, now," she added.

"Okay, Ma I'll be upstairs in five minutes," he replied.

Lynn turned to leave. "Rayshawn, can you answer one question for me?"

"Sure."

"Why is your dick still hard? You couldn't even make that shit go down before you got here?"

Rayshawn was humiliated. He couldn't believe his mother was even paying attention to him in that area. "It's a long story," Rayshawn said, sitting up on the bed.

"Let me break that shit down for you again like I always do. I better not be an early grandmother. These stank-ass girls fuck anything walking. But when they find someone who has potential of making something out of himself, they connect themselves and start dropping babies just to be a part of his life forever. That shit *is not* going to happen with you though. I raised you better than that."

Rayshawn sighed. "I already told you, Ma you don't have to worry about that."

Lynn was on her way up the steps when she suddenly stopped. "Oh, yeah, how is it going with Ko-Ko down at that magazine?"

Rayshawn jumped up. "What you mean? Why?"

"Well, I was just checking. I told her to take it easy on you."

"Oh, I kept up," Rayshawn said, feeling confident his mother had no idea of what he and Ko-Ko did the night before.

As Lynn made her way back upstairs, her cell phone began to ring. Rayshawn's heart began beating like a drum, once he heard his mother acknowledge Kiara. Creeping up the steps, he tried his best to eavesdrop and wait for the moment when his mother went ballistic, but that moment never came. His heart began to beat a hundred miles a minute. The increase of adrenaline had finally made his erection go down. *What the fuck is*

Kiara saying to my mother? Please Lord, don't let that bitch say anything about me having sex with Ko-Ko. I promise I'll stop.

Chapter Seven

When ten minutes passed, Rayshawn sat on the edge of his bed wondering what his mother and Kiara were still talking about on the phone. The pounding in his chest felt like the bass drum coming out the trunk of an SUV when Lynn yelled for him to come upstairs.

"Rayshawn, get up here now!" She sounded angry.

Not wanting to piss her off more than she already sounded, Rayshawn slowly walked up the basement steps like a punished three year old. When he made it upstairs, he turned to find his mother sitting at the dining room table tapping her foot against the floor.

"Yes."

"Is there something that you want to say to me?"

Rayshawn dropped his head. Even though he really didn't know how to answer her question, he still wasn't about to come clean about anything. Who snitched on themselves? "Ma, I don't know what you're talking about. What do I have to tell you?"

"Why is it that my phone is ringing off the hook and everyone is wishing me a happy birthday except for you? I can't believe you would forget my damn birthday. Now you're acting like a typical damn man."

Rayshawn started to laugh. He wiped his forehead and let out a sigh of relief.

"I'm glad you find amusement in my pain," Lynn said standing up.

"No Ma, you got it all wrong. I wasn't laughing at you. I was thinking about something else. I could never forget your birthday. I wanted to make you another special breakfast, but just lost track of time," Rayshawn replied walking over and hugging Lynn.

It seemed like Lynn was beginning to accept his apology, but the lost track of time remark really hurt her. Her eyes started to squint. She then balled her fist and began tapping them on her legs. "What the hell could you have been doing that was so important to lose track of time on my birthday?"

"It's no need to go over any specifics. They just had a lot of work for me to do. Can we leave it at that?" he replied.

"I mean…was she that good?"

Rayshawn hated when his mother acted like this. "Ma, please."

"If the roles were reversed and I missed your birthday, how the hell would you be feeling right about now?" Lynn asked walking over to him. "Besides, you smell like fresh soap, so I know what that means. I don't know why you think I'm one of those kids on the short yellow bus. Stop trying to play me."

Rayshawn started to laugh. He turned to walk away, but Lynn grabbed him by his right arm. Rayshawn looked back to see that his mother was still waiting for a response to where and what was so important that he'd forgotten her special day.

"You didn't answer me," Lynn said.

"I did. There's nothing more to say."

"You better say something."

Rayshawn pulled his arm away from Lynn's grasp. "Seriously Ma, you need to mind your business on this one. I was working real hard to make it through on my project and that's it," Rayshawn said with a stern look on his face.

"Did you just say mind my business?" Before Rayshawn could respond, Lynn smacked him across the face. It wasn't a hard slap, but enough to get his attention. "I know you didn't just get smart with me. Now, you've really lost your damn mind. I brought you into this world and if you ever talk to me like that again, I'll take your ass out," Lynn added on.

Rayshawn stood, holding his cheek. He was stunned over her reaction. "I'm sorry, Ma. I meant that I didn't do anything but work late. I'm trying to make you proud. I'll never let work come before you again."

Lynn eyed her son. "I hate the fact that you're working at that smut magazine. I hope Ko-Ko isn't working you too hard." She tried to change the tone.

Rayshawn reflected on his work with Ko-Ko and laughed. The pain immediately left his face with thoughts of her laying on top of him riding his dick like a rodeo girl going for a gold medal. *If only you knew just how hard she worked me last night it would send chills up your spine.*

"Please don't be mad. Trust me. I could never forget your birthday," Rayshawn pleaded.

"I should make your ass go in that kitchen and cook me that special breakfast again, but we need to get out of here," Lynn informed. "Oh, by the way, Kiara was nice enough to make all of us some plans for dinner at the Cheesecake Factory out in Tyson's Corner tonight. Everyone is gonna meet up at seven o'clock."

"Kiara made the reservations. When did you and her get so buddy-buddy?" Rayshawn asked. He was worried that Kiara would try and cause a scene at dinner.

"What are you saying? Kiara is like a daughter to me. Just like you're probably like a son to Ko-Ko. I mean, don't you think it's weird how she hired a rookie photographer as an assistant for the magazine when there were tons of people more qualified than you," Lynn replied.

"I don't believe she thinks of me like a son."

"Why you say that? Did something happen at work?"

"No, nothing happened. I'm just saying that I just don't think Ko-Ko sees me as a son."

"Boy you sounding real dumb. That woman watched you

grow up. You and Kiara were always together. We used to say
that the two of you would marry one another because you were
around each other so much." Lynn laughed, showing her one
dimple.

Rayshawn didn't want to hear any more. "I'll be a little
late getting to the restaurant. I have a few errands to run this
evening. Oh, by the way I'm no longer the assistant photographer. I already got a promotion."

Lynn couldn't believe it. "What? You just got there." She
then suddenly got suspicious. "Hold up…how did that happen?
Because you don't mind working late?"

Rayshawn grinned. "No, Ma. I'm just as surprised as you
are. The lead photographer left, so instead of replacing him with
someone else, I guess they decided to promote me."

"Well, I guess I need to say congratulations. But
wait…what do you mean you'll be late? What errands do you
have to do that would make you late for my birthday dinner?
We just had this long talk about not letting work come before
me. Did you forget that shit already?"

"I didn't forget. I just need to go pick up something that's
a surprise and I can only get it later on in the day. But don't
worry. I'll be there," Rayshawn said, before walking off so Lynn
couldn't respond.

He better not miss this get together or he'll get a fucking
surprise, Lynn said her herself.

"There's a forty-five minute wait," the hostess said to
Rayshawn as he entered the restaurant.

"I'm here with the McMillan party. They should be here
already."

The hostess looked at her laminated seating chart. "Oh,
yes I'm sorry. Right this way."

Rayshawn froze when they walked past the bar and he

saw Kiara, Ko-Ko, Tootie and Melyssa all sitting at the table with Lynn. The conversation came to a halt once he walked up and the hostess pulled back the last empty chair. He felt all the eyes on him.

This is going to be a very interesting dinner, he thought sitting next to Ko-Ko. *And why the hell is this the only available seat?*

"It's about damn time," Lynn said to her son.

Kiara let out a loud laugh that everyone knew wasn't necessary.

"I mean damn, can you at least sit beside me?" Lynn continued. She began to pout like a toddler.

"Please don't start, Ma. I told you that I had a few things to do before I got here. It took a little longer than I had expected downloading some pictures from my camera into the computer. This is my first time using one of those Apple Mac things. Plus, the guy was running behind as well," Rayshawn said.

"What guy?" Lynn asked.

Rayshawn pulled a dozen of orange Tiger Lillies from behind his back. He knew that they were her favorite. After that, he reached into his pocket and retrieved a little black box. "The jeweler in Georgetown was running behind with all his customers," he said extending his hand.

When Lynn opened the box her eyes quickly became glassy. Rayshawn had gotten her a white gold locket on a sixteen inch chain. It was exactly like the one she'd lost when he went away to college. Once she opened the locket and found a picture of him and her from his high school graduation, tears were already making their appearance.

"It's beautiful. I love it. Look at this!" Lynn said, in excitement as she passed it around the table. "My son is so thoughtful."

"I wanted to get it engraved, but I ran out of money, so you'll just have to wait until I get my first paycheck. Remember, you took my bank card," Rayshawn added.

Lynn wanted to ask where he even got the money to buy

the necklace, but refused to ruin the moment. "Hey Ko-Ko, does anyone else at that magazine work? I mean, you seem to be riding my son awfully hard," Lynn blurted out.

"I know what you mean, Lynn. She's riding him from sun up to sun down," Kiara said with a laugh.

Everyone looked over at Kiara. Rayshawn's jaw dropped to his chest. His heart rate increased, accompanied by a large knot in his throat.

"Did anybody ask your ass anything?" Ko-Ko shot back.

Lynn shook her head. "Well, don't get used to it. Rayshawn is going back to school, and finishing his degree. He's going to be a doctor or he'll need one, that's for sure."

"I know what you want him to be, but he's a grown man now. I'm sure he can decide on what he wants to do for the rest of his life," Ko-Ko said.

"I wonder if Rayshawn will be one of those doctors who makes house calls. I'm sure he'll be good at that. He can drop by and check on his patients then give them a little TLC," Kiara included.

Both Melyssa and Tootie laughed.

Lynn glanced over at Kiara and wondered what she was talking about, but quickly turned her head back toward Ko-Ko. *If she's not going to be part of the solution, then she's part of the problem,* Lynn thought. "Look, don't put any ideas in my son's head. I've worked real hard to have him make something out of his life and not throw it all away for a hobby job."

When the waitress walked up and asked Rayshawn if he cared for anything, he ordered his food along with a shot of Remy and another round of wine for the ladies to try and get the attention off of his mother's comments. They were finishing their appetizers of fried calamari and spinach dip when Rayshawn suddenly felt Ko-Ko's hand rubbing his leg under the table. He quickly grabbed a nacho and slid it in the dip to try and focus on something else.

As Ko-Ko slid her hand up his thigh to his crotch, the soft flicks on his dick made him choke on food. Ko-Ko laughed as she felt his manhood growing in size with every circular motion. Trying his best not to seem obvious, Rayshawn glanced around the table to make sure no one had any inclination what Ko-Ko was doing. His eyes locked on Melyssa, who sat directly across from him. At that moment, Rayshawn moved Ko-Ko's hand away, but seconds later it was back rubbing him even harder.

Kiara looked over and realized that Rayshawn was beginning to sweat and fidget in his chair. "So, Aunt Lynn, what's your thoughts about an older woman and younger man in a relationship?"

Ko-Ko yanked her hand from underneath the table and took a sip from her drink. She then looked over at Kiara and wondered where her daughter was going with the question. *Daughter or not, I will fuck Kiara's ass up if she says anything about me and Rayshawn in front of everybody*, Ko-Ko said to herself.

"I really never thought about it in a negative way. Hell, if it takes a young blood to rock your world and the woman is happy, then age doesn't really matter," Lynn responded.

"Not me. I have to know the age. Anything under ten years is nasty. I would feel like I'm sleeping with a baby. I'm too old to be raising a child," Tootie added.

"As old as you act, he probably wouldn't want to be with you anyway," Ko-Ko joked. "Look at you with that old-ass looking shirt. Are those shoulders pads that I'm looking at?"

"Fuck you, Ko-Ko," Tootie fired back. "Let's see what you're wearing tonight." She looked at her friend up and down. "Oh, a normal pair of thigh-high hooker boots. How lady-like."

Ko-Ko raised her fork and held it in a stabbing motion. It probably wasn't a good idea that they were sitting beside each other.

Kiara spoke back up. "Let's get a man's perspective. How do you feel about dating an older woman Rayshawn?"

Lynn squinted her eyes as Rayshawn thought about how to answer the question. "Well, I just love women in general so it really doesn't matter to me. I mean older women will obviously understand how to treat a man, so it's different but in a good way. Younger women are stupid," he said, giving Kiara a look that defined the last comment was meant specifically for her.

"Are you saying that a woman my age wouldn't know how to treat you? I know for a fact that there are some real mature women out here my age," Kiara replied. She looked over at her mother, who was obviously not interested in the conversation. She'd picked up her phone, tuning everyone out.

"I know that's right. Tell 'em," Melyssa chimed in.

Rayshawn jumped, when he felt Ko-Ko's hand back on his thigh. "I'm not saying that there aren't any women my age who know how to treat a man like me, but the probability of me meeting her is probably slim. Why are we talking about this anyway? Let's change the subject."

"It's actually interesting," Lynn stated.

"So, if your mother brought home a guy about your age and introduced him as her man, that wouldn't bother you at all?" Kiara continued to drill.

Rayshawn removed Ko-Ko's hand under the table once again. "I know it's not too many guys my age who would be able to handle my mother, so that thought never crossed my mind. But it's her call because it's her life."

"Speaking of a man, Lynn, when the hell are you going to go out with that cute doctor at the hospital who keeps flirting with you? Girl, it's time to put those batteries away," Ko-Ko said. "What's his name again? George?"

Lynn gave her friend the look of death. She was always uncomfortable talking about men or her sex life around her son. "It's Garrett, and I don't know when I'm going to call him back. Hell, maybe I'll call when I lose some weight." She played with her hair for a few seconds. "Can we talk about something else?"

Rayshawn was about to continue when his phone began to vibrate. He pulled out to find a text message from Ko-Ko:

I want u so bad. Don't u want me? Go to the bathroom now. I'll meet u. If u try to ignore me, I'll

keep texting!

Rayshawn quickly closed his phone, then excused himself from the table. "It's my boss Ms. Contour, I have to take this call outside," he announced.

"You know I'm really sick of that fucking job already, Rayshawn. Hurry up and come back. Our food should be here soon," Lynn stated.

Rayshawn got up and walked around the bar and out of their sight. He then dipped around the hostess and walked toward the bathrooms. He pretended to be on his phone as Ko-Ko stepped up to him moments later. She didn't give him any small talk though. Instead, she grabbed him and stuck her tongue in his mouth.

Ko-Ko backed Rayshawn into the women's bathroom still kissing him vigorously. She didn't even bother to see if anyone was already inside. She continued to kiss him as they stumbled into the last stall going at it like two high school seniors.

"I want to taste your dick. Take it out," Ko-Ko ordered.

"Are you serious? We're in the women's bathroom with my mother and your daughter outside in the restaurant," Rayshawn whispered then pushed her back. "Besides, they'll probably get suspicious if both of us are gone from the table."

"Don't worry about that. They think I'm outside smoking. Now, give me my dick." She had already claimed his manhood.

"I can't believe this. Are you joking?"

"Does it look like I'm joking? I want to feel *my* dick in my mouth right now," Ko-Ko said, pulling their bodies back together.

"I'm not sure about this."

"I said take my dick out. And since you wanna brag about being with older women and getting a call from Felice, I want you to call me mommy and follow my every command because you came off like a real momma's boy."

Rayshawn looked at Ko-Ko in awe. Realizing she wasn't going to give up, he fumbled with the zipper on his jeans then finally released his dick from his pants. Ko-Ko's eye's lit up as she squatted down and fully took him into her mouth. Rayshawn reached out his hands and held on to the sides of the stall watching Ko-Ko suck him like vampire at a blood bank. Ko-Ko then dug her nails into his butt cheeks as his dick pounded the back of her throat.

"I said call me mommy," Ko-Ko said, yanking his dick out her mouth.

"Don't stop. Keep going." At that point, Rayshawn could care less who was in the bathroom either.

"I want to hear you say thank you mommy for all that you do. Let me know how grateful you are for all that I do for you. You better make me believe that you think I'm the best mother in the world."

"Please mommy. I need you to keep going. You're the best mother in world. Thank you for all that you do," Rayshawn moaned.

Rayshawn reached down and grabbed the back of Ko-Ko's head. He began to push and pull her by the hair as her grip tightened. The tingling feeling began in his toes then moved up his legs like a plague. He felt the release of his thick juices reaching the tip of his dick. At that moment, he rammed his tool fully into her mouth and shot ounces of his cum into her mouth. He tried his best to hit her tonsils before his legs buckled and he fell back into the wall. Ko-Ko still continued to suck as his eyes rolled up into his head.

"Who's your fucking mommy?" she asked, jerking the last bit of cum out his shaft.

Rayshawn leaned against the stall door. He glanced down at Ko-Ko pulling on his dick. *She can't be serious,* he thought. *The role playing shit needs to be over.*

"I want you to tell me if mommy made her dick feel good."

"This had to be hands down the best head I've ever had in my life. My shit is still cumming."

"You see what happens when you find a real woman. I'm

sure you were fucking amateurs back in school, but now you've met a professional with years of practice on pleasing her man," Ko-Ko bragged.

Suddenly, the door to the bathroom opened, which instantly made Ko-Ko stop talking, especially, when she heard the voices of Tootie and Melyssa walking inside. Ko-Ko gestured for Rayshawn to climb up on the toilet so they wouldn't see two pair of shoes under the stall.

"Girl, I can't believe you're still with that man of yours," Tootie said.

"I know things are happening so fast," Melyssa replied.

"Are you sure you're doing the right thing? There are a lot of good looking men out here. How do you know you found mister right?"

Melyssa smiled. "I don't, that's what so funny about it. I'm just stepping out on faith."

"Speaking of stepping out, I wouldn't mind stepping out with Rayshawn. He's grown up to be one fine piece of ass," Tootie admitted. She looked in the mirror and touched the small mole on her cheek. A beauty mark just like the famous, Marilyn Monroe.

Rayshawn glanced down at Ko-Ko. He had a large smile on his face. Ko-Ko however, didn't find the comment funny in the least bit. She looked up at Rayshawn as too say, *I wish you would.*

"Girl, you ain't lying. I mean a sexy young guy like that saying that he doesn't mind dating older women is rare. If I wasn't already in a relationship, I'd love to take him on a test try," Melyssa admitted.

"I would fuck the shit out of his young-ass," Tootie added.

"You know what. I'm not sure, but I thought I saw Ko-Ko flirting with him back at the table," Melyssa said, washing her hands.

"You lying. Well, shit now that I'm thinking about it, that wouldn't even surprise me. You know her nasty-ass is always thinking with her pussy instead of her head," Tootie stated. "She been doing that shit for years. The bitch be on her back so much, I wonder what the hell her legs are for."

Both women burst out laughing.

Ko-Ko wanted to walk out and confront them both, but Rayshawn grabbed her arm. He looked at her and shook his head side to side moving his lips to say, "no."

"Ain't that the damn truth? Once a hoe, always a hoe. I mean shit, she fucked everybody in Berry Farm back in the day, so she's probably still up to her old tricks. I'm sure every man up at the magazine has tapped that ass," Melyssa said.

"Ko-Ko really needs to calm her ass down. If she's not careful, she going to catch something that a simple shot won't get rid of," Tootie agreed.

Melyssa made sure every strand of her pixie styled hair-cut was in place. "Remember when Ko-Ko fucked those three guys we met that night at Ben's Chili Bowl. Did I ever tell you that Lynn told me that one of them burnt her ass?"

"You and Lynn never told me that shit. That's one wild bitch. I feel sorry for whatever man tries to put a saddle on that pony."

They both began to laugh again. Rayshawn held Ko-Ko tight until they left the bathroom and he heard the door close. Rayshawn started laughing himself once he let her go and they exited the stall.

"What's so damn funny?" Ko-Ko asked.

"I'm not sure. If I didn't know better, I would think you were a little jealous because your girlfriends find me sexy and they want to fuck me. Either that or you're mad because they think of you as some little sex freak that can't control herself."

"Me jealous? Nigga please…you got the wrong woman. Besides, why should I care what a skinny bitch and a bitch who has no sense of style thinks of me. Shit, but don't get it twisted either. If you knew me and your mother back in the day then you would see how we were *both* freaky. We've shared a many of men. Maybe one night, I'll tell you about the men your mother and I have tag teamed. That's if you're old enough to handle it." Ko-Ko could care less about lying. She didn't want Rayshawn to think she was the only promiscuous one in the bunch.

"You got jokes. I don't wanna hear about my mother smashing some nigga. That shit is nasty."

As soon as Rayshawn finished his sentence, he could hear Lynn's voice coming down the hallway toward the bathroom. When the voice got closer, Ko-Ko and Rayshawn dashed back inside the stall. Just in time as the door opened and Lynn walked in with Melyssa and Tootie.

"Why did you pull us back in here, Lynn? We just left the bathroom?" Tootie asked.

"So what? Besides, I need to fix my make-up. Which one of you has black eyeliner?" Lynn asked. She fixed her bob in the mirror then played with the cow neck sweater she wore.

"So, girl, how's your birthday going so far?" Tootie asked, handing over the make-up case from her purse.

"It's going pretty good, but I don't feel like I'm thirty-eight. Where did all the time go?" Lynn asked. She pulled the pencil out and began applying it.

"How can we make this better for you, sweetie?" Melyssa asked.

"It's not you. I just wish my son would treat this like it's my special day and not just something he's obligated to do," Lynn replied in a low tone.

"Girl, you worry about that boy too much. You need to treat this day like it's special to you. What you need to be doing is going through your phone and finding a number that's guaranteed to make you wake up with back pains in the morning," Melyssa said.

"That's right. You're too overprotective of him. He's going to be okay. If he was a doctor, he'd tell you to find a man and fuck his brains out tonight. Hell, find two if need be and call us in the morning," Tootie added, then pushed her bangs out of her face. "Ko-Ko was right for once. Call Garrett or should I say call Dr. Feelgood."

All three of them started laughing.

"What I need to do is find out where Rayshawn went?" Lynn said. "He's been gone a long-ass time. That phone call can't be that important. And where is Ko-Ko? She didn't come to the bathroom with y'all?"

Tootie and Melyssa gave each other a funny look then shook their head.

"You know Ms. Thang. She's probably in the kitchen fucking the chef," Melyssa replied. "Maybe we can get our food for free."

As all three women laughed, Rayshawn cell phone began to ring. He quickly tried to shut it off before Lynn or one of the others heard it. Ko-Ko grabbed it and tossed it into the toilet.

Lynn stared back at her reflection in the mirror. "Hold up…that sounded like Rayshawn's phone."

"You're tripping, Lynn. Let's go back to the table because it seems like you've had too much wine. Why would he be in here?" Melyssa questioned.

"Yeah, you're probably right. Let's go," Lynn responded.

When all three women finally left, Rayshawn didn't waste anytime rushing out of the stall. He wanted to get out the bathroom before anyone else came back in. Ko-Ko on the other hand was pissed that she'd overheard Melyssa and Tootie's conversation. Even though it was a known fact that the three of them mainly just put up with each other most of the time, she had no idea that they talked that much shit.

When Rayshawn made his way toward the door, Ko-Ko grabbed his arm then kissed him forcefully on the lips. When she began rubbing on his dick once again, he quickly stepped back.

"We're not going to start this up again. Let me get out of here before they come back."

"Is it that easy for you to tell me no? If so, I'm gonna have to do something to change that."

After kissing one last time, Rayshawn was the first to

leave the bathroom and return to the table. His mother along with the rest of the ladies gave him a long stare…like they knew he'd been up to something. Rayshawn wondered if he had that *guilty* look on his face. Ko-Ko however never returned. She left without saying a word to anyone not even Rayshawn, which didn't bother him. He wanted to get through the rest of his mother's birthday peacefully. He just hoped no one asked to use his phone. Each woman had their own thought about why Ko-Ko didn't come back, but Kiara was the closest.

I bet she fucked the nigga outside in the car then left, Kiara thought. *Damn. Kourtney, one…Kiara zero.*

Chapter Eight

The forecast had called for sunny skies, but Rayshawn couldn't tell by looking up to see the thick clouds blocking any chance for the sun to come out and play. He drove to work the next day still thinking about his restroom rendezvous with Ko-Ko. It was the first time he'd ever gotten his dick sucked in a public place, and hopefully wouldn't be the last. Ko-Ko had proven that she had a hell of a sex drive, so he couldn't wait until their next encounter. The only problem he had was trying to find a way to tell Kiara her services were no longer needed. Somehow he had to smooth things over, so she wouldn't let his mother know what was going on. The task was going to be challenging, but had to be done. Sexing a mother and daughter long term, seemed fun, but he knew it couldn't go down like that.

As Rayshawn continued to think, he almost crashed his car when he caught a glimpse of Felice walking toward the building in her four inch stiletto boots. Rayshawn admired how her black bubble Bebe dress swayed in the light breeze. It was if the sun was held captive by the clouds until Felice decided to strut down the street. The bright rays seemed to inch its way out with each step, and by the time she reached the front door, it glared off her soft brown skin. Rayshawn laughed as several guys on the street tried to get her attention, but were instantly rejected by her complete lack of interest. Not only did she ignore them, but she never missed a step.

Rayshawn quickly pulled into an open parking space to try and catch up with her. After shutting off the ignition, he sprinted like Carl Lewis into the building and was glad to see her just stepping through the elevator doors.

"Hold the door, please!" he shouted.

When Felice stuck out her black briefcase to stop the doors from closing, Rayshawn stepped inside and thanked her for the help. However, when another person yelled for them to hold the door as well, Felice deliberately pushed the button to close them instead.

Rayshawn flashed a smile. "That was cold, Ms. Contour."

"I used my quilted Bottega Veneta to ride up with you alone. I couldn't risk damaging my two thousand dollar briefcase to share an elevator with anyone else. They can catch the next one."

When Rayshawn looked over to see what was so special that would make someone pay two grand for a bag to carry some files, he didn't get past Felice's thick thighs and tight work out ass. With long legs that ran for days, she was a full figured woman with enormous breasts and full lips. When Felice saw him staring, she bent over to rub her ankle as if she had an itch that had to be scratched just to give him a little tease. Rayshawn leaned back to get a look at her entire ass and not just the side shot. Either way, he enjoyed the view.

Once the elevator doors opened on the fourth floor, and Felice and Rayshawn walked inside the office, ironically Ko-Ko and two models were standing at the receptionist desk talking to Nikki. Anger was immediately expressed on Ko-Ko's face as she watched Rayshawn opening the door for Felice like a true gentleman. The slight smirk Felice gave even made Ko-Ko crack her knuckles. She looked like a warrior ready for battle once Felice stopped in front of them.

"Good morning, ladies," Felice said.

Everyone returned the heart warming greeting except for Ko-Ko of course. She was only interested in a staring competition.

Nikki decided to give Rayshawn a separate shout out. "Good morning, boo. You looking good as ever."

Rayshawn smiled. "Thanks."

"When are we going to lunch?" Nikki held one of her fire engine red fingernails in the air. "Let me just say this now. I asked him first, so y'all skinny b's better back up." She wanted to say bitches so bad, but knew Felice may not approve.

While the models laughed, Ko-Ko and Felice kept eyeing each other. Ko-Ko wasn't worried about Nikki. She wasn't a threat, Felice however was.

Rayshawn didn't want to ignore Nikki, especially in front of everyone. "We'll see. They keep me pretty busy around here."

"Excuse me, but is that a Bebe dress?" one of the models interrupted.

"Yes, it is," Felice answered.

"I thought so. I just saw it in the window at Pentagon City the other day. That's a bad dress. I wish I had your shape," the model complimented.

Ko-Ko couldn't take it any longer. "Oh, please. Okay, I'm going back to my desk."

"Actually Ms. Jackson, I need you to get the team together right away. We need to meet a little earlier this morning to discuss an upcoming event that I've worked out," Felice said before Ko-Ko could walk away.

"What event? Where…" Ko-Ko tried to say.

"No need in me going into details right now. Just get the team in the conference room in ten minutes and I'll break the news to everyone," Felice said cutting her off.

"Okay, but cutting me off wasn't necessary," Ko-Ko said, with an instant attitude.

Felice tried to be calm, but she was beyond tired of Ko-Ko's mouth. "Just get everyone assembled." After that she walked away…swaying her hips of course.

When Rayshawn finished watching Felice switch all the

way down the hall, Ko-Ko gave him a kidney punch to acknowledge that his actions were completely inappropriate.

He placed his hands in the air. "What?"

"You like what you see? I can't believe you find her ass sexy," Ko-Ko said walking away. "That bitch is far from that."

All the models eyes bulged, even Nikki as Ko-Ko quickly walked away with Rayshawn not too far behind. After following her into the break room, he ran up behind Ko-Ko and put her in a bear hug.

"What's the problem? I was just looking at her dress. I was trying to see what was so special about the outfit that had the model freaking out. That's all."

"Don't try to be nice now. Looking at another woman while I'm in your damn presence is unacceptable." When Rayshawn flashed a sexy smile, Ko-Ko couldn't help but soften a little bit. "If you really want to make it up to me then go gather everyone for this fucking meeting." She pushed his arms from around her before anyone could see them.

"Okay...*mommy*." Rayshawn smacked Ko-Ko's ass.

While watching Ko-Ko rub her stinging butt inside her David Kahn skinny leg jeans, his dick twitched as her hand seemed to circle in slow motion. Rayshawn had to adjust his penis as his erection began to grow. He then had to tell himself to calm down.

"Thanks, baby," Ko-Ko said, blowing him a kiss. While leaving the room, of course she had to sway her hips as well. She wasn't about to be outdone by any woman.

Fifteen minutes later, Felice sat at the end of the cherry wood conference table waiting for the technician to hook up the PowerPoint presentation. The team entered, wondering what the big news was and continued to whisper amongst themselves about what it could be. However, their private conversations came to an end as Felice stood and cleared her throat.

"Good morning everyone, we have a lot of work to go over today, no need to delay any longer. I have some very good news."

Ko-Ko sat at the other end of the table rocking back and fourth in her chair. Felice might as well been talking in French because she wasn't paying her any attention. Instead, she focused on critiquing Felice's little dress. *What's so special about that cheap shit anyway?* Ko-Ko said to herself. *Bebe...my dresses cost three times as much as that.* Her thoughts came to an end when the sound of Felice saying something about the islands echoed inside her head. Ko-Ko leaned forward and finally spoke up, "What did you say about the islands?"

Felice stopped and gave Ko-Ko a frown. *I know I told her on more than one occasion that I didn't like to repeat myself. Is she trying to be funny?* Felice wondered. "Mr. McMillan, can you please rephrase what I just said to Ms. Jackson who obviously wasn't listening."

Everyone turned their head toward Ko-Ko. Rayshawn and everyone else couldn't help but snicker as he flipped back his note pad to reread his notes. Ko-Ko felt the sting of Felice's comment, but kept her composure.

"The company is going to the Hedonism Resort in Negril, Jamaica for the upcoming anniversary edition of the magazine. The itinerary, which is already confirmed, is that we'll arrive on Wednesday, March 3rd and return on Monday, March 8th which is six days. The theme of this shoot is Girlz in Paradise. You said that we should be able to get the entire shoot done in three days and the team will be given the last three days to relax for all the hard work we've been doing. Did I leave anything out?" Rayshawn asked.

"You left out that you and I will be going down two days prior than anyone else to scout out potential locations for certain shots," Felice said with a huge smile.

"Hold up, what about me? I'm the one who selects the locations, times and sets for everyone," Ko-Ko informed.

Felice walked around the table and stopped behind Rayshawn's chair. She put her hands on his shoulder, giving him a light massage.

"Well, I've decided that I want this edition of Fantasy

Girlz to be my pet project. You will come down with everyone else. Mr. McMillan can brief you on our locations and if you have any concerns, then get them out of your head because I built this company from nothing. I'm more than capable of figuring out the best places to take pictures."

Everybody's head rocked from side to side as the conversation began to heat up.

Ko-Ko was furious. "I'm not saying you can't. I just don't understand why Ray…I mean Mr. McMillan is going in place of me."

"I want a pair of fresh eyes on this project. Your last few releases for the magazine have been kind of similar, so I think we need some outside the box ideas on this one." Felice began to massage Rayshawn's shoulder again.

"Well, that excuse is just not good enough for me," Ko-Ko countered.

The room went completely silent. Everyone couldn't wait for Felice's next reply or what was about to go down. The entire conversation was almost Jerry Springer material. Felice pinched Rayshawn's shoulder until he jerked, then walked back to the end of the table.

"We need a quick break. I need everyone to step out of the room for a few minutes except for you, Kourtney Jackson," Felice ordered.

The look on Felice's face made the team immediately get up from their seats and quickly exit the room. As everyone filed out, Ko-Ko continued to stare at Felice. The door hadn't even closed all the way when Felice immediately began shouting.

"How dare you challenge my judgment in front of my employees? I think you've forgotten whose name is on the bottom line of the checks being written around here. You need to think real hard the next time you open your mouth in front of everyone."

"Who do you think you're talking to?" Ko-Ko asked.

Felice looked around the empty conference room. "I must be talking to you, *Kourtney* because there's no one else in here but the two of us."

Ko-Ko hated when people called her by her government name, especially Felice. She preferred her nickname, which was given to her by her late grandmother. "I'll ask you as many questions about a photo shoot as I want. That's my job!" Ko-Ko banged her fist on the table. "I mean you must've forgotten that I'm the one who puts this magazine on the stands around the world every month."

"So, what the hell do I do? Just sit behind a desk and look pretty."

"You might do the first part of sitting behind the desk, but I don't know about the second part."

Felice didn't find Ko-Ko's sarcasm too funny. "If you ever pull a stunt like asking me why I made a decision or talking to me in that tone, I'll fire your ass on the spot. Are we clear on that?" Felice banged her fist on the table as well.

Ko-Ko laughed. "You'll fire who? Are you joking? Bitch did you forget who you're dealing with? Did you forget that we go way back? Don't make me pull your card." Ko-Ko had Felice's undivided attention. "Did you forget about the information that I have on you? Did you forget that I was the one you called when your ass got locked up for that call girl service you had? Did you forget that your broke-ass didn't have any money after that? You begged me to help you out. I'm the one who made you, and if you keep showing off, I'll be the one to expose your ass," Ko-Ko warned. "Shit, I really should be the CEO. I just let you be in charge."

"I know you're extra loud so you can try and embarrass me, but all that shit about the call girl service is ancient history. Tell the whole fucking world if you want. Nobody will care about my past as long as they're getting a paycheck. Go ahead and scream your head off. My future is pretty bright baby." Felice gave a devious grin. "Especially if Rayshawn is involved."

"All I know is that I have something in my bag of tricks that people won't let you slide by with so easily. You know if I tell the entire story that some folks will dismiss your future as a fucking nightmare. Let's not forget…I know your other secret, bitch!"

Felice's entire demeanor changed. "Don't go there."

"Let me see you up in Rayshawn's face again. Not only will I spill the beans, but I'll rock the very foundation that you think you built. You better stay clear of what's mine or else."

"Oh, so you're claiming him now?"

Ko-Ko nodded. "I guess you can say that. As a matter of fact, you can ask him for yourself."

"Well, if that's the case and he's so into you, why does he keep checking me out every chance he gets?" Felice inquired. "Maybe I'll ask him that."

"Whatever bitch. All I know is that you need to stay away. I mean seriously, Felice. You're not right for him, and you know that."

Felice frowned. "And you are?"

"Yes, I am."

Felice didn't respond. She just looked at Ko-Ko with a blank expression. Ko-Ko's expression on the other hand said that she wasn't playing. Ko-Ko glanced over at the door and could see the shadows of people's feet moving from the other side. She wanted to tell Felice, "*Fuck you and your company,*" but didn't want to give her the satisfaction of thinking she ran her out of there.

This bitch is really trying to play high post. I got her number now. If she thinks she's just going to pull up on my man and talk all big and bad, I got something for her. This shit is only the beginning and we'll see whose laughing at the end, Ko-Ko thought still staring at Felice.

"Do you need to say anything else?" Felice asked. She could hear whispering on the other side of the door.

"Actually I do. Now that I think about it you're right, Ms. Contour. This is your company and if you want to go pick out the locations then what am I complaining about? It's less work for me and if it turns out bad, then you have only yourself to blame," Ko-Ko said, storming out of the office.

Ko-Ko walked down the hallway with everyone's eyes glued to her like fly paper. When she went into her office and opened up her file cabinet, she pulled out her emergency bottle of Ciroc. Ko-Ko didn't even use her shot glass; she just took a couple of gulps to the head from the one liter bottle. Ko-Ko then went into the bathroom and splashed water on her face. She lifted her head to see her reflection in the mirror. *Am I losing it? What is it about that big bitch that Rayshawn seems to find more appealing than me? When she's around he doesn't even acknowledge my presence. I must need to do something shocking with this pussy to get that edge back. Fuck that, it will be a cold day in hell before that bitch gets the best of me again. Oh, she'll pay for this one. Fucking with my man right in front of me is unacceptable. Oh, she's going to pay big time.* Ko-Ko decided that she needed to get out of there and just take some alone time. She grabbed her Louis Vuitton Mahina purse and headed out the door.

Chapter Nine

Later that evening, Ko-Ko went home a made herself a hot bath with her Carol's Daughter Body Aches bath salts, then poured herself a glass of wine. She had just put out a cigarette and submerged her body in the water when her house phone began ringing. She reached over and grabbed her cordless off the floor.

"Hello."

"Damn, you sound awful. What's the matter?" Lynn asked.

The line went silent. Ko-Ko leaned back down in the warm water to switch the phone to the other ear. Lynn could hear the water splashing and the grunting noise Ko-Ko made through the phone.

"It sounds like you met your match last night, boo." Lynn laughed.

"Ha-Ha, everybody's a fucking comedian."

"I'm sorry that I seem so insensitive. I was only calling to find out how you were doing because Rayshawn called and told me to check on you. He said you had a little run in at the office today with someone named, Felice. Who's that?"

Ko-Ko let out a long sigh. "It's Rayshawn's boss, but the bitch ain't my boss. Actually, Rayshawn is the main reason I'm so stressed out to begin with."

Lynn stopped in her tracks then put the phone on speaker. "What did my baby do?"

Girl, your son is far from a damn baby, Ko-Ko thought. "She was trying to flex on me to show off for him. I think she likes him more than just on the employee level, but you know I had to check her."

"Really? Oh no, that's not going down. Maybe I need to take a field trip over to the magazine and get to the bottom of this shit. She doesn't know what a terrible idea that would be for all of us. That's why I need my son back in school and not falling for some hoe with a tight body and pretty face."

"Umm. That bitch ain't hardly pretty, and especially not prettier than me," Ko-Ko replied.

"You just love to toot your own horn, huh? I actually can't remember exactly how she looks. I saw her when we all went to Vegas when the magazine first started a few years back, but it was dark in that nightclub, and I saw her from a distance. I didn't get a chance to officially meet her. Even if I saw her on the street, I wouldn't know who she was. I remember her being tall though. Like a Wendy Williams type of chick." Lynn chuckled.

"That's exactly who she reminds me of so I can't see what people find interesting about her."

"Girl, you need to stop faking. Even fucking Stevie Wonder can see that that her body puts both ours to shame," Lynn answered. "Now, I do remember that."

Ko-Ko didn't respond. The last thing she wanted to hear was a compliment about Felice. "Please, that fake bitch. Everything about her is fake. Boobs, eyes everything." At that moment, her anger returned. Picking up her cell phone from off the floor, Ko-Ko went to Rayshawn's name under her address book, and hit the button to send a text to his new phone.

Felice may think she has her eye on u but that can't happen. I'll shut it down b4 people get hurt. U & her going to the islands early, huh? What u gonna do? Call me.

Ko-Ko was so into the text that she'd completely forgot that Lynn was still on the phone.

"Ko-Ko, what are you doing?" Lynn asked.

"I'm sorry girl. That was some dude I met a few days ago. I just had to curse his ass out for texting me for the fifth time today. He's getting on my nerves already, so he's out. Anyway, what were you saying about *my body*."

Lynn laughed. "Is that all your heard? I was just pointing out the obvious, Felice's body is like ours back in the day, especially mine."

"Shit, maybe yours but not mine," Ko-Ko replied. Speaking of her body and thinking about Rayshawn made her move her fingers down beneath the water and circle around her clit. Before long, she had her fingers inside her pussy moving it back and forth. Ko-Ko closed her eyes as soft moans began to escape her mouth

It made Lynn mad instantly. "Bitch, I know you're not doing what I think."

"What did you say sweetie?" Ko-Ko asked in a whispering tone.

"Never mind, you just go ahead and finish pleasing yourself and give me a call when you have some time. Bye."

Rayshawn deliberately decided not to respond to any of Ko-Ko's texts because he'd had enough drama for one day. After she sent the first one, four more texts followed with one crazy message after another. After being around two catty women all day, he decided to hook up with his two best friends at the gym for some male bonding. Growing up without a father, Rayshawn took the bonding with his friends seriously. Although they weren't exactly father figures, his friends were always there when he needed support, a shoulder to lean on or just to talk. Rayshawn commended his mother on an excellent job of raising him and always being his cheerleader, but some things he just couldn't share with her. That's normally the void his friends filled.

After arriving at Capital Sports Complex in District Heights, Rayshawn changed into his gym gear inside the bathroom, then headed straight for the basketball courts. Because his friends were on different teams, Rayshawn knew they would be playing a pick-up game, so he sat on the bench and began lacing up his shoes waiting for the current game to end. Once it was over, his boy's immediately walked over toward him to talk some trash.

"Shawn, what happened to you last night, nigga? You were supposed to meet us at the strip club after work," Damon said. "Trix was looking for you." Regardless of what day it was, Damon loved to make it rain on the local exotic dancers.

"His gay-ass probably found some guy model over at the magazine who took advantage of him," Gary said jokingly.

"Fuck you, nigga," Rayshawn shot back. "Besides, gay muthfuckas don't be at my place of business. It's only beautiful women who walk around naked all day. I mean the name of the place is Fantasy Girlz."

Gary's eye's lit up like the Fourth of July. "You lyin'. All day?"

"All day. Remind me to show you some pictures," Rayshawn replied.

"Damn, I bet it's a rack of phat-ass women down there," Damon chimed in. He rubbed his goatee like he was in deep thought.

"It's a few, but I'm actually tapping my mom's friend Ko-Ko," Rayshawn replied.

Gary threw the ball and hit Rayshawn on the arm. "Oh shit. Ray is fuckin' somebodies' great-grandmother. I'll put a dime on it that that nigga had to keep performin' CPR every time she had an orgasm. Either that or he had to clean out all the cob webs from her pussy just to go in."

Damon had to hold his stomach because he was laughing so hard. "All that young pussy at your job and you want to tap some old broad. Does she wear Depends?"

"You fools are real funny. Let's just play some ball."
Rayshawn said getting up. "Come on bright-light let's go." He
always made fun of Gary's pale complexion. He had a Chico
DeBarge thing going on with his bald-head and thin mustache.

The guys kept saying old women jokes as they walked
over to the court. Moments later, Rayshawn's cell phone rang so
he ran back see who was calling. It was Ko-Ko with another text
message.

**Why wont' u text me back? If u have a little
free time, Y don't u meet me at the Harbor- Mc-
Cormick & Schmick's bar-9 pm. I'm playin' wit your
pussy, but I really need to feel u.**

Rayshawn smiled. He had to admit, Ko-Ko had a way
with words, and could make his dick rise in a second's notice.
He quickly sent a reply.

**I'm at the Capital Sports Complex playing
hoops with the guys. Holla at you later.**

He could barely put the phone down, before she sent an
immediate reply:

**R u saying that u prefer 2 play basketball wit
your friends over this pussy? Yeah Ok. U do u then.**

Rayshawn laughed, then put his cell phone back on the
bench before heading for the court. In his short twenty-one
years, he'd seen this possessive behavior from women before.
Ko-Ko wasn't the first, and she wouldn't be the last. However,
in his mind she did need to pump her brakes a bit.

Rayshawn was in the middle of his third game when he
went up for a rebound and got knocked to the beige colored
paint. It was at that moment, when he rolled over to see a
woman who resembled Felice doing kick-boxing in one of the
group exercise classes. As the woman did several vigorous
kicks, he liked what he saw, especially when he realized it really
was Felice. Sweat looked good on her. Rayshawn got up, called
for a sub and took himself out of the game. He brushed the dirt
off his shorts, grabbed his cell phone off the bench and walked

over toward her.

"Hey nigga, where you going?" Damon yelled.

"I'll be right back. I'm going to talk to someone real quick," Rayshawn replied.

"How can pussy control like that? One day that dick is going to get you into some shit that you won't be able to get out of," Damon added.

"Knowing his dirty-ass, he's already puttin' his dick in some shit," Gary jumped in.

When the other guys on the court laughed, Rayshawn didn't respond…only smiled. As soon as he made his way toward her, he could tell that the class had just ended. When Felice went to get a towel out of her gym bag, Rayshawn walked up behind her.

"Ms. Contour, I didn't know you hung out in the hood."

Felice turned around and smiled. "Boy, please. I'm from the hood. What are you saying anyway? How do people look who hang out in the hood?"

"Maybe I shouldn't have said that," Rayshawn replied. "I've never seen you here working out before. You looked good doing that kick boxing stuff."

"Are you saying that you're here everyday to monitor when and how often people work out?"

Rayshawn smiled. "Let me stop while I'm ahead. You seem to be an expert at twisting shit around."

"I was just kidding. Hey, but on another note since you have that rock hard body, I was wondering if you could give me a few tips on using some of the equipment they have. I need to tighten these puppies up if sexy men like you are going to keep staring at them." Felice pushed up her sweaty breast.

Rayshawn grabbed Felice's right arm. "Sure, I would love to. Follow me." He led Felice over to a public work out area and over to the weight bench. "Lay down while I adjust the weights."

Felice slid her right hand across Rayshawn's chest, then slowly threw her leg over the machine. Rayshawn smiled as she scooted forward keeping her legs spread wide. Felice's pussy formed a fist as she laid back under the weight bar. It appeared that she was getting excited from the stiffness of her nipples. Rayshawn stepped over her, placing his pelvic region directly above her face. He then grabbed her hands and put them on each side of the bar. Moments later, Rayshawn lifted the steel bar of the hooks and assisted it down to her chest.

"I need you to squeeze your chest plates tight as you push the bar into the air. It's important to inhale when it comes down and exhale as you push up," he informed.

"I'm having a hard time concentrating with your dick in my face," Felice said laughing.

"I'm your spotter. I have to stand here so I can keep the bar from falling down and hurting you."

"I'm going to follow your directions because you're the boss. But believe me, the day will come when I'm on top shouting out directions and you better remember to be obedient just like I'm being now."

Rayshawn was shocked by her response. "I like the sound of that."

Felice continued to lift the weight with Rayshawn's help a few time before she got tired. She put it back on the hooks then raised her head and wiped her forehead on his crotch. Rayshawn looked down to see what she was doing.

"Is your dick supposed to be hard when you're my spotter?" she asked.

Rayshawn couldn't wipe the smile off his face. "Well, most weight lifters don't use the dicks of their spotter to get the sweat off their faces."

"Hey Ray, you gonna introduce us to your friend?" Gary asked walking up with Damon.

Rayshawn shook his head and sighed. "Fellas this is my boss, Felice. Felice these are my boys Damon and Gary."

"Damn baby girl, now I see why that nigga is always at work. You can be my boss any day of the week and twice as long on the weekend," Damon said winking an eye.

Rayshawn's friends were definitely blood hounds.

"If you would've spent more time in school instead of the street corner, you've known better than to try that weak-ass line on a woman like me," Felice said getting up.

"Damn," Gary chimed in.

The three of them watched as she got up and walked back toward the common area of the gym. Damon gave Rayshawn a little nudge with his elbow. Rayshawn looked over and gave him a smile and head nod.

"If you're hitting anybody at your job, it needs to be her," Damon said. "I like women who don't take no shit."

"Yeah, she tall as a muthafucka, but fine though," Gary added. "She's one of those pretty stuck up bitches. I bet she only suck the dicks of Bill Gate muthafucka's."

"All I know is if she keeps fucking around, I'm going to break her back one night. You know what they say, every women wants a little thug in them at some point and time." Rayshawn responded.

"Man, fuck that pipe dream. Let's go get another game in," Gary said, pulling on Damon. "You coming, Ray?"

Just when Rayshawn was about to answer, his cell went off. It was Ko-Ko…again

Are u going to meet me or what? I'm not playin' wit u anymore! No…no I'm sorry about that comment. I just miss u. Let me make it up.

"Go ahead and start without me. I need to take care of some business with my job," Rayshawn replied. He could see the disappointment in his friend's eyes.

"Alright, hurry up man," Gary said.

When they disappeared, Rayshawn decided to reply.

Not sure still playing hoops. Oh, and guess who's at the gym- your boss Felice. But don't get hype! It's just a coincidence that she's here.

Ko-Ko replied almost instantly.

U better not b n that bitches face. Fuck that…now I c y you acting funny. U need to have your

ass at the restaurant at 9pm sharp or else!

"Man, Ko-Ko needs to chill the fuck out," Rayshawn said to himself. He was just about to reply when he noticed Felice with her gym bag on her arm. She looked like she was about to leave so Rayshawn ran over to apologize for his friend's dumb-ass remarks. He was a little out of breath trying to catch up with her.

"Felice. Excuse my friends, they just like joking around."

"See, that's why I don't deal with young men. They're too damn immature," Felice announced.

"What about me? Am I included in that bunch?"

Felice paused for a few seconds. "You might be able to get a pass."

They both smiled. "Let's go back and finish the work out before you leave. I feel bad that we were interrupted."

She was hesitant at first but finally gave in. "Sure, why not."

They flirted with one another over the next forty-five minutes until Felice told him she had to leave. Trying to be a complete gentleman, Rayshawn carried her bag and escorted her to the parking lot so they could get as much small talk in as possible. However, once they reached her car, they stopped as if someone had put their feet in concrete. They couldn't believe their eyes. All four of the tires on her new E-Class Mercedes Coupe had been slashed. There were also several long scratches that ran like waves running from the hood to the trunk.

"What the hell happened to my fucking car?" Felice shouted. She looked around the parking lot like the perpetrator was still there.

"Damn. Who would do something like that to such a beautiful car? You must've pissed somebody off real bad."

"I can't understand why someone would do this to my car," Felice said shaking her head. Tears formed in both her eyes.

"Did you dump the wrong man or some shit? A crazy nigga like that is really dangerous. You might want to go get a restraining order on his ass," Rayshawn said, trying to come up with a solution.

Felice pushed him in the chest. "I don't have any psycho-ass dudes after me. I haven't had a man who thought I was his property in years and I doubt very seriously if he's still stalking me. It must've been some jealous bitch driving a Hyundai and can't stand to see someone doing better."

Felice reached for her bag on Rayshawn's shoulder then pulled out her cell and AAA card. She called for a tow truck to come and pick up her car and take it to the Mercedes dealership. Rayshawn waited with her until it arrived twenty minutes later. Felice pulled her famous two thousand dollar briefcase out of the trunk once the guy pulled her car on the flat bed.

"Do you mind giving me a ride to the airport? The Benz dealership is closed by now and I need to rent a car until I can get a loaner car from them. Shit. I still can't believe this."

"Let me run back inside to get my stuff and I'll take you wherever you want to go." When Rayshawn turned to run back inside the gym, he thought he saw a familiar face sitting in a black Honda Accord. The car sat in a parking space a few rows over right in the direction of where Felice stood. He eyed the car closely until he made it to the door. Once he came back out, he looked for the car again, but this time it was gone. *It couldn't have been her,* he thought.

After dropping Felice off at the airport, Rayshawn made his way over the Woodrow Wilson Bridge and contemplated about meeting Ko-Ko. After dealing with her crazy text messages, he really didn't feel like being bothered, but he was also curious why she was threatening him. He hesitated for a few more seconds, then finally took the Harbor exit ready for whatever she had in store.

Entering the newly congested waterfront attraction, Rayshawn made his way to one of the expensive parking garages. When he entered the nice seafood restaurant, he was surprised that Ko-Ko was no were to be found. He even gave a description of Ko-Ko to the hostess, but no one had seen her. Looking at his sports watch, it was only 9:05, so he doubted if she'd left that soon. Rayshawn sat at the corner of the bar so he could watch the basketball game on the 42 inch plasma hanging over the bar. After waiting for another thirty minutes, he was getting ready to leave when he finally heard her sweet voice.

"Only a fool would leave this pussy. I know you ain't even thinking of rolling out already," she whispered in his ear.

Rayshawn turned around. "Actually I was. You told me to be here at nine o'clock sharp and you weren't even here your-self. What's up with that? You got me sitting here looking stupid."

"Oh baby, I'm so sorry. I wanted to look nice for you." She turned around so he could see how good she looked in a black pair of leggings, thigh high boots and a smoke grey Dolce & Gabanna sweater. A sweater that barely covered her thick ass. "How do you want me to make it up to you? You know I will do whatever you want."

Rayshawn finally cracked a smile. "You'll do whatever. Okay, I'm going to remember you said that."

"Do you forgive me?" Ko-Ko said kissing his ear lobe.

"That depends on your smart-ass threat about being here or else. What the hell was that all about?"

Ko-Ko sucked her teeth. "I was just grand standing. I didn't mean anything with that text. It fucked with me a little that you were with that bitch instead of me." When she looked at his gym clothes, it reminded her about it all over again. "You couldn't even change your clothes before you came?"

"Look, I told you I was at the gym. I didn't have time to change my clothes, especially since you wanted to threaten a nigga." Rayshawn stared into Ko-Ko's seductive eyes. "Let me ask you something. You wouldn't happen to own a black Honda

Accord would you?"

"Please…don't be silly. You know I have a Range Rover. Why?"

He shrugged his shoulders. "I thought I saw you over by the gym just before I left that's all."

"No, I don't think so. Maybe it was someone who looked like me."

"Maybe so."

"Listen, I actually fought real hard with the idea of coming here or not. Then I thought it would be better to tell you face to face instead of through a text," she said, changing the subject.

"Before you finish, have a drink with me," he said tapping her leg. "Bartender two double shots of Remy."

After sitting down, Ko-Ko looked up to see who was playing when she felt something wonderful. Rayshawn had stood up and began massaging her neck and shoulders. She closed her eyes as his strong hands made delightful sensations over her body and moistened her pussy.

"You gonna start something that we can't finish," Ko-Ko admitted.

Rayshawn laughed. "You need to loosen up I just want to be your play toy. Nothing serious. Whenever you need someone who will pamper your every need, all you have to do is call," he said continuing to rub her back.

"That's what I wanted to talk to you about. The fact that I'm best friends with your mother, and I have a daughter your age is really bothering me. It's wrong for me to even be here."

"Look, I'm a grown ass man. My mother has nothing to do with who I see or sleep with. You're starting to give off the impression that you have to answer to someone. Maybe you're not the women I thought you were."

Ko-Ko smiled. She reached for her shot glass and tossed the Remy back then slammed the glass onto the marble bar. She gave Rayshawn a long look and yanked his head toward her before giving him a long kiss. She twirled her tongue inside his mouth several times then slowly pulled her lips back.

As a smile crept across her face, she thought about the lie she'd just told. The truth was, she wasn't bothered by Lynn or Kiara at all. She was just playing mind games to see if Rayshawn was feeling her or not. *Besides, having my own personal sexy ass play toy couldn't hurt any one especially if they never find out,* Ko-Ko thought.

She decided to keep the roll going though. "If we're going to do this we have to be respectful of other people's feelings and make sure that no one finds out about us," Ko-Ko stated.

"That works for me. How about dinner after work tomorrow?" Rayshawn replied.

"Why don't we do breakfast in bed after I feed you," Ko-Ko replied.

"Feed me what?"

Ko-Ko smiled again. "Me. We can go over to the Westin and you can eat me all night."

The two of them smiled. "Check please," Rayshawn said.

Ko-Ko began to nibble on Rayshawn's ear again when she suddenly spotted a familiar face coming into the restaurant. It was Melyssa and her boyfriend, Brandon.

"Shit!" Ko-Ko said. She quickly turned around as Melyssa and Brandon looked in their direction. "Rayshawn, we need to get out of here. That's Melyssa at the door. If she comes this way, we need to dip in the other direction."

Ko-Ko's trash talking still had him a little horny. "I'll hide you," he said.

Ko-Ko pushed Rayshawn off her. "Stop playing fool. I'm serious."

"You're right," Rayshawn put his head down, so he wouldn't be noticed.

When Ko-Ko noticed Melyssa pointing, it appeared as if they were about to make their way to the bar. "Oh, shit. What are we going to do now?" she asked, shaking her head. Ko-Ko had to think of an excuse quick.

However, a few seconds later, the hostess escorted the

couple to another area of the restaurant.

"Come on, we need to get out of here," Ko-Ko said.

"Can we get another drink first? I want to be good and ready to tear that ass up tonight," Rayshawn replied.

Ko-Ko grabbed Rayshawn by the arm and threw some money onto the bar for the bill before hauling ass out of the restaurant with her head down. Once outside and several feet away from the restaurant's windows, she gave Rayshawn a quick kiss.

"We're gonna have to reschedule. I know you only had one drink, but are you gonna be alright to drive?" Ko-Ko asked.

"I'm more than alright. I'm fine. Look at me," Rayshawn said laughing.

"I'm glad you can find humor in all this shit. Can't you understand that we almost got caught?"

I guess this is his immaturity coming out, she thought.

After kissing him one last time, Ko-Ko walked to her car in the opposite direction of Rayshawn. She didn't want to take any chances. As soon as she got inside, her cell phone began to go off. Thinking it was Rayshawn playing around again, she pulled it out of her purse and finally smiled. However, her smile was quickly replaced with a frown when she saw Melyssa's name pop up beside a message.

You should be ashamed of yourself. What are you doing with him? Does his mother know?

Chapter Ten

Two weeks later, Lynn, Tootie and Melyssa were all sitting around in Lynn's living room talking. They were also listening to Chrisette Michelle, sipping on a red Merlot and some leftover chicken skewers that Lynn had made the night before. The conversations ranged in all sorts of topics from sex, children and finally marriage. At that moment, that's when Melyssa finally stood up and cleared her throat.

"Okay ladies, I know I asked you all to meet me over here because I had a special announcement."

"Yeah, I've been waiting on you to tell us," Tootie said. "What's the news?"

"Wait, Ko-Ko's not here yet. Maybe we should wait for her a little longer," Lynn replied.

"Oh, hell no. Fuck that. We've been waiting for an hour. She should've been here on time. Go ahead Melyssa," Tootie said harshly. It was obvious she was a bit tipsy from the wine.

Lynn knew she couldn't defend her friend any longer as Melyssa began to jump up and down like an excited kid on Christmas morning.

"Brandon finally asked me to marry him at dinner the other night!" she belted. "And I accepted!"

Lynn and Tootie both began screaming at the top of their lungs. Lynn quickly grabbed the wine bottle and refilled all of their glasses.

"I can't believe you're going to get married. You're the

same woman who was anti-marriage just last year when I was talking about growing old and lonely without someone," Tootie said, grabbing her glass.

"I know right. This is happening really fast and he wants to get married in a little over a month," Melyssa announced. "March actually."

Lynn looked shocked. "March, why so soon?"

"Well, since both of Brandon's parents died, he wanted to get married on their anniversary. You know my man is into the sentimental things." Melyssa giggled.

"Wow," Lynn said. "I'm so happy for you."

Tootie held out her hand. "Where's the ring?"

Melyssa reached inside her purse and pulled out a baby blue box. A box that every woman recognized on the spot...Tiffany of course. When she opened the lid to expose the platinum two carat brilliant cut engagement ring, the other women couldn't believe their eyes.

"It's absolutely beautiful," Tootie said. "I guess Brandon's government job is paying off. Damn, I hate you. When the hell am I going to find somebody?"

Melyssa put on her sparkling beauty. "Oh, your day is coming. Trust me."

"Where the hell is Ko-Ko? She's going to die when she finds out you're getting married," Lynn said.

"Who knows," Tootie replied. "She's been real secretive for the last week or so."

"Yeah, too secretive," Melyssa said under her breath.

Suddenly, the doorbell rang. When Lynn went to go answer it, she returned with Ko-Ko just a few steps behind. It was as if she knew they were talking about her. Ko-Ko felt all eyes on her as she switched across the living room, stylish as ever wearing a studded Tory Burch tunic, tight jeans and a pair of Christian Louboutin Python Stilettos.

"The queen has arrived and she's in rare form tonight," Tootie said. "Oh, and very glamorous as always. I don't know where the hell she's going looking like that, but I guess she had to make a grand entrance."

No one really knew exactly who Tootie was talking to.

"Don't start with me, bitch. I don't even want to talk about that outdated Bill Cosby inspired sweater you're wearing," Ko-Ko countered. When she glanced over at Melyssa, she felt a little uncomfortable. Ko-Ko never responded to her text, and hadn't tried to get things straight. Up until now, she'd chosen to put the situation in the back of her mind.

"Where have you been? You're late," Lynn said sitting down. When Ko-Ko didn't answer, Lynn's tone got a little higher. "Ko-Ko, did you hear me?"

"Girl, stop and breathe, I'm here now and that's all that matters. What do you need for me to do?" Ko-Ko asked.

"First, you need some wine!" Lynn yelled. It wasn't long before she poured her friend a glass.

Ko-Ko looked confused. "What's going on?"

"Melyssa has something that she needs to tell you," Tootie said.

Melyssa waited for Ko-Ko to take her first sip then pulled her hand from behind her back, dropped her wrist and shook the ring in Ko-Ko's face. "I'm getting married."

"Who the hell wants to marry your crazy-ass?" Ko-Ko asked, even though she knew the answer.

Melyssa rolled her eyes. "Brandon."

"I guess people are right when they say there's somebody out here for everyone," Ko-Ko said, raising her glass of wine.

"Stop being a hater," Tootie chimed in.

"I'm not being a hater." Ko-Ko looked at Melyssa and finally smiled. "Congratulations, Chica."

"Thanks," Melyssa said as she sat back down. After reaching inside her bag, she pulled out a stack of bridal magazines. "Now, remember he wants to get married soon so I need a little help going through all of these to find the perfect dress. I also need for you all to help with bridesmaid's dresses. Because I don't want any drama, I'm not having a maid of honor. I want everyone to be equal so, just bridesmaids."

The thought of putting on a hideous bridesmaid's dress made Ko-Ko's stomach crawl. "If I'm gonna wear a bridesmaid's dress, it has to be sexy. Don't pick out shit Tootie would wear."

As a comeback, Tootie held up her middle finger high in the air.

Lynn shook her head. "Damn, I thought we were all gonna be cougars together. Now, Melyssa is leaving us."

"Speaking of cougars, did Ko-Ko tell you gals?" Melyssa said, looking around at the bewildered expression on everyone's face.

All eyes were staring at Ko-Ko. "Excuse me, told who, what?" Ko-Ko inquired.

"Did you tell them about that young boy I saw you drinking with at the bar over at McCormick & Schmicks a few weeks ago? Melyssa indicated.

I know this bitch is not about to bust me out right here and now, Ko-Ko thought.

Tootie took another sip of wine. "Was he fine?".

Melyssa paused and stared at Ko-Ko. "I didn't get a real good look at him, but he appeared to have it going on."

"So, who is he?" Lynn asked. "Since, I'm not getting any on a regular, I need to live through your sex life."

Ko-Ko shook her head. "It's no big deal. Just some guy I met." She paused. "Can we move on?"

"Are you sure you don't want to tell us about the young gentleman?" Melyssa questioned.

Ko-Ko frowned. "Yes, I am Melyssa, so drop it. It was nothing." Ko-Ko refilled her glass and swallowed it in one big gulp. She couldn't believe Melyssa would go there without talking to her first. She wanted so badly to curse her out, but knew that couldn't happen. Until she just didn't give a damn who knew about her and Rayshawn, she would have to kiss Melyssa's ass until then.

The ladies began going through the magazines, tossing back glass after glass until they were on their third bottle. After looking at what appeared to be a hundred dresses, Ko-Ko began to get bored. Not to mention, the wine was making her feel kind of freaky.

I wonder where the hell Rayshawn is. I know he's home because I saw his car out front when I parked, Ko-Ko thought. She began thinking of ways to go downstairs without looking too suspicious. Ko-Ko pulled out her cell phone and sent him a text message saying that she was upstairs and wanted him badly.

After finishing her fifth glass of wine, Ko-Ko realized that he still hadn't texted her back. She intentionally spilled her next glass of wine onto her three hundred dollar shirt, in order to get up.

"Damn…clumsy me. Lynn, do you have anything to get this out before it's ruined?" Ko-Ko asked.

"I think I have some Shout downstairs in the laundry room," Lynn answered.

Melyssa gave Ko-Ko a strange look as she stood up and walked toward the basement steps. Even after she'd seen them together, Melyssa thought Ko-Ko had a lot of nerve to try and pull off any type of stunt. "Try not to disturb Rayshawn. He probably needs to be left alone."

Ko-Ko could've killed her friend. "I'll try."

"And why are you taking your purse. What…you think we're gonna steal from you or some shit?" Tootie questioned.

Ko-Ko ignored her friends and kept walking. Once she got downstairs, she tiptoed over to Rayshawn's bedroom door and put her head up against the door. All Ko-Ko could hear were moans of a woman coming from inside. *I know this nigga ain't fucking some bitch with me and his mother upstairs,* she thought.

Instantly, Ko-Ko got upset and was about to bang on his door to fuck up his groove, but had another idea. She quickly took off all her clothes and softly knocked on his door. Ko-Ko could hear Rayshawn tell her to hold on. Seconds later, the moaning stopped and she could hear him moving around inside. Rayshawn opened the door to find Ko-Ko standing in her birthday suit smiling.

"Where the fuck is she? I know she's in here some-where," Ko-Ko said, bursting past him. "If you're gonna be in here fucking somebody it's gonna be me."

His eyes enlarged two times their normal size. "Where is who? What the hell are you doing down here with no clothes on? Are you crazy?"

Ko-Ko began looking around the room like a crime dog. She then started laughing when she noticed that Rayshawn had been watching porn on his television. Ko-Ko looked back at him standing in the door stunned.

"Wow. I'm sorry baby. When I heard some moaning coming from here, I guess I just went ballistic. Please forgive me. I just wanted to taste my dick for a second. It seems like forever since I felt him," Ko-Ko pleaded.

Rayshawn shook his head. "I'm really starting to think you're special. You need to take some anger management classes."

Ko-Ko quickly grabbed her clothes along with her purse. She then went inside her purse and pulled out a small bag of sex toys. "Hurry up and lock your door so you can Tea Bag me a couple of times," Ko-Ko replied trying to change the subject. "By the way, I got some new toys."

"Hell no. What about my mother?"

"Don't worry about her. They're up there talking about some boring-ass wedding invitations." Rayshawn gave her a puzzled look. "Don't ask me anymore questions. Just do what I said," Ko-Ko ordered.

Rayshawn turned to lock his bedroom door, but won-dered if the door at the top of the stairs was closed as well. At that point, he left his room and bolted up the steps to check the door at the top of the steps, quickly realizing it had been left open. Just when he reached for the knob to pull the door shut, someone appeared. It was his mother.

"Why are you hiding in your room?" Lynn asked. "We have company."

"Ma, I don't wanna sit around listening to you and your girlfriends," Rayshawn answered nervously.

"Hey Lynn, didn't you remodel the basement?" Tootie asked walking up behind her.

"Yes, I did. Come on…let me show you what I had the contractor do for Rayshawn's room."

Rayshawn eyes almost popped out of his head and his chest was beating like a drum. He shook his head back and forth watching them walk down the steps past him. "No. My room isn't clean!" he yelled. However, his distraction didn't work.

Lynn kept on walking. "Boy, please. What else is new?"

Once they made it to the bottom, Tootie let out a loud scream. "Oh, my God!"

The scream quickly made a vision enter into Rayshawn's head. He imagined Ko-Ko laying on his bed totally naked with her legs spread open wide. Rayshawn quickly ran down the steps.

He got to the bottom of the steps only to find Tootie, and his mother looking around like two tourists. Ko-Ko had some-how disappeared. Rayshawn looked around realizing that Tootie's screams were about the new bathroom with ceramic tile floors, a pedestal sink and a fancy light fixture. Wondering ex-actly where Ko-Ko was hiding, he followed both ladies around, crossing his fingers as they expected almost every corner.

"Where's Ko-Ko?" Lynn asked.

Rayshawn displayed a puzzled look. "I…have no idea. I haven't seen her. Did she come down here?"

"Yes, she spilled something on her shirt and was sup-posed to be cleaning it in the laundry room," Lynn answered.

"Maybe she went outside," Tootie suggested. Luckily, Lynn had just installed the walk out patio door, which led to the back yard during her renovations.

"Yeah, maybe so," Lynn replied.

Rayshawn sat on the edge of his bed as Lynn kissed his forehead then led Tootie back upstairs. Rayshawn scratched his head. *Damn, where did she go?* he wondered. Suddenly, a hand grabbed his foot causing Rayshawn to almost jump out his skin.

"Can you help me up? That was awfully close," Ko-Ko said, trying to crawl from under his bed. "You need to clean up. It's all types of shit under here."

After closing his door, Rayshawn dropped to his knees in front of her fully exposed body, opened his zipper and pulled out his erect penis. Rayshawn dangled his shaft in circles right in front of her mouth.

"Get out my way so I can get up," Ko-Ko said in a low tone.

Rayshawn moved his dick closer to Ko-Ko's face. "Are you sure you want me to move? You said you wanted me so badly, so you gotta pay the toll to exit the tunnel," he said wiggling the tip of his dick near her mouth. Now that they had just dodged a major bullet, he suddenly felt comfortable.

Ko-Ko stared up at him and couldn't help but laugh. It didn't take long for her to slowly take his dick into the palm of her hand. She moved her tongue all around his shaft until she could no longer resist. With one quick swoop, all of his manhood splashed around inside her moist mouth. Rayshawn leaned his head back. He loved how Ko-Ko engulfed him. He then closed his eyes and relaxed his muscles so he could fully enjoy her soft lips twirling over him.

"Rayshawn are you descent? Lynn wanted me to see what she's done to the basement. I've already seen up here!" Melyssa yelled walking down the steps.

"Huh…ah hold up. Give me a second," Rayshawn yelled in return. He quickly pointed at Ko-Ko. "Shit. Get back under the bed."

Melyssa could hear a lot of wrestling going on. "I can come back if it's not a good time. I didn't mean to intrude."

Rayshawn knew if he didn't let her come inside, his mother would've wondered what he was doing. Privacy obviously wasn't a strictly enforced rule.

"No, no…it's fine. Just…just give me a second."

When Rayshawn finally told her to come in a few seconds later, he looked as if he'd lost ten pounds from all the sweat that ran down his forehead.

"Oh my," Melyssa said, with a startled expression.

"What's wrong?" Rayshawn asked. Paranoid was an understatement at the moment.

Melyssa didn't respond. She only walked past him and motioned with her eyes for him to look down. Her awkward expression caused Rayshawn to glance down and look at Ko-Ko's wine stained shirt lying on the floor next to his bed.

"Oh yeah. She spilled something on it, and was trying to get it out before getting a phone call. I think she's outside. My mother was looking for her, too."

"Right," Melyssa said looking around. She peeked in closets, opened the door that led to the laundry room and tapped on newly painted walls. *I know that bitch is down here. Plus I can smell her perfume. I wonder where she's hiding,* Melyssa thought.

"Whoever Lynn used did a good job. I love the faux paint," Melyssa said, pretending she didn't know what was going on. "Well, I see that you're busy so I'll let you get back to whatever you were doing."

Rayshawn adjusted the collar on his shirt. "I'll make sure you get the guy's name and number."

Melyssa displayed a fake smile. "Thanks." She walked back up the basement steps, but instead of going back to join her friends, she waited until she heard Rayshawn close his door, then snuck back down like a trained ninja. Tiptoeing across the floor, she placed her ear up against his bedroom door and waited until she heard what she knew all along.

"Ko-Ko, the coast is clear. You can come out now," Rayshawn said quietly.

"Damn, I thought that bitch would never leave," Ko-Ko said a few seconds later.

Ko-Ko wiggled out from beneath the bed. She was getting ready to respond when Rayshawn covered her mouth. He put a finger over his mouth to acknowledge that she needed to be quiet.

Rayshawn walked over to his bedroom door when he heard footsteps going back up the steps. He knew someone had been down there, just wasn't sure who. He quickly went back to his room. "You gotta go. I think someone knows you were down here. Plus, Melyssa saw your shirt."

"That bitch needs a life. She saw us the other night at the restaurant too, so at this point she wants to fuck with me."

"Are you serious? Does my mother know?"

"If she did, wouldn't your ass be on her shit list by now?" Ko-Ko had a point.

Rayshawn went to his closet and gave Ko-Ko one of his jackets. "Go out the patio door down here and just make up some shit when you go back inside. You know how my mother drills people, so be ready."

She walked closer to him. "I can't keep hiding like this. I'm starting not to care if everyone knows about us."

"Have you lost your mind? My mother will fuck both of us up if she finds out. I'm not ready for that type of shit. Besides, you're not worth it."

Ko-Ko frowned. "What the fuck is that supposed to mean?"

Rayshawn knew he had to get her out of his room, before anymore surprises emerged. "Nothing. You really need to leave."

Trying to put up a front like Rayshawn's comment didn't faze her, Ko-Ko slipped her clothes on, then made her way out the back door. She rung the front doorbell like she'd been outside the whole time, and told herself that she was ready for another Academy Award performance.

"Where the hell you been, Ko-Ko?" Lynn asked as Ko-Ko walked inside.

"I got locked out when I went out back door to smoke me a couple of cigarettes," Ko-Ko answered.

"What did you do with your blouse?" Melyssa questioned.

"It's down in the basement soaking in some cold water and Shout," Ko-Ko replied.

"Hmm…did Rayshawn give you that little jacket?" Melyssa, asked being a little more sarcastic.

"I saw this jacket in the laundry room and put it on to go outside. Why are you so worried about what the hell I'm wearing anyway? Damn, shouldn't you be looking at flowers or some shit. I'm not your man, so stop questioning me," Ko-Ko stated.

Melyssa bit her bottom lip. "Oh, you wanna talk shit?"

"Okay ladies, I think we had just a little too much wine. Why don't we call it a night and hook up on Wednesday for dinner," Tootie said, jumping in to break up a potential fight.

"Whatever! I need a plastic bag to take my blouse home," Ko-Ko said, thinking of a way to get back downstairs to say good night to Rayshawn.

Melyssa looked directly at Ko-Ko. "Before we all go, I have one last announcement. I have to tell you all this right now or it'll kill me if I don't."

Chapter Eleven

Rayshawn opened the basement door to find his mother and her friends jumping up and down. They were hugging one another shouting. "Congratulations!" Everyone except Ko-Ko, of course. She was looking at them like they were crazy. However, she was glad that Melyssa's big news wasn't the fact that she was fucking Lynn's son.

"What did I miss?" Rayshawn asked.

"Melyssa is getting married in the islands and she just told us that her man is flying us all down for the wedding!" his mother shouted.

"Oh, that's cool. Congratulations," Rayshawn said.

"I bet you can't guess when and where it's going to be." Ko-Ko said to Rayshawn.

"I don't know. When?" he questioned.

"Her date is on Saturday, March 6th in Negril, Jamaica. That means we'll all be down there at the same time. Since the wedding party will be flying out on that Wednesday, now I'll be down there while you and Felice are trying to find locations for the shoot. How's that for coincidence?" Ko-Ko asked with a slight grin.

Rayshawn nodded his head. "Yeah, that's a real coincidence for sure. Well, I'll let you ladies continue to celebrate. I'm about to leave."

"Where are you going?" Ko-Ko questioned before Lynn

could. It was at that moment when she realized that Rayshawn had cleaned up well. He looked handsome in his camel colored Polo sweater, jeans and a nice pair of Kenneth Cole shoes. He even smelled good.

Melyssa glanced over at Tootie as Lynn's face frowned up.

"You heard your other mother. Where are you going?" Lynn repeated.

"Well, if you all must know. I'm going to a fraternity party over on New Jersey Avenue in D.C. I'm hanging out with Damon and Gary. We probably will go out to get a bite to eat after it's over and then who knows," Rayshawn replied. "Don't wait up, Ma." He walked up to his mother and kissed her on the forehead.

"Where on New Jersey Avenue?" Ko-Ko questioned.

Melyssa and Tootie both had dumbfounded looks on their faces.

Rayshawn stalled for a minute. "Umm…by Dunbar High School, why?"

"Nothing just curious," Ko-Ko said shaking her head.

"Be careful, son," Lynn replied in a motherly tone.

"Yeah, be *very* careful," Ko-Ko co-signed. She wished that he would kiss her as well, just not on the forehead. Anything below the waist would've been preferred.

Rayshawn had no idea what Ko-Ko meant by that comment, and honestly didn't want to. After saying goodbye to the women one last time, he left. Ko-Ko and the other ladies left minutes later. Ko-Ko hadn't even started her engine before she started texting Rayshawn. She had to let him know that he was expected at her house by twelve a.m. He didn't text her back as usual. Once she got pissed off and cursed him out to herself, Ko-Ko drove straight to her house to find Kiara asleep on the couch.

"Wake up. You need to take your ass in your own room. I'm expecting company in a few hours." She shook her daughter several times.

Kiara rubbed her eyes and sat up. "Who's the company?" She hoped Rayshawn's name wouldn't come up.

"Maybe if a bill came to this house with your name on it, I might feel the need to explain myself to you. All you need to do is get your ass up off my couch, pick-up all these dirty dishes and go to your room."

Kiara looked at the clock on the DVD and realized that Ko-Ko had actually done her a favor. She needed to get dressed anyway. Kiara had plans to go to a party in the city. "I needed to get up. I'm going out to some party tonight with a couple of my girlfriends."

"Oh, really." From Ko-Ko's response, it was clear that she wasn't anyway near interested in her daughter's where-abouts. As long as Kiara didn't come home pregnant, Ko-Ko could care less. She wasn't about to be anybody's grandmother. All she cared about at the moment was Rayshawn. She checked her phone again before walking over to one of the kitchen draw-ers where she kept the tea light candles. After grabbing at least six, she began placing them all around the living room.

"I see it's going to be one of those wild nights. I'll spend the night over at Aunt Lynn's tonight," Kiara said, walking to-ward the steps. Staying at Lynn's was perfect. Her goal was to get close to Rayshawn to see if they could patch things up. She didn't want to be outdone by her own mother.

"You better call her first because Rayshawn said he was hanging out all night, so she might be trying to find some com-pany of her own."

Kiara agreed, then ran up the steps jumping two at a time. By the time Ko-Ko finished decorating the house and turn-ing on the living room fireplace, Kiara made it back downstairs with a face full of makeup, lots of accessories and a pair of jeans that looked entirely too small.

"Damn. Are you gonna be able to move in those things?" Ko-Ko asked. "Looks like an instant yeast infection to me."

"I don't plan on moving that much until I take them off."

"Shit you gotta walk, right? Ain't that moving? You

might as well make your doctor's appointment."

Kiara grinned. "I'll take my chances. Besides, men like tight jeans. You should know that."

"They might like tight jeans, but don't no man like pussy that's out of order. Now, that I do know." Ko-Ko stood in the living room reflecting back on when she was Kiara's age, and all the men she had giving her major dough. Due to Kiara's lack of funds, it was obvious that she hadn't been blessed with Ko-Ko's automated teller skills.

Ko-Ko waited for Kiara to walk out the door before she went to her room to put on a sexy costume for Rayshawn. Not sure what she wanted to be for the evening, Ko-Ko first tried on her red and white nurse uniform that stopped right above her ass cheeks. Not satisfied with that look, she switched to her two-piece school girl uniform. The red cropped v-neck sweater lifted up her breasts and exposed her naval ring at the same time. She then slid on her white knee-high stockings, and put her hair in two ponytails. Ko-Ko modeled back and forth in front of the full length mirror on the back of her bedroom door.

"Now, all I need is my backpack with all my toys in it and I'm good," she said, giving herself one final glance.

The candles had completely gone out and BET had started showing a re-run of the crazy show, *Frankie & Neffe* before Ko-Ko looked at the time and realized that it was almost twelve-thirty in the morning. *I can't believe that motherfucka hasn't gotten here yet*, she thought throwing her glass of wine into the dining room wall.

Ko-Ko walked over and grabbed her black trench coat, car keys and stomped out of her house toward her car. She didn't even think about how Rayshawn might react as she drove to D.C. at top speed. She also had no idea exactly where on New

Jersey Avenue the fraternity party was, but at least Rayshawn had given her a landmark. After arriving at her destination, Ko-Ko slowly drove down the street, and stopped in front of a row house on the seventeenth hundred block after noticing several drunk looking party goers hanging out on the front porch. Once Ko-Ko paralleled parked her car, she jumped out and headed straight for the front door. Several people standing outside couldn't believe their eyes as she walked past.

"What the fuck is that bitch wearing? I didn't know this was a costume party. Are you trying out for the Matrix movie or something?" one girl yelled out.

Ko-Ko's five inch black patent leather boots with two zippers on the side made her ass jiggle with each step. When the wind caught her trench coat and blew it behind her like a cape, her short argyle printed skirt and fish net stockings managed to grab everyone's attention.

"You don't have to go any further. You've found what you're looking for right here," a guy said as Ko-Ko got to the top of the steps.

"I doubt that shit very seriously," she returned.

"Why do you say that? Just give me a second to prove it to you," the guy fired back. "Trust me. I'm the right guy."

"The right guy wouldn't use some corny-ass line to pick up a woman like me, so fuck off," Ko-Ko said stepping into the house.

She walked around to find a bunch of drunk girls being sexually assaulted by even drunker dudes. "I better not find Rayshawn touching any of these bitches when he has all this body waiting to fulfill his every desire," Ko-Ko said, as she strutted through each room.

Rayshawn was walking down the steps when he noticed Ko-Ko turning the corner by the kitchen moments later. He couldn't believe his eyes. Suddenly, he ran down the rest of the steps and tried to close her coat immediately.

"What the fuck are you doing here and what are you wearing?" Rayshawn shouted.

"Oh shit. Who is this?" Gary asked. "Is this the broad you told us about?"

"I'm sure I am," Ko-Ko stated like a proud parent. The fact that Rayshawn had mentioned her to anyone was exciting.

"What about the girl at the gym?" Gary continued.

Ko-Ko's face looked like the little girl in the Exorcist movie. "Yeah, so what the fuck happened to the bitch at the gym?"

Damon was so in shock, he couldn't even say anything. Ko-Ko didn't look anywhere near as old as he'd pictured her. Not to mention, her body didn't read a day over twenty-three.

"What are you doing here?" Rayshawn repeated. "How the hell did you find me anyway?" Then it dawned on him that Ko-Ko had asked about the whereabouts of the party earlier.

Ko-Ko placed her hands on her hips. "I had to see why you weren't replying to any of my messages that's why."

"You drove all the way down here dressed like that because I didn't answer my phone. Are you high?" Rayshawn asked.

"I'm standing here damn near naked and all you can do is ask me if I'm high. No, I'm not but you must be," Ko-Ko stepped back and whipped off her coat. "How can you stay at this kiddy party when you have all of this wanting you? I was dressed like this so we can have some fun. I wanted you to play my naughty school teacher."

"Damn!" both Damon and Gary said in unison.

Rayshawn grabbed her coat off the floor and tried to wrap it around her body. By this time, Ko-Ko and Rayshawn had every pair of eyes in the party locked on them. Rayshawn grabbed Ko-Ko by her arm.

"You need to take your ass home. You're embarrassing yourself and me!" he yelled. "This shit ain't cool."

"I'm sorry baby. I just miss you. Is that wrong?" Ko-Ko asked, trying to put her arms around his neck.

"Hell yeah, it's wrong! I can't believe you're here dressed like that. What were you thinking? Get your hands off me and carry your ass home. You're too fucking possessive. I'm not your man."

"I'll be your man!" Gary yelled, rubbing his pale hands together.

"Please Rayshawn, don't be mad at me. I guess I just wasn't thinking straight. I thought that this could be like one of those amazing gestures to sweep you off your feet. Let's go to my house so we can work this out," Ko-Ko pleaded.

"I'm not going anywhere with you. Don't you get it…you were just a piece of ass. It seems that you want more than what I'm ready to give. Showing up here dressed like a fucking prostitute has made it very clear for me. This shit seems to be getting out of hand. I'm done."

Ko-Ko grabbed Rayshawn's arm. "Noooo. Don't say that. I'm sorry. I just wanted to do something shocking to prove that I want you. I love you."

Rayshawn looked around the room. Everyone in the entire house was staring in their direction. It felt like he was on a reality show. "And you thought this would do that? How can you love someone after fucking them for a short period of time? You're really crazy."

"So, what was that at your house earlier today, huh? You were dangling your dick all in my face. Now, you standing here acting like you aren't feeling me," Ko-Ko stated.

"Look, you should've never brought your ass down in my room anyway, especially with my mother right upstairs. So, no…I wasn't feeling that shit just like I'm not feeling you right now," Rayshawn fired back.

"Mom, what the hell are you doing?" Kiara shouted as she walked into the house. "What the hell is going on?" She looked back and forth between Rayshawn and her mother. She knew whatever it was, it couldn't be good.

"Rayshawn, please give me a chance to make this up to you," Ko-Ko said, ignoring Kiara's question.

Rayshawn smacked Ko-Ko's hands off him. He turned and headed for the door. "You need to take your mother home," he said walking past Kiara.

"Why is she here and what the fuck did you do to her?" Kiara asked.

Rayshawn smiled, then whispered in Kiara's ear. "The same thing I did to you, but for much longer."

Kiara was heated over his sarcastic remark. "What the fuck did you just say?"

"You heard me. Take your mother home. Both of y'all are fucking sick. Acting all crazy over some dick," Rayshawn said before stepping out the front door.

"Damn!" one person yelled.

"I need to be like that nigga when I grow up," another person commented.

Ko-Ko was speechless. She'd never let a man talk to her that way and get away with it. Rayshawn wasn't even financing her pockets like most of her men did. He obviously had something on her that she couldn't shake.

Gary looked at both women. "Hey, if he don't want y'all, I do." He handed Kiara a piece of paper with his name and number on it. It obviously had been pre-written. "Call me…anytime." He then turned around to catch up with Rayshawn while Damon followed.

With everyone looking at her with all kinds of crazy smirks, Kiara wanted to say something slick, but staring at her mother standing in the crazy outfit, made her dismiss Rayshawn's disrespect…for now. She walked over and picked up the trench coat and covered up her mother's half-naked body.

"Don't worry about him. He's going to get his soon enough," Kiara warned.

Chapter Twelve

Lynn sat on the edge of her bed thinking about what Tootie, Melyssa and even Ko-Ko had said to her at her birthday dinner. After watching her friends and Rayshawn leave her house for another exciting night on the town, she couldn't help but to sigh several times. *Everyone seems to be living their life except for me,* Lynn thought. Even if it was only for one night, Lynn realized that for once she had to live her life. After years of trying to please her son or everyone else, she rarely made time to please herself. Hell, most of the time she ignored herself, except for when she pulled out the double-A batteries, of course. However, all that needed to change. It was time for her to consider her own needs, and right now, she needed a stiff dick. Grabbing her cell phone, Lynn began searching through her phone book for the only person to end her drought.

After hesitating for what seemed like an hour, she finally got up the courage to call Garrett, the handsome doctor from her job. He'd given her his phone number at least three months prior, but for some reason she hadn't felt the urge to use it until now. When Garrett didn't answer, Lynn left a short but sweet message to call her back. The last thing she needed was to sound pressed even though she was. Much to her surprise, Garrett called back within five minutes. Lynn mouthed the words, *Oh My God* at least three times before she finally answered.

"Hello, Dr. Hines."

"Hello, Ms. McMillian. Is everything okay?"

"Ahhh, yes. Everything is fine. Sorry, I know it's late. I hope I didn't wake you."

"No, I was up actually. You've never called me before, so I'm in a bit of a shock."

Lynn wiped the sweat off her hand on the comforter. "I know. I actually didn't want anything. I just called to say hello." After looking at the clock that read 1:25 a.m., Lynn realized that what she'd just said was dumb. She was obviously rusty in the conversation area, and booty calls weren't her specialty.

Garrett laughed. "Oh, really. Well, even though it's late, I'm glad you called. I've been waiting on this for three months, so I actually wouldn't have cared what time you called." His deep baritone voice sounded like Ving Rhames.

"Would you like to come over," Lynn blurted out. She didn't feel like beating around the bush, and definitely didn't have time for games.

There was an uncomfortable silence for a few seconds before Garrett responded. "Of course. Give me your address."

After talking for a few more minutes, Lynn hung up then ran straight to her bathroom. You couldn't wipe the smile off her face as she quickly jumped in the shower and scrubbed her body down in every area, especially between her legs. Minutes later, she was out of the shower, and sporting a new cranberry tunic that enhanced her breasts. Lynn thought it would've been too typical to be in lingerie, so she decided on something a little less obvious.

Once her hair and makeup were in place, Lynn went downstairs to make herself a glass of wine to calm her nerves, but all her bottles were empty.

"Shit," she said, picking up one bottle after another. She and her friends had demolished every one. "I gotta go get another bottle."

Lynn grabbed her purse and quickly headed outside to her car. She knew that it was a liquor store not too far from her house that stayed open until two-thirty. With Garrett coming from Brandywine, she still had a little time to spare before he arrived.

When Lynn pulled back into her driveway fifteen minutes later, Garrett's old apple red Z28 was parked across the street from her house. She could spot his car a mile away. As soon as she put the car in park, Garrett was already walking toward her. He reached out and tried to open her door when she shut off her engine. Lynn laughed to herself thinking, *is he crazy. Not only is it late, but I live in Prince George's County. Does he think I'm trying to get jacked?* She clicked the button and he pulled for the second time.

"Have you been waiting long?" she asked.

"No, I just pulled up actually. How are you? You look gorgeous. It's good to see you out of those scrubs."

Lynn smiled. "Thanks. You, too." Garrett closed the car door after Lynn got out and gave her a warm hug. A hug that immediately made her juices begin to flow. "And you smell good, too." She looked up at his 6'4' frame. She loved tall men, just like her son.

"Thank you."

"Well, we can't sit out here and compliment each other all night. Let's go inside," Lynn suggested.

"I'm so glad you called me. I was a little surprised that you did but happy none the less," Garrett said entering the house.

Lynn hadn't even put her purse down before she decided to change her clothes. Her lingerie theory had quickly been changed. She wanted to feel a little sexier. "Make yourself at home and fix us a couple of glasses of wine while I go slip into something a little more comfortable," Lynn said, handing the liquor store's infamous black plastic bag to Garrett.

He smiled, showing a perfect pair of expensive veneers. "Sure, no problem."

Garrett was working on his second glass when Lynn returned wearing a red silk robe with a lace babydoll set underneath. The sweet smell of Halle Berry's new perfume filled Garrett's nostrils as soon as she turned the corner. Lynn slowly walked over to the coffee table and grabbed her glass of wine then opened the robe a little so her well defined thighs that she had just oiled up could be seen. For once, she didn't feel self conscious about her body.

Remembering what Ko-Ko had taught her a while back about seducing men, Lynn made her butt cheeks jiggle as she switched over to the stereo and turned on the radio. She then began to pop her fingers as the sounds of Frankie Beverly and Maze's, *Golden Time of Day*, oozed out of the speakers. It wasn't long before she was doing a little two-step.

You could see the excitement on Garrett's Hershey chocolate skin as he refilled his glass, then sat down on the couch to watch the show. Lynn looked back to find his eyes staring at her like she was the winning numbers on the daily lotto show. Lynn loved his nicely trimmed beard and hazel colored eyes, which brought out the bold features in his face. Garrett was a very attractive man, but Lynn often worried about Rayshawn liking him, which was the reason why she never tried to get serious with him in the past.

Lynn sat down next to him as the song went off and they began to catch up on lost time. No matter how hard Garrett tried to steer their conversation, Lynn would find a way to make a reference about her son. It wasn't until Lynn's third glass of wine that she even leaned over to kiss Garrett. He assumed that was his cue that Lynn was heating up, but the next words that came out her mouth were about Rayshawn once again.

"I wonder if my son took his big coat. He can't afford to get sick," Lynn said.

"I'm confused. Did you call me over so we can talk about your son all night or did you have another thought in mind?" Garrett asked, putting his glass on the coffee table.

"I'm sorry. I didn't ask you over here so you can hear me talk about my son. I called you over to do what you do best and break me off until my body shakes or the bed breaks. Which ever one comes first," Lynn boldly stated.

Glad to finally get the green light, Garrett didn't waste

another second. He snatched Lynn up into his arms and began carrying her up the steps. Lynn felt her juices swirling around between her legs as his strong muscular arms held her tight. She rubbed her hands across his chest as they entered her bedroom and Garrett tossed her onto the bed.

Lynn bounced a couple of times, laughing at the thought of falling off the other side. She looked up to find Garrett opening the buttons on his shirt. She licked her lips as his chiseled six- pack was revealed. Goose bumps ran up her legs acknowledging that she was a little nervous. It had been some time since she'd been with a man.

Garrett threw his shirt on the dresser behind him before dropping down to his knees and grabbing Lynn's legs. As he slowly pulled off the robe and lace thong, Lynn made a gesture to hold on to them for a brief moment then allowed him to take them off. Garrett then balled them up into a ball, brought them to his nose and inhaled.

Damn, he's freaky, she thought.

Lynn closed her eyes as she felt his thick tongue sliding up her right leg headed for her dripping pussy. The warmth of his breath sent an immediate chill racing up her body. Her hands clamped the comforter as he began to tickle her clit with tiny jerks of his tongue.

It's been way to long. I'm ready to cum already.

As the warm cum began to rush into his mouth, Garrett began to lick faster as if he was trying to get to the center of a tootsie pop. Lynn started to moan louder until another orgasm had come and gone. Garrett slid his nose down to rub against her clit as he nibbled on her pink lips. Garrett stood up to finish undressing so he could take their session from second base to third. When Lynn opened her eyes to see him fussing with his belt, she rushed over to give assistance and removed his black slacks. Once his pants dropped to his ankles, Lynn pulled out his dick and quickly wrapped her throbbing lips around his erect penis.

"Whoa! You need to pull back on the teeth," Garrett said,

jerking his body back. "That hurts."

Lynn pulled his dick out of her mouth and looked up at him. "Sorry. It's been awhile since I've done this. I'm a little rusty."

"Its okay sweetie, I know it won't take long for you to remember how to do this," Garrett replied in a comforting tone.

When Lynn eased his shaft back into her mouth, she paid extra attention to relaxing her gums so that her teeth didn't touch his dick. Lynn had just found a nice groove when she heard the sound of keys and the front door opening.

Lynn stopped immediately, "Oh shit, I think my son is coming in," she said, holding Garrett's dick in her hand.

"You don't have to stop. He's not going to come up here, is he?" Garrett asked, feeling the tingling in his feet starting to disappear.

"I don't know, but I'm not willing to take that chance. Hurry up and put back on your clothes. I don't want my son to find us up here undressed in my bedroom," Lynn whispered.

"How old is your son again? You're whispering as if he's a little child," Garrett said, reaching for his shirt.

"What difference does that make? I just don't want my son to see his mother with a man up in her bedroom. Since you have a problem with doing what I asked, you can leave," Lynn's tone had changed drastically.

Rayshawn walked into the house. "Hey mom, you home?"

"Yeah, baby I'm home. I didn't expect you back so soon. Do you need something?" Lynn shouted.

Rayshawn looked over and saw the two empty glasses on the coffee table and smiled. The music coming from the stereo and the darkness coming from upstairs told him that she wasn't alone.

"Naw, I'm going to bed. You go ahead and enjoy the rest of your night," Rayshawn yelled as he quickly ran downstairs to his room.

Garrett smiled. "You heard your son. He said enjoy the

rest of your night,"

"Do you expect me to fuck you with my son in the house?" Lynn asked.

"Yeah, I do."

Lynn was heated. "Absolutely not. I should've known this wasn't going to end right. This was a big mistake. Please get your stuff and leave." She pointed toward the door.

"Are you serious? You're acting like your son is a little damn boy. I'm sure he knows that his mother had to have sex before. That's how he got here," Garrett said, putting on his shoes.

"Look, not that I owe you an explanation, but my son means everything to me. The way he thinks about me is very important. I don't want him to think his mother is a whore."

"I don't understand. Can you at least finish giving me head until I bust a nut?" Garrett asked, rubbing his still erect dick.

"What? You need to get your shit and get out. You've just ensured the fact that I'll never call you again. I need you to leave right now."

Without hesitation, Lynn slipped her robe back on then walked Garrett to the front door. After stepping onto the porch, he turned back around. "Lynn, I'm sorry. I didn't…"

She didn't even wait for him to finish before she slammed the door in his face and quickly put on the dead bolt lock.

"Loser," Lynn said to herself then walked into the living room to turn off the stereo. It wasn't long before she grabbed the two wine glasses and headed to the kitchen. "I wonder if Rayshawn noticed these when he came in," she mumbled. "Oh well, I guess I'll have some explaining to do." She then opened up a drawer and pulled out a few packs of Double A batteries. For her dildo of course.

Chapter Thirteen

The weekend seemed to creep by and all Ko-Ko could think about was Rayshawn. She'd left him several text and voice messages on his phone, but as usual got no reply. Of course she knew he was ignoring her, but Ko-Ko wasn't the type of woman to give up easily. Her plan was to keep stalking her prey until he finally surrendered. She was more than determined to make things the way they used to be.

When Rayshawn got back from lunch on Monday, Ko-Ko was waiting for him outside. He'd been avoiding her all day, so she decided to try another option. Once he walked toward the building, she plucked the butt of her cigarette, then jumped up to block his way. Ko-Ko looked him up and down then leaned over to sniff him.

"What the hell are you doing?" Rayshawn asked.

"Just seeing if I could still smell some bitch on you."

"I'm serious Ko-Ko, you need some psychological help. Nobody walks around sniffing people and shit," Rayshawn said, stepping back. He shook his head in disbelief that she was still making a fool of herself.

Ko-Ko put her hands on her hips. "All I need is you." When Rayshawn tried to move toward the door, she blocked him again. "I really need for you to take some time out for me."

"Look, you need to really get it in your head that we're done. It was fun while it lasted, but shit is getting way out of hand, and I don't need that right now. Plus, you and I both don't want my mother to find out, so it's best that we go back to the way things use to be."

Ko-Ko was relentless. "If you just give me one day, I'm sure I can make it up to you for my behavior the other night. Please Rayshawn, I'm only asking for just one day. I think I deserve that." She wasn't use to being turned down by any man. Let alone, someone almost half her age.

Just then Felice walked up toward the door in her normal sexy stride. When she saw Ko-Ko and Rayshawn outside talking, she smiled. It definitely looked like a lovers quarrel. "Hello."

Rayshawn returned the smile. "Hey, you."

Ko-Ko didn't.

"Hey Rayshawn, I need to go over some details regarding the trip. Can you meet with me right now?" Felice inquired.

"Yes, Ms. Contour," Rayshawn answered. Once Felice walked inside, he turned to Ko-Ko. "I guess our conversation is just like our non-existent relationship…over."

"I'm telling you this and you better take my warning seriously. You don't want to start no shit with Felice. You'll regret it for the rest of your life. Shit ain't what it appears to be. Besides, this situation ain't over until I say it's over," Ko-Ko said, before storming off.

He couldn't figure out what Ko-Ko meant by saying things weren't what they appeared, but didn't entertain the thought for too long. Refusing for her to ruin the rest of his day, Rayshawn entered into the conference room and sat on two chairs away from his boss. Felice sat at the head of the table ordering some dinner over the phone.

"I hope you like Chinese food," she said hanging up.

"How long do you expect us to be here?"

"We really need to get a jump on this project so that we'll have a little free time to enjoy ourselves before everybody else gets down there. Do you have a problem with that or should I cancel your ticket and take Ms. Jackson instead?"

"No, not at all. There's no problem. I'm the right person

for this project," Rayshawn confirmed.

Felice and Rayshawn sat next to one another going over the schematics and looking at pictures from different beach fronts around the island. They were down to six locations when the night security guard rang the phone in the conference room. Felice put it on speaker.

"Yes."

"This is Fredrick from downstairs, Ms. Contour. Your food is here. Would you like me to bring it up?"

"Oh, my goodness, it's 7:30 already?" Felice asked looking at her Chanel watch. "No, that's okay. I'll get someone to come down." She hit the speaker button again.

"I'll go get it," Rayshawn offered.

"Thanks," Felice reached in the pocket of her cardigan sweater she wore around the office and pulled out a twenty-dollar bill. "You're working late, so it's on Fantasy Girlz."

"Are you sure? I can pay for my own food." Rayshawn didn't want to feel like a loser.

"Positive. Oh, and when you come back, go to my office instead. It's too cold in this room."

Rayshawn chuckled. "Okay."

Once Rayshawn went downstairs, Felice gathered up all the notes and headed toward her corner office. However, as she got closer to the door, she noticed the receptionist, Nikki coming out. Felice stopped in her tracks. "What are you doing?"

Nikki immediately dropped the stack of papers she was carrying. "Oh shit, you scared me."

"It's after hours? What are you doing here and what are you doing in my office?" Felice's eyebrows began to scrunch up.

"Well, since I know how to do the expense reports and the accountant has been out sick with the flu, I decided to stay late and do them. I know how important it is that they get done before you all are off to Jamaica. I put them on your desk." Felice still seemed uneasy. "If I'd known you were here, I would've brought them to you."

"Oh…oh okay. Well, thanks for doing that, but don't think your ass is getting a raise or something. We don't have any money for that."

Nikki laughed. "Girl, ain't nobody thinking about a raise. I just did it to help you out. Shit, this let's me buy some time anyway since I gotta go get my mama's ass from bingo."

After some brief small talk, Nikki made her way back to her desk, then packed up to finally go home. When she saw Rayshawn come back in the office with the white plastic bag, she rolled her eyes. "Punk-ass. You should've gone out to lunch like I asked," she said walking out.

"Boy, this world is full of fucking haters," Rayshawn said out loud.

Minutes later, Felice began talking about a few excursions she wouldn't mind going out on in Jamaica as they ate greasy Orange Chicken straight from the paper cartons. During that time, Rayshawn caught Felice staring over at him from time to time.

"Rayshawn, you've done a wonderful job with the pictures I've seen so far. You started off with some major concerns, but you were able to prove yourself and then exceed my expectations. I can see you running this project and many others in the future."

"Thank you, Ms. Contour."

"Stop being so damn formal. Oh, and speaking of something else you need to stop doing. Stop arguing in front of the office with Kourtney. As my grandma use to say, don't let that woman get you burnt under the collar," Felice said smiling.

Rayshawn stood up to stretch. "Now, I wouldn't say her childish actions burnt me. I just thought more of her and less of her behavior."

Felice watched as Rayshawn's muscles tightened in his arms under his shirt as he reached for the ceiling. She then noticed the bulge in his slacks.

"My back is so tight. We need to think about buying some better chairs around here. Even the ones in the conference rooms aren't that comfortable," Rayshawn continued.

Felice slowly twirled her torso, twisting both shoulders and rotating her chest and stomach. "My back is a little tight, too. A massage would be just what the doctor ordered."

"You want me to give you a back massage?" Rayshawn asked wanting clarity.

Felice stood up. "I actually want a little more." Pulling her skirt up and exposing a pantiless crotch, her neatly trimmed pussy grabbed his attention. Especially her long thick vagina lips that seemed to mesmerize him.

Rayshawn smiled before walking closer to her. Just like actors always did in the movies, Felice got onto her desk and pushed all the paperwork and photos to the floor. She then removed her blouse and unhooked her royal blue lace bra. Rayshawn noticed that the cool breeze had made her nipples harden.

"This might not be an award winning massage since I don't have any oil or lotion," Rayshawn said getting closer.

"Well, if you walk over to my file cabinet, you'll find some baby oil in the bottom drawer. I'm sure you'll be just fine."

Although he wondered why she had baby oil in her cabinet, Rayshawn kept his mouth shut, retrieved the oil and slowly walked back over toward Felice. Her flawless body was stretched out as if she was at a nudist beach. He cracked his knuckles as he made his way over Felice's body, using several fingers to dig into the deepest areas of her tense back. The more she let out soft moans, the more his dick began to grow and poke her.

Felice sighed. "How many hands are you using? This is already making me feel much better."

Rayshawn opened the oil and poured a nice amount down the middle of her back then sat back to watch it run down to the crack of her ass. He stared at the tattoo of some lips with a tongue hanging out at the lower portion of her back before continuing to massage. That is until he felt his fingers cramping up.

At that moment, he paused to flex his fingers and get the blood flowing again. Felice began to roll her hips to feel his dick against her lower back.

"What are you waiting on? You know I'm not wearing any panties and I want to feel you inside of me. My pussy is throbbing and wet beyond belief."

"You want me to take you right here, right now?" Rayshawn asked. He looked around nervously. "What if someone comes?"

"You're talking too damn much. Everybody is gone. Give me that dick or you're fired," Felice responded with a smile.

Rayshawn didn't hesitate any longer. He kicked off his shoes, removed his pants and ripped away his boxers. Rayshawn looked to find Felice face down and ass up on the desk. She reached back, and spread her butt cheeks wider.

Rayshawn slid between her legs then flicked the tip of his penis against her clitoris. *Oh my, she wasn't lying. This pussy is extremely wet...and tight,* Rayshawn thought. Using a figure eight twirl, he maneuvered all around her erogenous zones.

Felice's pussy dripped over his shaft and onto the desk. "My kitty is ready. Give it to her!" she shouted.

Rayshawn arched his hips and dove fully inside her. His penis rubbed against her clit, pressed both outer and inner lips, as her vagina canal exploded from the might of his thrust. *Damn, this pussy is like a suction cup. It feels like it's never been used before,* he continued to think.

"Yes! That's how you fuck," she said.

"When's the last time you made love, baby? It's so tight. It's so good," Rayshawn said in return.

The high degree of friction rubbing on her clitoris increased the pleasure for Felice. He pumped harder and deeper as her head shook repeatedly from side to side and up and down. Felice's hair swung all around as if she was in a violent storm. She began to buck like a bull in a rodeo while her pussy filled with more warm cum, then began to smack his right hip as his dick found her unsuspecting G-spot.

"Don't stop. You better not fucking stop. I'm about to cum," she warned.

Rayshawn felt an orgasm of his own approaching, but he needed to prolong it. Felice's pussy reminded him of straight up virgin. He'd definitely hit the jackpot. Rayshawn pulled back, leaving the top still inside her. He then grabbed his dick to press against the thick vein running up his shaft. He kept it clamped until the ejaculating sensation passed.

Felice looked back at him. "Stop teasing or I'll fire your ass for real."

Rayshawn laughed. He reached around her hips with his right hand and pinched the tip of her pussy before ramming his erected dick back to that special spot that caused Felice to shake and tremble.

"Shit! Not so hard!" she yelled. "I'm not going anywhere!"

Ignoring her cries, Rayshawn grinded his dick inside Felice until she fell flat, face first on the desk. Moments later, he leaned over and twirled his tongue down her lower back, through the middle of her ass, and stopped at her butt hole. His dick dripped with her juices while he played with her anus. Rayshawn slid his body up her oily back, then positioned his dick directly over her ass hole and jammed it inside. She dug her nails into the wood, letting out a loud porno star moan. Rayshawn felt her ass cheeks tighten then quickly relax as his shaft entered deep inside her.

Felice pushed her body off the table and stopped when she got into the true doggy style position. Rayshawn grabbed her hair with one hand and her left breast with the other. He began banging his dick in and out of her ass until her moans became one steady scream.

"You still want to fire me?" Rayshawn asked.

"Hell yeah, especially if you don't stop pulling my damn weave!"

Rayshawn reached down and grabbed both sides of her hips, then began diving his dick inside like an Olympic swimmer while pulling her ass back with all his might. Felice's long arms began to buckle with the force of Rayshawn's pelvic area banging into her.

"Yes! Yes! Don't stop. I'm about to cum again!" Felice screamed.

Rayshawn pushed Felice's face down to the table and lifted her hips so his dick reached the deepest parts of her ass. *Damn I've never met someone who can take it in the ass like this*, he thought. He began smacking her cheeks with all his might. Then suddenly, Rayshawn's legs began to shake. He was about to unload inside her.

"No, wait," Felice said pulling away. Much to his surprise, she quickly made her way toward his dick and inserted it in her mouth.

Rayshawn was in heaven as he released all of his thick cum into her mouth. Felice continued to suck until every ounce ran down her throat. Rayshawn fell back onto the table completely exhausted. However, the break was just long enough to catch his breath. All night, they fucked on every chair, against the file cabinet, on the window seal and even against her water cooler before they finally fell out from exhaustion.

"The janitor is going to really earn his pay tonight when he comes to clean this office," Rayshawn joked.

When Rayshawn looked at the clock on the wall, and realized it was after ten, he decided it was time to go home. Not to mention, he was beyond tired. They both began slipping their clothes back on, eyeing each other every few seconds.

"I hope you're not going to be acting weird around the office after this," Felice said, as they walked out of her office.

Rayshawn took a deep breath. "I'm cool. There won't be a change on my end. I hope you can say the same thing."

"I agree. Besides, I would hate to spread a few nasty rumors about you to all the nosey people around here. This time I'll make you gay with a crush on Fredrick the security guard," Felice joked.

Rayshawn placed his hand on Felice's butt as they walked to the elevator. They kissed a couple of times on the ride down, then both said good night to the security guard who gave them a strange look. After walking Felice to her car, Rayshawn waited for her to drive off before he jumped into his car and pulled off as well.

Little did Felice and Rayshawn know, as they made their way home, Nikki made her way back into the building. She'd been waiting outside for hours. By the look of the guards face, he knew something wasn't right, but couldn't figure it out. Nikki was upstairs at Fantasy Girlz at least twenty minutes before coming back down holding a black bag. She and Fredrick eyed each other closely before Ko-Ko walked into the lobby. She quickly motioned for Nikki to meet her outside.

"Did you get it all?" Ko-Ko asked.

Nikki nodded her head. "I'm pretty sure I did. I make tapes at home all the time with me and all my niggas, so we should be good." She reached in the bag and pulled out a Sony camcorder. After ejecting the DVD, she handed the disc to Ko-Ko. "That bitch almost caught me too, but I handled it."

"Good. Here's what we agreed on." Ko-Ko placed six crisp one-hundred dollar bills in Nikki's hand. "Oh, the extra hundred was for letting me borrow your car that day." Ko-Ko smiled as she thought about the look on Felice's face when she noticed her car had been vandalized in the parking lot.

"No problem. You can borrow that piece of shit Honda Accord anytime, especially if I can floss in your Range. Let me know if you need anything else. I like this type of shit." Nikki could care less if Felice found out about her secretly placing a camera in her office. Fantasy Girlz had been her third job in six months, so getting fired wasn't an issue.

Once Nikki left, Ko-Ko had one last thing to do. She walked into the building and headed straight for the security guards booth. Fredrick smiled as she placed both her hands on his desk.

"Is everything okay?" he asked. "I've never seen any of you all here this late."

Ko-Ko held a stern look. "Do you like working here?"

"Yes, of course," he replied with a puzzled expression on his face.

"Well, if I even hear a whisper about anything you saw us doing tonight, I promise you that your ass will be fired. Not only that, I know people…and not the nice kind of people. The ones who like to hurt folks. Are we clear?"

He shook his head. "Yes, Ms. Jackson, not one word."

Just to be on the safe side, Ko-Ko slowly eased around the security booth, turned Fredrick around and dropped to her knees. He watched as Ko-Ko began to open his button and pull down his zipper. Ko-Ko yanked out his dick and locked eyes with him.

"This is a little bonus for doing this for me, and a little incentive for you not to say a word to anyone," she said, just before placing his entire dick into her mouth.

It didn't take long for Ko-Ko to make the security guard bust a quick one. Afterwards, she stood up and wiped the little bit of cum off the corner of her mouth leaving Fredrick in a complete daze.

Ko-Ko pulled out the DVD. "Can you make me a few extra copies of this?" When Fredrick didn't respond, Ko-Ko began to yell. "Hello, did you hear me?"

"Umm…yes…yes. I can." He took the DVD and placed it into a small black box then quickly burned Ko-Ko two more copies.

Ko-Ko reached inside her Yves Saint Laurent bag, gave him a hundred dollar bill then blew him a kiss. "Thanks, boo."

Watching Ko-Ko make her way out the door, Fredrick had no idea what the DVD was all about, but hoped like hell she would need his help again.

Chapter Fourteen

Lynn sat on her couch drinking a cup of coffee and watching the early morning news when she heard a faint knock on her front door. She put her feet into her slippers, turned down the volume to the television and closed the front of her robe. She wondered who could be knocking on her door that time of morning, 5:15 a.m. to be exact. It was moments like this that she wished Rayshawn was around. Over the past week, he'd been staying out late every night and sometimes not coming home at all, which almost had Lynn in a state of depression. She knew he'd obviously met some girl, but every time she asked him any type of information, he wouldn't give her any leads. Lynn was determined to find out who had her son's attention though because she just wasn't ready to give him up yet.

Daylight still hadn't made an appearance, so Lynn turned on the porch light and peeped out the blinds to find Ko-Ko and Kiara standing outside like two homeless women. She couldn't open the door fast enough.

"What are y'all doing?" Lynn asked. "Is everything okay?"

"We went to this crazy party out in Rockville, and I think we had a little too much to drink. We didn't want to drive all the way home when we saw all the police out pulling cars over," Kiara informed.

When Kiara mentioned something about Rockville, Lynn hoped Ko-Ko hadn't taken her own daughter to that crazy swingers place, Taboo. "Don't say anymore. I know exactly what you mean. You definitely don't wanna get pulled over in this state of mind," Lynn said, after the strong smell of alcohol hit her nose. "Come on in."

"Do you have any aspirin?" Kiara asked walking inside.

"I think it's some beside the refrigerator," Lynn said, locking the door behind them. "I'll get you some."

Kiara sat on the couch as Ko-Ko walked over to the dining room table and sat her purse down. Lynn had left a bottle of wine open, so she immediately went to pour herself a glass. After downing it, Ko-Ko was getting ready to pour another one when Lynn peeped her head from inside the kitchen.

"You need to slow down! Damn didn't you all already have too much to drink at the restaurant?"

Ignoring her friend, Ko-Ko took her glass and the bottle into the living room then sat on the love seat and curled her legs up on the plush cushions. She adjusted the pillows so that she could see the television. "What are you doing watching this shit? All they talk about is who got killed in South East."

"What did you say sweetie?" Lynn called out.

"Nothing," Ko-Ko answered.

Kiara got off the couch and joined Lynn in the kitchen. She walked up next to her and leaned on the counter. "Why did my mother have me?"

Lynn displayed a confused expression. "What do you mean?"

"You know my mother better than anyone. Why did she have me? I can tell by the way she looks at me that she hates everything about me. Nothing I do is good enough for her. The things I think I do right, she tries to outdo me just to make me feel bad." Kiara wiped her eyes.

After grabbing a bottle of water, Lynn closed the refrigerator. "I don't think Ko-Ko hates you. Your mother has always been a pistol. I'm the only one in our little group who gives her the benefit of the doubt. Ko-Ko means well, but she just doesn't know how to let her feelings show without feeling vulnerable to others." Ko-Ko handed Kiara the aspirin along with the water.

"She keeps throwing it up in my face that I ruined her life when I was born, but I tried to tell her that's no reason why she should treat me so bad. I didn't ask to be here. Rayshawn's situation is worse than mine. I mean he's the product of you being raped and you don't treat him like shit," Kiara said, taking the medicine.

Lynn cleared her throat. For years, she'd told everyone that she was raped by Rayshawn's father, and had no idea who he was, but that wasn't the case. Lynn knew exactly who he was, and what she was doing at the time. Even though she was young, she was in love. Things just didn't work out as she planned. "You can't use my situation to try and compare or justify your relationship with your mother. Rayshawn and I just share a special bond that's hard to explain," Lynn went back in the refrigerator and pulled out some turkey meat. She planned on making her two sandwiches for lunch. "What brought all these emotions out of you tonight anyway? You need to tell me what's really bothering you." She wasn't sure if the alcohol had anything to do with Kiara's Dr. Phil moment.

Kiara turned to face Lynn. "Rayshawn forced me to have sex with him the night before he left for college a few years ago."

Lynn's eyes almost bulged out of her head. "What?"

"I'm tired of holding all this stuff in. I'm tired of carrying it around."

"You told Rayshawn to stop and he didn't!" Lynn screamed.

Kiara began crying even harder. "I'm sorry. It's just that I had to tell someone. When he started going inside of me, I told him to stop, but I guess he didn't want to. I just wanted to please him and show him that I really loved him."

Lynn now had tears in her own eyes. "So, are you saying he raped you?"

Kiara lowered her head. "I guess you could say that."

"Why? Why are you telling me this now? Why didn't you tell me this before?"

"I was afraid to tell anyone. No one knows. Not even my mother."

Lynn was beyond shocked. "But how could you continue to be around Rayshawn knowing what he did to you?"

"Because I love him, and I didn't want to see him get hurt. Even now, I still don't want him to get hurt. I know he's getting involved with the wrong woman who's going to hurt him in the long run. I just can't stand on the sidelines and watch him mess up his life."

It was hard for Lynn to even look at Kiara, but she had to find out what the hell was happening with her son. "What woman?"

"She works with him, but I don't know exactly who she is. I just know when I saw his text messages one day that she's a real freak and she's playing games with him."

"Do you remember the woman's name?"

"I think one of the text messages ended with Felice," Kiara responded.

Lynn placed her hands on both of Kiara's arms. "Listen, I don't want you to worry about anything. We're gonna get through this. And don't think that the whole rape issue was your fault either because it wasn't. Trust me, I'll handle Rayshawn." She gave Kiara a huge hug before walking back into the living room. Ko-Ko had dozed off, but Lynn wasn't about to let her get any beauty rest.

She looked up at Lynn. "What?"

"Why didn't you tell me my son was fucking that woman named Felice at your job?"

Ko-Ko sat up like she was surprised even though she wasn't. She and Kiara had been putting on a performance from the start. There was no late night drinking and they definitely weren't drunk. In fact, the alcohol smell came from them dabbing some Vodka on their clothes. They were however, actresses for the moment. She looked at her daughter. "Kiara, why did you tell her?"

"Why didn't you tell me?" Lynn snapped.

Ko-Ko hunched her shoulders. "I just didn't want to get involved. I didn't want Rayshawn hating me for being a snitch, and I didn't want you mad like you are now."

Kiara snickered as Lynn began to pace back and forth. *We've got her right where we need her.*

"Ko-Ko, you know I'm not gonna sit back and allow my son to date a woman who's my fucking age," Lynn stated in a matter of fact tone.

"I know. Felice is indeed too old for him," Ko-Ko agreed. "Is Rayshawn here? Maybe we all can talk about it?"

Lynn shook her head. "Hell no. His ass has been staying out late all week. I haven't even seen him." The more Lynn talked about Rayshawn's whereabouts, the angrier Ko-Ko got.

"Oh, I saw his car when we pulled up," Kiara said.

"No, for some reason he wanted to take mine last night. Said he had a special date. If I had known it was with an old-ass woman, and he was gonna be out all night, he wouldn't have taken shit of mine. That's okay though. I'll catch up with him sooner or later. I'm getting ready to text his ass and see if he responds," Lynn informed. "I'm going to my room to get ready to work another twelve hour shift. The guest room is already made up whenever you two are ready to lay down."

"Sorry for being the bearer of bad news, Aunt Lynn," Kiara said, before walking over to Lynn on the steps. "Thank you again for not being mad at me, too. I wish at times that you were my mother instead," she whispered so Ko-Ko couldn't hear.

"Don't you ever let me hear you say that again. Your mother means well, but you need to know that she's had to live a very hard life."

I wonder if you'll say the same thing when you find out that she's fucking your son and smiling in your face day in and day out, Kiara thought.

Thirty minutes later, the sound of the front door opening made Kiara wake up. She obviously must've dozed off after watching the movie, *Burn Notice* on HBO. Once he heard the television on, Rayshawn just knew that his mother had fallen asleep in the living room, so he gently closed the door trying not to disturb her. However, when he walked around the corner to find Kiara on the couch and Ko-Ko balled up on the love seat, he started to turn right back around. It was if he couldn't get away from them.

"Good morning," Kiara said.

"What the fuck are you two doing here?" Rayshawn whispered.

"We were over here having a drink with your mother and we had a little too much," Kiara lied.

"I knew I should've stayed where I was at a little longer," he said, walking toward the basement.

"Would you like some company since I'm already here?"

Rayshawn wasn't in the mood for that shit. "Kiara, I need for you and your mother to get a life."

"Fuck you, Rayshawn."

"What are you saying?" Lynn shouted from the top of the steps.

"Oh no, I wasn't talking to you Aunt Lynn," Kiara replied in a sweet tone.

Ko-Ko rolled over when she heard the yelling to see Rayshawn standing near the kitchen. Popping up like toast, she immediately began to fix her hair.

"Who are you talking to then?" Lynn asked.

"She was talking to me, Ma," Rayshawn chimed in.

"Rayshawn, get your ass up here right now!" Lynn roared.

Rayshawn looked over at Kiara who had a devilish little grin on her face. *What the fuck did they tell my mother?* Rayshawn wondered. He held up his arms to silently ask Kiara what did she say, but Kiara only shrugged her shoulders and laughed. He didn't even bother to ask Ko-Ko.

Rayshawn kept looking back at the two women as he walked up the steps in a slow pace. From Lynn's tone, he knew whatever it was she wanted, couldn't have been good. Lynn was putting on her Crocs when Rayshawn entered her room. He sat down on the edge of the bed.

"Yes."

"I think the roller coaster ride is coming to the end for you. You're taking your ass back to school. I'm going to let you keep working until we all come back from Melyssa's wedding since you're going to be down there with the job anyway, but as soon as we get back, you're going back to New Orleans."

"So, I don't have a say in this matter?" Rayshawn asked.

"No, you don't!"

"Ma, I already told you. I don't want to me a doctor. You can't make me be something I don't wanna be."

"Well, do that photographer shit while you're in school then. I'm not saying that you have to totally give the idea of being a photographer up. You just need to get your degree then see where you feel from there."

Rayshawn didn't respond. He sat there trying to figure out if this was the real reason that she called him up or was this just the warm-up. Lynn ran her fingers through her hair then sat next to him.

"So, is there anything exciting going over there at that magazine? Is there something you want to tell me?"

"Like what?" Rayshawn felt her real reason coming on.

"I was just interested in what and who you're doing over there at the magazine. Are you doing something that you know I wouldn't approve of? Just let me know if I need to come down there with my knife and slice me up a hoe or two." She rubbed his back to try and gain some trust. To make him feel more comfortable.

Rayshawn realized that his mother was on a fishing exhibition. "There's nothing going on at the magazine except work and getting ready to go shoot the anniversary issue down in the island's."

"Are you sure?"

"I'm positive. There is nothing to tell you."

"Not even about Felice?"

He stared at his mother for a few seconds. "Felice? What about her?" He wanted to go downstairs and beat the shit out of Ko-Ko and Kiara. He knew what they were trying to do.

Lynn could no longer withhold her sweet demeanor. "Why the hell are you seeing someone almost half your damn age? Are you crazy?"

"Ma, it's not that serious."

"Yeah right, something tells me that bitch got you following her ass around like a sick little puppy, and I don't like it. You haven't even been coming home at night."

Rayshawn hated to admit it, but his mother needed a man...a life...some dick. She sounded more like his wife. "Can we talk about this when you get home or something. I'm really tired right now."

"Yeah, okay sure." Lynn turned around and looked at her Garfield printed scrubs in the mirror one last time, then grabbed her purse. She hadn't even brought up the Kiara situation yet, so they definitely needed to have a one on one when she got back. "Give me my damn car keys."

"So, when are they leaving?" Rayshawn handed Lynn her key ring, then pointed downstairs.

"No time soon. They've been drinking, so I don't want them to drive. I'm sure they'll leave once the alcohol wears off."

"Oh, hell no. I don't want them here!" he shouted.

"Boy, you better calm your ass down, and who are you cursing at? This is my house, and they are my guests. What the hell is wrong with you? They're like family."

Rayshawn shook his head. In his mind, if anything those bitches were shady. He couldn't believe that the two people who were obviously out to get him, had his mother damn near wrapped around their finger. If Felice hadn't told him she had several errands to run that morning, he certainly would've left and went back to her condo in Crofton. Deciding not to respond,

Rayshawn went back downstairs, and headed toward his room. As he passed Ko-Ko and Kiara, they were both acting like they were asleep, but he knew it was just a hoax. Once he was in the basement, Rayshawn didn't waste anytime getting undressed. After having sex with Felice all night, his body was worn out. Getting in the bed, he punched his pillow a couple of times then drifted off to sleep within minutes.

Rayshawn was in the middle of a good dream when he felt a soft pinch on his dick. He raised his head to find Kiara sucking on his tool and massaging his balls as Ko-Ko was tying his leg to the foot posts with several of his old neck ties. Rayshawn tried to move his arms to push her off him but couldn't. Ko-Ko had already managed to secure them to the lower part of his headboard. It wasn't exactly a MacGyver type of solution, but it definitely worked.

"What the hell? Y'all crazy bitches better untie me right now. I'm not playing with either of you," Rayshawn ordered in a stern voice.

"You just lie still baby. I heard you calling my name in your sleep. Don't worry, I'm here to take care of you," Kiara replied.

Rayshawn kept tugging trying to free his arms, but the knots were too strong. Changing his approach, he pleaded with Kiara to stop, but she didn't listen. Rayshawn's legs started to shake as Kiara's tickled the tip of his penis with her twirling tongue. It felt so good. He closed his eyes and began to pump his dick upward into her warm mouth. When he opened them a few seconds later, he was surprised to see that Ko-Ko was now sucking his dick and Kiara was taking off her tight jeans and boy shorts. He began to wiggle his body and pull on the ties with all his might when he realized she was about to ride him without putting on a condom. Not that he'd used them with her before, but he knew this time she had an agenda.

"Get off of me!" Rayshawn shouted. "Ma!" He knew he sounded like a little bitch by screaming, but it was all he could think of at the moment. Hell, Rayshawn would've screamed out for the mailman if he knew it would get him away from the crazy situation.

"You can scream all you want, Mama's boy. Lynn left about thirty minutes ago to go to work. She won't be home anytime soon," Ko-Ko said laughing.

At that moment, Kiara walked out and headed straight for the laundry room. She came back a few seconds later with wash cloth. Rayshawn continued to fight with the tight binds, but couldn't get free. He was about to yell for help again, but Kiara stuffed the wash cloth in his mouth and secured it with another neck tie. Kiara used her tongue to lick all around his face as her mother continued to suck and lick his dick until it was fully erected. She rubbed it up and down her pussy lips until her juices were running all over his shaft. Kiara stared deep into Rayshawn's eyes as Ko-Ko inserted his dick inside her. She began riding him with tremendous force then grabbed the top of the head board to get leverage to pound him even harder. Rayshawn looked up to see Kiara's breast bouncing all around smacking him in the face.

"So, you thought you were running shit, huh?" Kiara asked.

Rayshawn shook his head up and down. He mumbled something, but Kiara wasn't paying him any mind. Ko-Ko started to grind her pussy harder and harder on Rayshawn's dick.

"You did the same shit to my mother, but for much longer. You thought that shit was cute when you told me that at the frat party. Right now, you belong to us. We're going to find out just how many hours you can go," Kiara taunted.

Rayshawn's dick was getting ready to explode. He tried thinking of sports, motorcycles, food and everything else so he wouldn't come inside of Ko-Ko without a condom on. Just before he unloaded, Ko-Ko quickly jumped up. Kiara moved in and took her mother's place. As she began to pick up the pace again, Rayshawn couldn't fight it any longer. He clinched his butt cheeks and released all his cum inside of her. Even though Kiara knew he'd busted a nut, she still didn't stop. She continued to grind his dick over and over again until his shit was hard again.

Suddenly, Ko-Ko began sucking on Rayshawn's nipples. His eyes even tightened as Ko-Ko dug her nails into his chest. Deciding to change positions, Kiara climbed off his dick and sat her pussy over his face. When she reached her climax, she squirted cum all over his mouth. Normally, Rayshawn would've probably enjoyed a threesome with two beautiful ladies, but this sexual escapade was even too much for him. He was convinced now more than ever that both Ko-Ko and Kiara needed to seek professional help. Disturbed minds definitely ran in their family.

They kept taking turns to ride Rayshawn all morning. Whenever he would cum, they quickly worked to get it back hard. When the orgy was finally over, Ko-Ko and Kiara got dressed, kissed his forehead, and headed out the door without untying him. They did do him a favor by removing the wash cloth from his mouth though.

"When you mother comes home, be a dear and tell her we said thanks for having us over. You were such a good host," Ko-Ko joked before walking up the steps.

Chapter Fifteen

"Rayshawn? You down there?" Lynn yelled downstairs.

"Yeah, Ma," Rayshawn responded in a weak tone. He couldn't believe he'd been tied up for over twelve hours with nothing to eat or drink. He was beyond weak and famished.

"Good, we need to finish talking," Lynn said already heading downstairs. "I can't believe you're home. Normally your ass is out…" She stopped in mid-sentence then immediately dropped the laundry basket full of clothes on the floor. Standing in his doorway, Lynn clutched her heart like Fred Sanford used to do all the time. "What in the hell?"

All Rayshawn could do was shake his head. He was so embarrassed that his mother had to come downstairs and find him like that. At the same time, he also felt a little relieved because his dick wasn't hard, but more like a limp spaghetti noodle. "Can you please untie me?" he pleaded.

Lynn finally caught her breath. "What the fuck are you doing? Your ass is in my house performing some type of wild sex shit!" She walked toward the bed, and stopped when she saw a note written in red ink on the night stand. When Lynn picked it up and read it, her body temperature seemed to rise about ten degrees.

Thanks for the dick, Ray. I can't wait until I can cum over again and taste you.

Love, Felice

Lynn went ballistic. "So, I'm at work trying to save money and keep your ass in school, and you have the fucking nerve to have that bitch in my house!"

"What are you talking about? Ko-Ko and Kiara did this to me!"

Lynn threw the piece of paper in his face. "Stop lying. She wrote a note thanking you for the sex!"

Rayshawn couldn't get over how far Ko-Ko and Kiara were willing to take this. "I'm not lying. I haven't seen Felice. I haven't seen anybody. I've been down here tied up all day. I'm surprised I haven't died from dehydration." Lynn's face said that she still didn't believe him. "Check my phone then, Ma. I'm sure Felice has been calling me."

When Lynn grabbed his phone, the only missed calls that appeared where from Gary and Damon. "I don't see any calls from her."

"Ma, I'm telling you, Ko-Ko and Kiara did this. Please just untie me."

Lynn walked up to the bed, freeing his hands. "You really need to take your ass back to New Orleans now."

Rayshawn quickly covered his penis and untied his legs himself.

"You don't have anything I haven't seen before." *I don't remember it being so big though*, Lynn thought. She quickly shook her head to get those thoughts out her mind before she watched him scramble to put some gym shorts on. "If you've supposedly been down here that long, you really do need some water," she suggested. Lynn turned around and made her way back upstairs with Rayshawn following close behind. She went to the refrigerator and pulled out two bottles of water then handed him one. Lynn was still a little uncomfortable that she'd seen her son's dick. She felt little heat flashes running through her body as the water descended down her throat. *I really need to get a man in my life*, she thought. She eyed Rayshawn for a moment. "I'm starting to really worry about you."

"You don't have to. I'm going to take care of this. There's nothing going on that I can't handle," Rayshawn replied.

"Why would I? First I hear that you're fucking some woman at your job. Then I hear about Kiara, and now I come home and find your ass tied up to your bed, by the woman who you're supposed to be fucking might I add?"

He was shocked to find out that his mother still didn't believe him. "Ma, I told you, Kiara and Ko-Ko were the ones who did this."

"How? Kiara called me on my cell phone by ten this morning, and said they were already home. Did all the tying up shit happen in two hours?"

"No, because they didn't leave until it was night fall. Don't you see? It's obvious that they're lying."

Lynn felt it was time to get down to the bottom of a very important issue. "So, did you force yourself on Kiara a few years ago?"

Rayshawn eyes widened. "What? Hell no. I've never forced myself on anyone."

"Well, she told me this morning that you did, and I couldn't believe it."

"And you shouldn't. I've told you more than once that she's lying. I've had plenty of girls, and don't need to force myself on anyone. What Kiara didn't tell you is that we've been having consensual sex since high school. She was even the girl who I had sex with on your bed that night."

Lynn didn't know what to believe. "So, if you lied to me that night about it being some girl named, Asia how do I know you're not lying now?"

Rayshawn was tired of repeating himself. He could feel himself getting angrier by the minute, and didn't want to snap. "I need to get out of here." Without waiting to see if Lynn had anything else to say, Rayshawn made this way back downstairs and grabbed his cell phone.

He began dialing Ko-Ko and Kiara's cell and house number

with the intention of cursing them both out, but neither one answered. He imagined them somewhere laughing at how they just got the best of him. Rayshawn was so upset that he couldn't think straight. He decided to call Felice after all his calls to the two lunatics had failed.

"Hello, handsome," Felice said answering the phone.

"Hey you. Did I catch you at a bad time?"

"No, not at all. I meant to call you today, but I've been so busy I didn't get a chance. What's wrong? I can tell that something is bothering you by your tone. You sound down."

"I need to see you. Is it alright if we meet for a drink or two at The Game Room over in Fort Washington?" Rayshawn asked.

"Sure baby, give me about an hour and I'll be right there," Felice replied.

"See you then."

Rayshawn quickly showered using hot water as if he was trying to burn the smell of Ko-Ko and Kiara off his skin. Minutes later, he got dressed, threw on some cologne and proceeded to head out the door.

"What's the backpack all about? We still need to talk. I'm not done with you," Lynn informed.

"Yeah. I gotta take this bag to Damon. He's borrowing it," Rayshawn lied. The truth was, he had no intentions on coming back anytime soon.

Rayshawn rode out to The Game Room in complete silence. The thoughts in his mind seemed to be fighting with the emotions he was feeling about what had gone down. Rayshawn felt taken advantaged of and used. However, when he thought about Felice he smiled. Being around her was drama free, and that's the route he wanted to travel these days. Fifteen minutes later, he pulled into the parking lot and noticed Felice's car parked up front. He walked into the spot and quickly found her sitting at the bar talking with some guy. *Please let that conversation be innocent. I don't need anymore shit tonight.*

"Hey, thank you for meeting me," Rayshawn said, walking up and kissing Felice on her cheek. She looked sexy in a black sweater dress with a thick leather belt going around her waist, along with some tall leather boots.

"Dude, can't you see that I'm talking to her?" the guy said, staring at Rayshawn.

"Well, I appreciate you keeping her company while she was waiting for me, but your conversation is no longer needed," Rayshawn answered.

Felice looked at Rayshawn with a look of surprise. She'd never seen him like this before. It was something about his tone that immediately made her become aroused. Felice stood up between the two men and placed both her hands on Rayshawn's chest.

"Okay baby, you need to calm down. We were just talking until you got here," Felice tapped his chest then looked at the other guy. "Thank you for the small talk, but my man is here now and I can't let you disrespect him."

"Your man, hell, I thought that was your son or something," the guy replied before getting up from his bar stool.

Felice glanced over at her and Rayshawn's reflection in the mirror behind the bar. She tilted her head from side to side as she tried to see what the guy was insinuating. "Damn, do I look that old?"

Rayshawn shook his head back and forth. "Not at all, baby."

"So, are you gonna tell me what's wrong now?" Felice asked, sitting back down.

"It's nothing. I just wanted to see you. I needed to get out of my house and get some fresh air so I called and hoped you would come out and keep me company."

"That's kinda sweet. You wanted to get out and thought of me, huh? I don't know what to say."

"No need to say anything other than you're glad I did."

Rayshawn and Felice ordered a few drinks and talked about a few things that were going on in each of their lives and the upcoming shoot in Jamaica. Rayshawn wanted to tell Felice about Ko-Ko and Kiara, but decided it was best just to keep it to himself and deal with the two of them on another day.

Chapter Sixteen

Felice and Rayshawn were spending a lot of time with one another during the weeks prior to them leaving for the photo shoot in Jamaica. In that time, Rayshawn had escorted her to a high-end industry party that took place in Crystal City every year. It was strange for some of her associates to see Felice with a younger man. She was usually escorted by men who looked like they owned Fortune 500 companies or hustled at the Stock Exchange. To them, Rayshawn looked wet behind the ears, but to her he was the complete package, especially since the older men couldn't keep a stiff dick like Rayshawn. To her, Rayshawn was not only great in bed, but was also confident, extremely knowledgeable in many areas, charismatic, and thoughtful. Not to mention, his appearance made her the envy of all the other women. Even on Valentine's Day, Rayshawn surprised Felice with a romantic getaway to a quiet little bed and breakfast in Pennsylvania. He went the extra mile to decorate the room with red and white rose petals for them to make love on, scented candles, and several slow song mix CD's that played her favorite music for hours. They made love until the sun would set and rise again.

The day of the trip, Felice made arrangements for a driver to pick her and Rayshawn up and take them to the airport. Rayshawn sat next to her staring out his window as they drove down I-295 to BWI International. Felice kept herself busy by talking on her cell phone to several distributors in New York until they got to the departure corridor.

Rayshawn sat patiently waiting for the driver to open the rear doors then got out, stretched his legs and watched as two sky caps unloaded and checked their luggage. After getting their boarding passes, Felice led the way over to the Gold Club Lounge, so they could have a cocktail before their flight. Rayshawn smiled. He'd flown out of BWI on several occasions going back and forth from school, but never knew this place existed.

"What can I get for you, Ms. Contour?" the bartender asked when they sat down.

"I'll have an Apple Martini, Matt," she replied.

"And you, sir?"

"Can I have a Corona with a shot of grenadine?" Rayshawn answered.

Matt nodded. "Sure."

Felice removed a piece of lint off the new Rock N Republic leather jacket that she'd just bought him. One of the many gifts she'd purchased for her new man. "I've never heard of anyone taking their beer with a shot of grenadine. You're full of surprises aren't you?"

"The grenadine takes the edge off the beer," Rayshawn said, grabbing her hand. "I see that you're a regular around here. The bartender knows you by name."

"Well, not only do I like to have a drink before I fly because it calms my nerves, but I also travel a lot for the magazine. I'm in New York and Colorado quite often."

"Colorado. That's an odd place to go. Do we have a lot of readers there?" Rayshawn questioned as the bartender returned.

Felice took a sip of her drink. "No, I'm mostly there for personal reasons."

"Oh yeah, like what?"

Felice didn't want to get into that at the moment. "We have all the time in the world to talk about me. For now, let's talk about us. I'm so happy that you've been staying with me lately.

It's nice to have someone to wake up to."

"I agree," Rayshawn said, taking a huge gulp of beer.

They were almost finished with their second round when the bartender told Felice the plane would be boarding shortly. Felice gave him her American Express Black Card and told him to include a twenty dollar tip for himself. After signing the receipt, Rayshawn held the door for Felice as they exited the club area.

"We are now boarding Delta flight 6869 for Montego Bay, Jamaica," is what Felice and Rayshawn heard as they walked up to the gate. "We're taking all first class and passengers who have small children or need assistance at this time," the ticket attendant said over the mic.

"That's our call," Felice informed.

"We're flying first class?" Rayshawn had never even bothered to look down at his seat assignment.

"Where else would a woman like me fly? Wait, don't answer that," she said with a laugh. "You're with me now. You just continue to knock my back out on a regular and take those wonderful pictures. I'll take care of everything else," Felice said, giving him a kiss.

He smacked her ass in return.

"Welcome aboard," a young stewardess said when they boarded.

Rayshawn nodded his head and flashed a quick smile. As Felice slid into her plush leather seat next to the window, Rayshawn quickly grabbed a pillow and blanket from the over head compartment, ready for the four hour flight. Felice cuddled up next to Rayshawn once he sat down and fastened his seat belt.

"You're too good to be true," she whispered.

Rayshawn brushed her hair off her forehead and gave her a small kiss. "I happen to think you're pretty special yourself. This feels right."

The two of them sat holding one another, while sipping complimentary champagne and watching passenger after passenger get onto the plane. Once all the other passengers were finally on board and the stewardess was about to close the door, they heard someone yelling.

"Wait, we're here. This is our plane!" a women's voice shouted.

The flight attendant looked out the door to find four women running down the corridor. "Slow down ladies, we won't leave without you," she said.

"Thank you so much," the woman replied.

Rayshawn recognized the voice immediately. Before he even had a chance to tell Felice to brace herself, he looked up to see his mother, Kiara, Ko-Ko and Tootie all walking through the door. Kiara was the first one to lock eyes on Rayshawn sitting in first class next to Felice.

"Oh, my goodness. Look who's on our plane and flying first class no less," Kiara informed.

All the women's heads turned to see Rayshawn and Felice all snuggled up like a bonafide couple. Rayshawn smiled as they stopped right in front of him. He handed his glass to Felice and tried to stand up to hug his mother.

"Sorry ladies but I need for all of you to find your seats. The captain has just been cleared to taxi to the run way," the flight attendant announced.

"When they turn off the fasten seat belt sign, you need to come talk to me," Ko-Ko ordered Rayshawn.

"I'm a little tired. I had a long night," Rayshawn replied, looking over at Felice. "I'll holla at you when we land."

Ko-Ko's face frowned. She was about to go off when the stewardess stepped up. "I need you ladies to find your seats. The captain is ready to taxi from the gate."

"You and I need to talk," Lynn said, walking past Rayshawn.

Rayshawn shook his head. "Okay."

"I'm not talking to you. She knows who I'm talking to," Lynn responded.

For some strange reason, Felice snatched her arm away

from Rayshawn as the flight attendant continued to direct the ladies into coach so they could find their seats. *This is going to be a long flight,* Felice thought before closing her eyes and laying her head back.

Rayshawn asked his flight attendant for another drink, but this time he wanted something stronger. After being told he had to wait until they got in the air, he sighed and placed his head back on the seat as well. He wondered how bad his mother was going to act up.

"Try not to let my mother get to you. She's just extremely over protective that's all," Rayshawn whispered.

"I know your mother," Felice told him.

Rayshawn looked completely surprised. "Really? Oh, shit don't tell me y'all are friends, too. How?"

"We all grew up in the same neighborhood, I was Kourtney's neighbor. We used to hang out back in the day, but she probably doesn't recognize me now. It's been years since I've seen her."

"You're not going back there are you?" Rayshawn questioned. He had that, *I wouldn't do it if I were you* look in his eyes.

"Absolutely not. When we take off, and the stewardess closes the black curtain, I'm taking a beauty nap so we can get our trip started as soon as we get to Negril. If you want to go back there that's on you, but I don't do coach for anyone," Felice advised.

"I'm not going back there either. How about if I work it out with the flight attendant so we can join the mile high club? I'd much rather do that when they turn off the fasten seatbelt sign." He reached over to grab her breasts.

"Those bathrooms are way too small for us to do anything inside of them. You can barely get one person inside."

Rayshawn was shocked. She'd never turned him down before. "Wow, I've never gotten an excuse. What happened? You can't focus because my mother is on the plane and she just might come up here and beat both of our asses?" he teased.

That was exactly the reason, but Felice wouldn't dare confess. "Your mother being on the plane has nothing to do with it. You know what…on second thought go ahead and work out the deal so they won't lock our asses up when we land."

After Felice handed him a piece of paper out of her purse, Rayshawn wrote down a couple of sentences then wrapped the paper around two hundred dollar bills. Bills that he'd just received from Felice. After that, he pushed the button for the flight attendant and waited. When she came over to check, Rayshawn slipped her the paper. The fight attendant read the note and gave Felice and Rayshawn a smile then nodded her head up and down.

After taking off, everyone waited patiently for the captain to turn off the glowing red fasten seatbelt sign. When they finally reached thirty-five thousand feet, the light turned off and all the passengers began taking out their electronic devices and pushing their seats back to get comfortable. Once the stewardess gave them the signal, Rayshawn and Felice made a b-line straight to the bathroom and locked the door. Knowing they didn't have much time, Felice quickly maneuvered her body so that she could ride his dick as Rayshawn sat on the toilet. She locked her legs around his back and allowed the motion of the plane to push his dick in and out.

"I'm about to cum already," Rayshawn whispered, trying not to alert the other passengers of what they were doing.

Felice lifted her pussy off his dick and slid down to her knees to suck his throbbing shaft then clamped his balls with one of her free hands. A move that made Rayshawn's entire body began to tremble. Moments later, he shot a large amount of cum into Felice's mouth. Felice began to choke but Rayshawn wouldn't let her pull back her head so she could swallow.

"I can't believe we're on the same flight as Rayshawn. Out

of all the flights going to Jamaica, we chose the same one. I guess Felice is taking him first class in every way," Kiara said to Ko-Ko. "It looks like he really likes her."

"Shut the hell up. You don't know what you're talking about. Rayshawn doesn't like her, Ko-Ko responded in a sharp tone. She was trying to make Lynn feel better. *Besides he's just doing this shit to make me jealous. We'll see what happens in Jamaica,* Ko-Ko thought to herself.

As Ko-Ko and Kiara went back and forth, Lynn continued to stare at the black curtains to see if Felice was going to walk out from behind them. After growing impatient, she tapped Ko-Ko on the leg. "Do me a favor. Go up there and stick your head through the curtain and tell that old-ass bitch I'm still waiting for her," Lynn demanded.

A large smile quickly popped on Ko-Ko's face. She leaped to her feet and began walking toward first class, happy to start some shit. However, when Ko-Ko stuck her head through, she noticed that Rayshawn and Felice's seats were empty. She actually didn't see either of them anywhere.

"I'm sorry miss, but you can't be up here without a ticket," a flight attendant said.

Ko-Ko scanned first class one last time, then turned to go back to her seat. When she sat down, Lynn had a look like she was ready to pop. Ko-Ko had no idea how her friend was going to react.

"So, did you tell her what I said?" Lynn asked.

"I couldn't."

"Why the hell not?" Lynn said getting upset.

"Well, when I got up there and looked around, they were gone. It's the weirdest thing. I mean they couldn't have gotten off, I don't think."

Lynn thought for a second, then realized there was only one other place they could be. She leaned over toward Tootie, who sat in the window seat. "You think they went to the bathroom to do you know what?"

"And what if they did? You really need to stop babying

that man, Lynn. Your son is no longer this helpless little boy who needs his mother to still fight his battles. Let him get his rocks off if he wants. If you go up there and embarrass him, he'll never forgive you. What you need to do is find a man and do the same. I haven't seen or heard you talking about getting some in a long time," Tootie answered. "You doing the same shit Usher's mother did to him and he still married Tameka's ass."

Kiara started laughing.

"And you see they got a divorce, too," Ko-Ko butted in.

Tootie threw up her arms. "It don't matter. That just goes to show that a man is gonna do what he wants."

Ko-Ko smacked her teeth. "Shut up Tootie. How is Lynn gonna take advice from somebody who can't even keep a man?"

Lynn couldn't believe how blunt her friend was, but still didn't let up. "See, you don't understand, Tootie. I can't let him do anything like that. What kind of mother would I be if I just let him do whatever he wanted? He's making a bad decision." She stood up and did a pushing movement. "Let me out, Ko-Ko." She hated being in the middle seat.

"Shit, I'm going, too," Ko-Ko co-signed. There wasn't any drama if she wasn't involved.

"I'm going to kill that no good slut when I get my hands on her," Lynn said to herself.

"Attention passengers. The captain is turning back on the fasten seatbelt sign due to some turbulence we're approaching. We need for everyone to return back to their seats and fasten their seatbelts until further notice," another flight attendant said over the intercom.

"I'm sorry, Miss but you'll have to take your seat and put on your seatbelt," a stewardess stated to Lynn.

Lynn however, didn't pay the flight attendant any mind. She continued to walk down the aisle like she owned the plane with Ko-Ko right on her heels. The flight attendant asked her to stop and go sit back down, but again Lynn ignored her. The two women were almost to the black curtain when an undercover Air

Marshall grabbed Lynn's arm.

"United States Air Marshall, do we have a problem here?" the geeky looking white man questioned. Just by looking at him, you would've thought he worked at Home Depot instead.

Lynn made a motion for Ko-Ko to keep going. "Get your hands off of me. I was just going up front to make sure my son was okay. He gets real bad headaches when he flies," Lynn spoke loudly so the focus wouldn't be on Ko-Ko going through the curtains.

With a pace that demanded attention, Ko-Ko walked straight to first class and up to one of the bathrooms. She put her ear to the doors and listened for any activity. Suddenly, she heard some faint moans coming from inside. Ko-Ko began banging on the door with all her might.

"I know you're in there, Rayshawn!" she yelled.

Everyone in first class was startled.

At that moment, the Air Marshall quickly pushed Lynn aside and burst into first class to stop Ko-Ko from banging on the door. He hurried to restrain her. When the bathroom door opened a few seconds later, a young white guy in a business suit walked out.

Ko-Ko and Lynn looked at one another with perplexed expressions.

"Ma'am you need to calm down now!" the Air Marshall demanded with authority. He held on to Ko-Ko with a tight grip.

"I needed to check on my son, but now I don't know where he is," Lynn said.

"If your son is that gentleman over there, you have nothing to worry about. He's taking a nap with his lady friend," the stewardess in first class answered. Luckily she'd been the one who Rayshawn and Felice had paid off earlier. When she realized there might've been a problem, the stewardess knocked on the bathroom door and told them to come out just minutes before.

Ko-Ko looked over at Lynn "I just walked up here and both those seats were empty. Besides, I'm not buying that sleep routine. How is he gonna sleep through all that?"

"Can I talk to my son?" Lynn asked the Air Marshall.

"No Ma'am. You've caused more than enough chaos." He turned to the stewardess. "We can always alert the captain and have him return back to Baltimore. We haven't been in the air very long."

"No, just escort them back to their seats. I'm sure everything will be fine now," the stewardess said in the ladies' defense.

The Air Marshall finally released Ko-Ko's arm. "I'm going to lock both of you up if I have any more problems for the rest of the flight. Is that understood?"

"Yes," Lynn and Ko-Ko said like two disciplined kids.

As they were being escorted back to their seat once again, Rayshawn and Felice who really were pretending to be asleep finally lifted their heads.

"That was close," Rayshawn said.

Now, he really needed that drink.

Chapter Seventeen

Rayshawn and Felice exited the plane first, while all the coach passengers were held up due to everyone getting their carry-on luggage from the overhead bins. By the time all the ladies made it to baggage claim and through customs, Felice and Rayshawn were already gone. Lynn and Ko-Ko were furious. They couldn't even enjoy the island's sunny eighty-three degree weather because they were so pissed. As they walked outside the airport and boarded the shuttle bus designated to take them to the resort in Negril, Ko-Ko assured her friend that everything would work out.

"Don't worry. We'll catch up with them. You must've forgot that not only am I here for the wedding, but I'm also here on business. They're staying at the Hendonism II, which is right beside our hotel. I'll actually be staying there myself on Friday."

Tootie chuckled. "Hendonism? The infamous swinger's hotel, huh? That's the perfect spot for a nasty-ass magazine. It's the perfect spot for you too, huh Ko-Ko?"

"You love to be funny. Too bad you're not," Ko-Ko shot back.

Lynn stared out the window. "As soon as we check in, I'm going to find that bitch and give her a piece of my mind."

"Well, I'm going with you. You might need a little back up if shit gets ugly. You know how anal you are when it comes to your son, so I don't know how this is going to turn out," Ko-Ko replied.

Lynn grunted. "You ain't seen nothing yet. I wish she would act brand new. I'll stomp her a new asshole.

"Lynn, I still don't understand why you don't just leave Rayshawn alone. Who cares who he's fucking anyway?" Tootie mentioned. "Let him live his life."

Ko-Ko jumped to Lynn's defense. "Did anybody ask you anything old lady? You don't have any kids, so I guess it's hard for you to understand."

Tootie got hyped. "What the hell was the purpose of coming down here if you weren't gonna help Melyssa? She still needs help finalizing the flowers for the bouquet, the menu for the reception and some other stuff. She's so nervous that all she has so far is jerk chicken and oxtails."

"Didn't I basically tell you to stay out of this? Melyssa is just gonna have to wait," Ko-Ko responded. "Me and Lynn got better shit to do."

"Shut up, Ko-Ko. Your ass needs to stay out of it, too. Even though you probably wanna fuck him, Rayshawn ain't got shit to do with you either."

Lynn looked at Ko-Ko sideways, while Kiara snickered. "Don't listen to her dumb-ass," Ko-Ko reacted. "I love Rayshawn like a son, and just don't want to see him get hurt, that's all."

I hope you're right because I would hate to beat your ass, too," Lynn thought.

The remainder of the forty-five mile ride was quiet. While some people slept, others listened to their Ipods or read magazines. Lynn however, thought about her son all the way to the five-star Breezes Grand Negril on Norman Manley Boulevard, formally known as Grand Lido. It was a beautiful all-inclusive hotel with tropical gardens, manicured grounds and irresistible amenities.

After checking into one big suite for all of them to stay in, Tootie decided to hook up with Melyssa who was already there, while Lynn, Ko-Ko and Kiara, made their way to the lobby.

They power walked over to Hedonism, which was right next door. Ironically, as soon as the ladies entered the front entrance of the hotel, Rayshawn and Felice were pulling out the driveway in a black Lincoln Towncar on their way to go scout out locations.

"I hope you know that my mother won't give up when it comes to me. You can't keep avoiding her this entire trip," Rayshawn said, looking out the tinted window.

"I'm not avoiding her. We just got here and I have a magazine to run. Besides, I know her a little better than you think," Felice said, leaning back and closing her eyes.

Rayshawn looked over at Felice and wondered what she meant by that. *What am I getting myself into,* he thought. Felice had no plans on dealing with Lynn or anyone else while she was there. She just wanted to please her man.

Rayshawn and Felice woke up after having hours of hot steamy sex on their third day in Negril, hyped and ready to get started. By noon, all the other staff from Fantasy Girlz and the models were already checked in and were eager to get started as well. Rayshawn had selected Bloody Bay Beach as the first location, which had a beautiful half moon shape and provided the perfect ambiance for what he wanted to accomplish. At one-thirty sharp, the models were laying out in the Jamaican sun with their semi-nude bodies spread across the white sands, ready for Rayshawn to arrive. As they sipped on water and fresh pineapples, Ko-Ko fussed with their animal print thongs, and Jamaican flag colored string bikinis.

Minutes later, several of the models rushed over to Rayshawn when they saw him walk up. When Ko-Ko heard his named being called, she slowly walked from behind the clothing rack wearing a Brazilian micro blue bikini with a matching sarong. Her body glowed from laying out the last two days on the beach. As Ko-Ko strolled across the sand, she truly believed that Rayshawn wouldn't be able to resist how she looked. She was already mad that Felice and Rayshawn had been locked up in Felice's room for two days. No matter how hard she, Lynn or Kiara tried to catch them coming out to even to get a soda, their plan was never successful.

Not even acknowledging her presence, Rayshawn walked right past Ko-Ko and headed toward some big rocks. "Sorry, I'm late ladies. Now, let's get this shoot going. We'll start over here!"

I know that nigga didn't just play me like that, Ko-Ko wondered. He'd walked right past her as if she was invisible. *I'm not going to trip though. He's got a lot on his mind with this big shoot, so I'll give him a pass for now.*

A short time later, Rayshawn was hard at work posing the girls and snapping pictures. Frame after frame, Ko-Ko stared at him as he controlled the shoot like a professional. A couple of hours had gone by when Ko-Ko suddenly saw Rayshawn taking pictures in the opposite direction of the models. She turned her head to find Felice's tall frame standing near the fruit table eating grapes.

Ko-Ko became extremely upset as Felice smiled and posed seductively in her short terry cloth skirt and a rose colored bikini top that made her breast perky. She even had large white shells around her neck that complimented her newly tanned skin tone. Felice continued to pose in different positions holding the grapes, then placing her thick painted lips around the bunch and slowly biting one off at a time. Rayshawn seemed to forget that everyone was around him watching. He snapped until the camera's memory card was full. Ko-Ko couldn't believe that Rayshawn was memorized by Felice of all people.

"This location is a wrap. We've got enough pictures of a fucking rock. Let's pack up and move this shoot to the second spot!" Ko-Ko barked.

Everyone started to move except for Rayshawn. Ko-Ko lis-

tened as the models whispered things about Rayshawn and Felice as they walked past her. Rayshawn still seemed to be locked
in his trance until Ko-Ko yelled to get his attention.

"Earth calling Rayshawn, come in Rayshawn. Did you
hear me? I said that we're done here. This shoot is history. You
need to get all your equipment together and let's go."

Rayshawn paused before finally taking his eyes off of Felice. "Calm down, Ko-Ko."

As Rayshawn began to gather his stuff, Ko-Ko walked toward Felice. Felice was still playing with fruit when Ko-Ko
stopped in front of her, blocking Rayshawn's view.

"What the hell do you think you're doing?" Ko-Ko asked.

"What are you talking about?" Felice responded.

Ko-Ko looked over her shoulder then nodded toward
Rayshawn. "Are you sleeping with him? I can't begin to acknowledge how wrong that would be on so many different lev-
els. What ever happened to all that shit we talked about?"

Felice didn't feel like the drama so she quickly denied
everything. "I'm not fucking him, he's one of my employee's. I
just enjoy hanging out with him. It's something about him that
makes me feel real comfortable."

"You're just hanging out with him. And you're positive
that the two of you have never gone past the boss and employee
level?" Ko-Ko asked in a harder tone.

Felice's facial expression changed. "What if I was fucking
him? What business is it of yours? What's wrong, Ms. Jackson?
It sounds like you're mad because I got to him before you."

Ko-Ko laughed. "I ain't mad at shit. You just need to know
that Rayshawn is off limits. Just remember that your ass was already warned before, and since you didn't listen, it's on." She
adjusted her new Chanel sunglasses then walked off.

Rayshawn poked his chest out as he walked over to Felice.
"What was that all about?"

"Oh, don't worry about that. Kourtney's bark has always
been bigger than her bite," Felice answered. She reached over
and fed him a few grapes. When she pulled her hand back,

Rayshawn had a large smile from ear to ear. Felice paused for a second and stared at him. She wondered what he was thinking. "What's that look for?"

"You're just so beautiful. Please be my date to my mother's friend Melyssa's wedding tomorrow."

Felice disagreed. "I can't go to her wedding. I wasn't invited, so I wouldn't feel right being there. Plus, with Kourtney's ass running around acting dumb, and your mother trying to kill me, I probably wouldn't enjoy myself anyway. "

Rayshawn stepped closer to her. "You wouldn't want me to be all alone would you? If you go with me to the wedding then I'll protect you from Ko-Ko and my mother. Plus, I'll be your slave for the rest of this trip? I'll do anything that you want, no questions asked."

Felice closed her eyes as Rayshawn brought his soft lips toward her. He wrapped his hands behind her back and kissed her gently. When he released her, Felice kept her eyes shut as chills ran up her body.

"I'll go with you but you better not renege on your promise. You better get a lot of rest too because Big Momma is gonna put your ass to work all weekend."

When Rayshawn turned to leave, he glanced up the walk way and saw Ko-Ko staring at them like a killer in a horror movie. *I sure hope that bitch's bark is bigger than her bite because she's barking loud as shit right now*, he thought.

As the Jamaican accented DJ announced the bridal party, Tootie, Kiara, Lynn and Ko-Ko were escorted out to the poolside reception by the groomsmen. Felice sat next to Rayshawn admiring all the beautiful decorations that were selected for the reception. Elegance was the key word as she eyed the floating candles in the pool along with the submerged flower centerpieces, and personalized menus. Each table was covered with specialty linens that blew in the cool Jamaican breeze, adorned with votive candles and personalized CD wedding favors, which featured the couple's favorite tunes. Even the three tiered, gift box shaped wedding cake stood out. The entire ambiance of the reception seemed grand.

"Everyone please stand on your feet and welcome for the first time, Mr. and Mrs. Brandon Townsend," the DJ said, announcing the newly married couple.

They circled around the dance floor before stopping in the middle as the calming voice of Luther Vandross made his way through out the speakers. Swaying from side to side with the ocean as their backdrop, Melyssa and her new husband danced to the song, *Here and Now* with huge grins.

Rayshawn glanced over to see both Ko-Ko and Kiara staring at him and Felice with stern eyes. He tried not to look in their direction, but couldn't help wondering what they were up to. He also wanted to know why Ko-Ko had decided to invite several people from Fantasy Girlz to the wedding. They didn't belong and looked out of place, especially the models in their skimpy, cheap dresses that barely covered their asses. *I wonder if Melyssa knows she did that*, he thought. His eyes continued to travel around the room until they stopped on Lynn. She too had that mean mugging thing going on.

Rayshawn leaned over to Felice. "You think my mother's bark is bigger than her bite, too?"

"I'm not quite sure about her," Felice admitted. "You know what, I'm gonna go talk to her. I need to get this over with." Felice stood up wearing a multi print Arden B. maxi dress, and made her way over to the wedding party table and asked Lynn if she could talk to her in private. When Lynn agreed, the two women made their way over toward the heart shaped ice sculpture before giving each other full eye contact.

"I see you've put on a bit of weight," Felice said, breaking the ice.

Lynn pulled on the strapless lavender bridesmaid dress. *See, I told Melyssa that I should've worn the halter top dress.*

That made me look a lot slimmer. "What are you talking about?"

"You've gained weight since the old Berry Farm days. You were what a six, back then? You're still beautiful though."

Lynn took a step back. For one, she was shocked that Felice knew her and secondly the way Felice eyed her, she wondered if she was gay. *Is this bitch trying to hit on me now*, she thought. "You lived in Berry Farms? I don't remember you." She wondered why Ko-Ko never mentioned that.

"Yeah, I did. I remember that you even used to date Raymond Wilson."

Lynn eye's widened. "How do you know that? Who told you? What...you used to date him or something?" No one knew she used to date Raymond. "Besides, I wouldn't necessarily call that shit dating."

Felice smiled. "Yeah, I guess you could say that I use to date him, too."

"Well, I tell you what. We might have that shit in common, but we'll never have my son in common. Don't you think you're a little too old for him?"

"No, not really. He's really mature for his age actually. I didn't even know you had a son. He's handsome. You did well...very well."

Lynn hated the way she talked about her son. "Out of respect for my friend and her wedding, I'm not gonna get ugly, but trust me, it's best for everyone if you leave him alone. He's going back to college soon, and doesn't need these types of distractions."

"That's funny. He told me last night that he wasn't going back to school, and that he wants to move in with me."

When the first dance was over, the DJ began playing a song by the O-Jay's, as several bowtie wearing servers started passing out the dinner plates. At the same time, Rayshawn continued to stare at the two women wondering what was going on.

"Well, I think we should end things here," Felice suggested. "I see food, and I'm pretty hungry."

I guess so. From your size bitch, it looks like you don't ever miss a meal. "Don't think this is over because I'm not done," Lynn warned.

Felice laughed. "Trust me, I've heard that before."

Leaving Lynn alone, Felice made it back to her table as Brandon's best man stood up and started to tap a spoon against his champagne glass to get everyone's attention. Once the room got quiet, he asked for Brandon and Melyssa to stand to their feet. It was time for the toast. Lynn looked over at Felice again. This time Felice held up her glass and gave Lynn a little head nod with a large smile. Lynn felt little chills run up her back as she went to rejoin the wedding party.

"This is in hope that you may never swear, steal, lie, cheat or drink. But if you must swear, swear by all that is good and holy, if you must steal, steal away your cares, if you must lie, lie in the arms of one another, if you must cheat, cheat death. And if you must drink, then raise your glass and drink with us because we love you so much. May the both of you live as long as you want and never want as long as you live," the best man said.

All the guests, family members and wedding party members began to clank their glasses together as many of the women had tears in their eyes. Even Melyssa's mascara began to run when a few tears strolled down her cheek.

"That was such a wonderful toast," Felice said to Rayshawn.

"Women are such saps when it comes to love. I heard that same toast on that movie, *Hitch* with Will Smith," Rayshawn said.

"You're missing the point. It's when and how it was said. He selected the perfect moment to deliver the perfect words at the perfect occasion."

"Yeah…yeah. So, what happened with my mother? What did she say?"

"Same warning. Different day. Oh, do you have any idea why the Fantasy Girlz crew is here?"

Rayshawn shook his head. "I have no idea. Who knows why Ko-Ko does these silly things."

Suddenly, Brandon walked over to the DJ booth and grabbed a cordless mic. He then made his way toward his new wife and kissed her. "I have a special surprise for you."

Melyssa buried her head in her hands. "I don't think I can take anymore surprises."

"Too bad." When the crowd let out a slight laugh, he continued. "I know how much you love Raheem DeVaughn, so I tried to get him to fly over here and sing, but he had a prior engagement that he couldn't get out of. But...he did have time to do the next best thing." When Brandon gave the DJ the queue, the LCD image projector flashed onto the white canvassed projector screen. "I asked him to sing one of your favorite songs and dedicate it to our long and happy life," Brandon spoke into the mic.

Melyssa sat down on her chair. She placed her face inside her hands again and began to cry. The smile on her face acknowledged that this was indeed a very special surprise. Everyone turned their chairs so they could see the screen. However, when the video popped up, it wasn't Raheem DeVaughn singing. Instead it was Rayshawn's big dick pounding deep inside Felice, which made everyone's eyes widen and their jaws drop. All of the guests sat watching the two of them having sex on her desk at Fantasy Girlz.

Melyssa yelled for the DJ to turn it off, but he'd mysteriously stepped away. At that point, Lynn rushed over to the machine and began pushing buttons trying to get her son's dick off the big screen. When her efforts went at no avail, she yanked the black cord out of the surge protector. As the projectors light went off, the homemade porno tape disappeared as well. The guests began looking at one another then all eyes stared at Rayshawn and Felice. The Fantasy Girlz models all had their mouths wide open. Rayshawn looked around in amazement as well. When he saw Ko-Ko sitting at her table with a deceitful grin over her face, he knew.

Chapter Eighteen

Lynn stomped over to where Rayshawn and Felice were sitting like a raging bull. "Do you think this shit is funny? How dare you ruin Melyssa's wedding with a stunt like this?" Lynn looked over at her friend as her tears of joy had switched to tears of anger mixed with a little sadness.

"Are you serious? Why would I mess up this wedding by playing a tape like that in front of all these people? Most of them I don't even know. I'm just as shocked as you are," Rayshawn tried to explain.

"The whole world doesn't need to know that you're fucking this woman!" Lynn turned and stared at Felice. "How old are you any damn way? Actually don't answer that because it doesn't matter. You're way too old for my son!" Lynn went to swing on Felice, but Rayshawn quickly blocked the blow.

Felice was beyond embarrassed. The last thing she wanted was for her employees to see her ass up in the air. It was a private moment that should've stayed private. Not to mention, she constantly preached about office affairs being totally unacceptable, so now she looked like a hypocrite "Lynn, I had nothing to do with this!"

"Bitch, don't call me by my name. You don't know me. Get out of here! You've caused enough trouble." Lynn tried to get to Felice again, but Rayshawn just wouldn't get out the way. She felt bad that she'd caused a scene at Melyssa's wedding, but now the damage was already done.

Felice looked over at Ko-Ko, who had her head back laughing like she was at a comedy club. At that moment, she jumped up, causing Lynn to take a boxing stance. However, Felice wasn't interested in her. She walked right past Lynn and straight over to Ko-Ko. Without much notice, Felice grabbed Ko-Ko by the front of her dress and yanked her right out of the chair. "It had to be you. How could you do some trifling shit like this just to get back at me?"

The Fantasy Girlz models looked on in awe like they were at a real boxing match.

"Bitch, you better get your construction size hands off me. I have no idea what the hell you're talking about," Ko-Ko tried to reply in an innocent tone.

"Y'all better get this freak a nature off of me!" Ko-Ko screamed.

Lynn, Rayshawn, Tootie and Kiara began pulling the two women apart. Melyssa and her husband couldn't believe how their special day had spiraled out of control so fast and quickly, became a living nightmare. The guest continued to watch the soap opera that was increasingly growing in front of them.

"You need to leave!" Lynn yelled at Felice once the two separated.

"Hold on Ma, if any one should be leaving, it should be that no good Ko-Ko," Rayshawn said stepping in. "She's the one doing all of this."

"Ko-Ko is like family. She's not." Lynn pointed to Felice.

"If Felice has to leave then I'm leaving, too. She's here with me, I invited her," Rayshawn said.

Melyssa walked over to the group. "I don't know whose idea it was to show that fucking DVD, but when I find out, it's not going to be pretty. I need for you to get control of this shit right now Lynn or all of y'all have to leave." Melyssa then looked over at Ko-Ko like she knew the entire episode was all her fault.

"Yeah, why are y'all taking such an interest in what happens between Rayshawn and that woman? I told y'all to leave that shit alone earlier. Now, look what happened!" Tootie included.

Lynn looked at both her devastated friends. She then turned back to Rayshawn and shook her head. "Well, I guess it's time for *both* of you to go." She hated saying that to Rayshawn, but knew it was best.

"You're right, I'm leaving. This was a bad idea. I should've known better," Felice admitted.

"Bye!" Ko-Ko yelled out.

Lynn and Felice both looked over at Ko-Ko. The smile on her face was devilish. Ko-Ko even had the audacity to wave her hand as if she had won a beauty pageant as Felice walked away. However, when she saw Rayshawn collect his belongings and follow her out the double doors, the smile on her face disappeared. "Rayshawn, where are you going?" she called out.

"What does it look like? With my woman!" Rayshawn belted.

Lynn called for him, too. Even Kiara, who'd just walked back to the table yelled out his name a couple of times, but he ignored them both and chased after Felice. Ko-Ko and Lynn looked at each other. *I know you had something to do with this, it's just like you to fuck up something special, especially when the focus is not on you,* Lynn thought.

Felice slowly walked in front of Rayshawn without saying a word to him. Rayshawn stayed on her heels until she got back to her hotel room. At that moment, he immediately went over to the mini bar and popped the top on the miniature Hennessey bottle, and turned it upside down. Felice walked into the bedroom, disgusted at the entire episode that had just transpired. She looked on the bed and saw a folded note lying on her pillow.

It's amazing how you wouldn't listen. You were warned about fucking with people who belong to others. I bet you'll listen to people in the future. Just be glad I didn't let them know about your other secret. When do you think I should let Rayshawn know about that?

Felice walked out to see Rayshawn finishing the third little bottle. She balled up the note and threw it in the trash then went to sit down on the couch. She closed her eyes as Rayshawn sat beside her.

"I'm not sure if we should continue to see each other. Things have become very complicated. In fact, they're too complicated. I think we've rode this train to the end of the line. Now, it's time for us to get off," Felice said.

Rayshawn looked over at Felice. With the light reflecting off her face, she'd never seemed more beautiful than she did at that moment. When he scooted over to get closer to her, the amazing scent from her expensive perfume caused his heart to pause.

"I don't want this thing we have going to stop. I've never felt this way about anyone before. I'm the happiest when I'm with you. You're the first thing I think of when I wake and the last thing on my mind when I go to sleep."

Felice opened her eyes to see Rayshawn only inches away from her face staring at her with his nicely shaped eyes. She felt him leaning toward her, but slowly pulled back. "I'm serious Rayshawn. I don't think I can handle this anymore. Besides, I haven't told you the absolute truth about me. There are some things in my past that you probably won't like when you find them out."

"There's nothing you can tell me about you that would change my feelings. I know what I want and it's you."

Rayshawn leaned in again and started to kiss her neck. He twirled his tongue up and down in a circular motion until he could feel her body responding. Rayshawn moved up to her lips and kissed her. Every ounce of passion he felt inside came flowing out through his lips and tongue.

"Stop Rayshawn" Felice whispered.

He continued to kiss her. "Are you sure that you want me to stop?"

Felice mumbled something just before she grabbed the back of his head and pressed her lips against him. They began to rub one another until their breathing increased. Felice tried to pull away, but her emotions got the best of her and she finally submitted and gave in.

The next day, Lynn and Ko-Ko tried desperately to find Rayshawn or Felice, even searching some of Negril's local clubs and popular restaurants. Ko-Ko's reason was to stir up some more trouble. Lynn's was to stir her son away from a woman she knew was no good for him. Whatever the reason was it, didn't matter because the two love birds were nowhere to be found. Rayshawn and Felice had changed their tickets and left a day earlier.

When Lynn finally made it home herself, she rushed down the basement steps looking and calling for Rayshawn, only to find a deserted room. To make matters worse, she noticed several empty dresser drawers and a closet full of abandoned wire hangers.

Chapter Nineteen

Ko-Ko entered the Fantasy Girlz office Thursday morning, with a serious chip on her shoulder. She'd deliberately called in sick for the past two days trying her best to piss Felice off. Unfortunately while in Jamaica, a special shoot at The Caves Resort got rained out, so the plan was to make up for it on set once the staff returned. Being that Ko-Ko had all of the model's clothing with her, they couldn't move forward as planned when she didn't come in, especially since the brand new custom made gold digger costume was to be included. Several people had called and left messages with her asking to come and pick the costume up, but of course Ko-Ko didn't return a single call. While they thought she was sick, Ko-Ko had spent the last two days watching Oprah, eating popcorn and masturbating.

After putting her purse, clothing rack and garments away, Ko-Ko headed into the conference room where everyone was passing around an advanced copy of the anniversary cover. Walking up to the table, Ko-Ko took a seat and reached for the photo paper. *Damn, Rayshawn really out did himself on this shoot*, Ko-Ko thought looking at the beautiful picture of one of their best models covered in green, yellow and black body paint. To make it even more special, Rayshawn had managed to capture the perfect sunset.

Several models and a few other employees began clapping when Rayshawn and Felice stepped into the room. When Ko-Ko turned her head to see what all the commotion was, she rolled her eyes in disgust. Her emotions were sent over the edge when Felice held Rayshawn's arm as if they were Barack and Michelle Obama going to a State Ball. It looked as if they didn't even care about being embarrassed at the wedding anymore.

"Fantasy Girlz employees listen up. I know by now you've seen the draft for the anniversary issue of the magazine. I would like for everyone to join me in celebrating what I know will be an award winning issue. I give you the man who is going to take our company to a whole new level, Mr. Rayshawn McMillan," Felice announced.

The roar of the crowd had that stadium feel. Rayshawn wiped his face to hide the embarrassment, then noticed that Ko-Ko wasn't clapping. She even held a cold blank stare as Felice leaned over and kissed Rayshawn on the cheek.

"Speech, speech!" the crowd began chanting.

Rayshawn held up his hand to quiet everyone down. "I just want to thank every single one of you for helping me in Jamaica. It was so easy to create this issue when you have the hardest working people in the business and the most gorgeous models on the east coast." He looked directly at Ko-Ko. "I would also like to thank someone very special because if it wasn't for her, I would've never gotten the chance to explore my dream."

Ko-Ko was just about to smile when Rayshawn turned his head to look at Felice.

"Thank you, Ms. Contour. If it wasn't for you, I don't know if anyone else would have given me such an opportunity," Rayshawn said, squeezing her hands.

Ko-Ko's pulse increased significantly. "What?" It felt as if her heart had been pulled out of her chest.

Everyone turned in her direction.

"What the hell are y'all staring at me for? It wasn't because of her that he has this fucking job. I'm the one who hired his ass. I'm the one who had Sammy show him the ropes. Hell,

I'm the one who came up with the body painting idea!" Ko-Ko grabbed the advanced cover and ripped it into tiny pieces. "When the fuck am I gonna get credit for something around here?" Pushing her chair back, Ko-Ko stormed out of the conference room at high speed.

"You didn't let me finish, Ms. Jackson!" Rayshawn continued.

Ko-Ko stopped in her tracks immediately. "Don't fucking call me Ms. Jackson like I'm an old lady. That store bought pussy got you tripping right now!"

"Ms. Jackson, you need to report to my office immediately!" Felice jumped in.

"Who the hell do you think you're talking to? This ain't the damn principal's office. I've told you about trying to flex in front of people and act like my boss. You may be able to tell everybody else in this company when and what to do, but don't forget who the fuck got this magazine started," Ko-Ko retorted.

The employees heads bounced back and fourth as if they were watching the Williams sister's at the U.S. Open. They all waited for Felice's response, but nothing came. Ko-Ko turned, walked into her office and slammed the door. There was a dead silence throughout the room.

"Hey, there are refreshments and sandwiches in the break room. This is a celebration so go eat up," Felice finally said. She turned around and walked out with Rayshawn not too far behind.

"Are you going to be alright?" Rayshawn whispered.

"Of course."

"You still think her bark is worse than her bite? That woman is very unstable and I wouldn't put anything past her. You need to deal with her crazy-ass now before it manifests into something major."

"That's what I plan to do." Felice could feel the almost every employee's eyes staring at her as she walked past the break room and into Ko-Ko's office. They wanted so desperately to ear hustle, but knew Rayshawn would snitch.

"You've lost your fucking mind talking to me like that in front of everyone!" Felice shouted.

"It ain't nobody in here for you to show off for. You need to save all that bullshit drama for somebody that'll care," Ko-Ko replied. "Plus you need bring your voice down another notch."

"You may have put up the front money for this magazine, but it was still my business sense that made all this shit come together." Felice sat her purse on Ko-Ko's desk, took out her check book and began filling out a check. "Matter of fact, I'll double the money you put up and we can call it even."

Ko-Ko got up and walked over to Felice. She snatched her check book out of her hand and threw it on the floor. "Please, the shit I got on you is priceless. Besides, you're not buying me out of this fucking company."

"Trust me, I have my lawyers working on that as we speak."

"Are you still forgetting about all the shit I know about you," Ko-Ko said, tapping Felice's shoulder.

Felice pushed Ko-Ko's hands off her. "That won't be your little ace in the whole on me for long."

"I told you to leave Rayshawn alone. Not only did you not listen to my warning, but now you're flaunting him all in my face. I guess I'm going to have to teach you and him another lesson."

"You conniving bitch. Why the fuck would you ruin your friend's wedding just to expose me and Rayshawn?" Felice asked.

Ko-Ko laughed "Who said I did that? You didn't hear me say that. I know you don't think I had anything to do with that."

"Trust me, Kourtney. Your day is coming. You just remember that shit." Felice bent down to pick up the check book then walked out the door.

It was only a matter of seconds before Ko-Ko realized that Felice had left her purse. When another crazy idea quickly popped into her head, she quickly closed her door, then went in Felice's purse to retrieve her cell phone. *I wonder if Rayshawn is in the mood for a little day time getaway*, she thought. *He's gonna be with me one way or the other*. Knowing Felice would be back, she placed the slim I-phone into her pocket then walked back behind her desk acting as if she had work to do. Just as she suspected, not even a minute went by before Felice barged back into her office.

"You don't know how to knock?" Ko-Ko taunted.

"No, and didn't plan on it," Felice responded, then grabbed her purse.

As soon as Felice closed her door and made her grand finale for the second time, Ko-Ko pulled out the phone. Luckily she had an I-phone herself so operating it wasn't a problem. Just as she was about to hit the SMS Text icon, a message from Rayshawn came through.

You were in there a long time. How did it go? he wrote.

Ko-Ko replied: **I handled my business like u know I can. Wanna play a game?**

When Rayshawn answered with, "sure," Ko-Ko could only imagine the cheesy grin he had on his face. She also knew she had to hurry up before Felice either realized her phone was missing or walked up to Rayshawn while they were going back and forth. She decided to push the envelope.

U have exactly ninety minutes to get over to Doubletree Hotel-Rhode Island Ave. If u are one second late, you'll miss the greatest sex in your life. Bring toys. Leave now!

A large smile overcame Rayshawn's face as he jolted out the break room like a bolt of lightening. Deciding to document the event, he grabbed his camera bag, headed downstairs and jumped in his car. He sped down the street, heading for his mother's house where he knew Ko-Ko had accidentally left her small bag of sex toys under his bed the day she had to hide from all her friends. He'd been meaning to go and get the bag when he knew Lynn was at work, but just hadn't gotten the chance. Rayshawn was at a red light when he received another text message.

A key will b at the desk. Don't worry about showing ID. Nikki from the office has a sister who works there. Have a room number already- 619.

Rayshawn stuck his phone into his jacket pocket then continued to push the speed limit in order to make it home. Luckily, it wasn't even lunch time yet so traffic was nonexistent. Twenty minutes later, Rayshawn parked his car as if Stevie Wonder had been driving then jumped out,   taking two steps at a time up to the front door. Anytime he could save was helpful.

"Where's the fire?" Lynn shouted as he burst into the house.

Rayshawn threw his jacket on the couch before hurrying down the basement steps to grab the bag. However, after reaching under the bed several times, he didn't feel anything. He even climbed under the bed just to make sure, but again nothing was there.

"Hey Ma, have you been in my room? I can't find some of my stuff!" he yelled upstairs.

Lynn didn't respond. After waiting all of two seconds for her to answer him, Rayshawn went back upstairs. "Ma, did you hear me?"

"Did you fucking speak when you came in my house," Lynn replied with an attitude. "You just walked your ass up in here and didn't say a word."

He wasn't in the mood to argue or bicker. "Sorry, Ma. Have you seen a small black platic bag that was under my bed?"

"Yeah, you mean the one with all those ass beads, dick rings and shit? Yeah, I saw it, and I also threw it away."

"Come on, Ma. This is not a time to joke around. I need to meet someone and my time is running out," Rayshawn said.

"Who said I was joking? I threw that shit away!"

Rayshawn was heated. "Ma, why did you touch my stuff? It was in my room. Not yours!"

Lynn had to pause before responding, so she wouldn't slap the shit out of her son. "First of all, you better stop disrespecting me in *my* house. You're the one who decided to move your shit out without saying anything to me, so I threw the rest of your shit out."

Rayshawn had to calm himself down as well. "But you didn't have to throw my stuff away. Why didn't you just call? I would've came and got it."

"Call? You won't answer the damn phone!" Lynn screamed. She looked at her son whose wardrobe seemed to have gotten an upgrade. "I can't believe this woman is taking you away from me like this. You were always considerate of my feelings until she came into the picture. I didn't raise you to be an asshole."

Rayshawn looked at his new Cartier watch that Felice bought him. In a way he felt bad, but didn't have much time to express his feelings. "Ma, don't blame Felice for anything. It's not her fault. Did you throw away my throwback Redskins jersey, too? The one I kept at the top of my closet? I left that here."

Lynn forced a smile. "No, I wouldn't dare touch that. You have some other things still down there as well. I lied…I didn't throw away everything."

Rayshawn leaned over and kissed his mother on her forehead. "Thanks. I'ma go get it along with whatever else I left and head back to work. I promise. We'll talk later."

As Rayshawn ran back downstairs, his cell phone began to ring inside his jacket pocket. Being nosy, Lynn walked over and picked it up. She began to shake her head back and forth after reading the recent and previous text messages. By the time Rayshawn came back upstairs a few minutes later, the television set was on but his mother was nowhere in sight. The front door was even open, but when he looked outside Lynn's car was gone.

"Where the hell did she go?" he asked himself.

His question was answered almost instantly when he saw his phone on top of the couch pillow. He grabbed it and saw Felice's had sent another message.

I'm turning my phone off – Hurry time is run-

ning out. My pussy is waiting and screaming to be kissed.

Rayshawn knew that his mother was on her way to the hotel. He needed to get there before she did something crazy. Rayshawn hurried to his car and sped off, trying to intercept his mother. But as his luck would have it, that was going to be difficult with his gas needle kissing the E. "Shit!" he yelled.

Chapter Twenty

Lynn came to a screeching halt when she arrived in front of the Doubletree. A young man working valet came to give her assistance right away, but Lynn quickly whipped open her door, jumped out and ignored him entirely. She didn't even turn the car off or close the driver's side door before running inside.

"Miss, wait for your ticket," the guy shouted. "It's $30.00 a day!"

Instead of stopping, Lynn kept power walking into the doors and up to the front desk. "I believe that a key was left for me at the desk. Room 619," she said out of breath. It had been years since she ran that fast.

"What's your name?" the heavy set women replied. "I was supposed to give the key to a gentleman."

Lynn didn't want to mess things up, so she decided to put on her best acting role. She also hoped that she remembered everything from the text. "Hey, girl. Are you Nikki's sister?" Lynn looked at her name tag, which read, Nivea.

"Yeah."

"Well…Neeva. Is that how you pronounce your name?"

"No, it's N-i-v-e-a. You know, like the lotion? My mama must've loved that stuff," she said with a smile.

Lynn smiled as well, hoping the small talk would help smooth things over. "Oh, that's actually a pretty name. Listen, I'm here to pick up the key. I gotta hurry up and put some toys in the room before Rayshawn gets here."

Nivea remembered Ko-Ko telling her what the guy's name was, so she figured Lynn must've known what was up. "Oh, okay cool. I can't wait to see this Rayshawn guy. My sister talks about him all the time. He must be fine," Nivea said, handing Lynn the key.

"He is…thanks." Before leaving she said to Nivea, "You may want to call the police and an ambulance in about ten minutes."

Nivea made a strange frown. She had no idea what that last statement meant as she watched Lynn run to the elevators and get on. "I'm so glad I'm about to get off. I'm staying out that shit."

When Lynn exited the elevator doors, she turned down the hallway and made her way to room 619. Saying a quick prayer before she went in, Lynn used the key to open the room door. With the lights off and the thick curtains drawn, only the flames of several candles made it visible for her to maneuver further into the room.

"Glad you could make it. You only had ten minutes left on the clock," Ko-Ko said. She was lying on the bed in a silk black teddy with her fingers in her dripping pussy.

Lynn recognized her voice instantly. "What the fuck are you doing here?"

When Ko-Ko heard Lynn's voice, she jumped up and turned on the light. "Lynn."

"I thought Felice was supposed to be meeting Rayshawn here."

"Umm…she was."

At that moment, all the things that Rayshawn had been telling her about Ko-Ko danced around in her head. "I know you're not fucking my son, too!" Lynn shouted.

Ko-Ko prepared herself for Lynn's attack that she knew was coming. "Give me a chance to explain," Ko-Ko said, getting up.

"Explain. Explain what? Bitch you've been playing me this whole time. How could you?" Lynn asked. Before Ko-Ko could say anything else, Lynn charged at her, connecting her right fist with the left side of Ko-Ko's check. "I don't wanna hear nothing you have to say to me right now!"

Ko-Ko began swinging wildly. They both hit each other with punches until Lynn got close enough to grab Ko-Ko's hair. Lynn yanked a handful of the thick strands and began hitting Ko-Ko with body shots, Mike Tyson style. She then pushed Ko-Ko into the nightstand and the lamp smashed against the wall, shattering it into several pieces. Lynn had a nice chunk of hair still in her palm as Ko-Ko managed to stand on her feet.

"Wait…let me explain. It's not what you think. I really love Rayshawn!" Ko-Ko pleaded.

"Shut up!"

Rayshawn got off the elevator to hear screaming in the distance. There were many other guests standing in the hallway trying to figure out what was going on as he made his way toward the room. The screams were clear, the sounds of breaking furniture were evident but the door was locked.

He began to bang on the door. "Mom, Felice, stop! Please open the door." Rayshawn begged for someone to call the front desk to get a master key. When the elevator doors opened moments later, two hotel security officers and the desk manager ran down the hall.

"I'm gonna have to ask everyone to go back inside their rooms for security reasons please!" a guard shouted.

Rayshawn continued to bang on the door as the other guests slowly followed the guard's instructions.

"Sir, I'm going to need you to step back from the door," one guard instructed when he walked up.

"Open the fucking door. My girl and mother are going to kill each other!" Rayshawn yelled. The banging grew louder from inside the room

"Let us handle this," the manager responded pulling out his master key.

Rayshawn stepped back as the guards took the master key from the manager to swipe the door key card. When the little light on the key pad turned from red to green and they cracked the door open, Rayshawn blasted past everyone.

Rayshawn could see his mother and Ko-Ko rolling around on the floor. The broken lamps, turned over chairs, and blood on the carpet was evidence that a major battle had transpired. Rayshawn was surprised that Felice wasn't anywhere to be found. He ran over and grabbed his mother by her shoulders and tried to pull her off of Ko-Ko's neck. It took one of the security guards to help get her arm off. Lynn continued kicking at Ko-Ko until she was across the room.

"Get your hands off of me!" Lynn screamed. "Bitch, I'll kill you. I can't believe you've been fucking my baby all along," Lynn said, breaking away from Rayshawn.

Rayshawn was so confused. He couldn't figure out where Felice was and how Ko-Ko even ended up at the hotel room to begin with. It was a major question running through his mind. Rayshawn grabbed Lynn again just before she could swing. He wrapped his arms around her. "You need to stop, Ma. I'm no longer your baby. I'm a grown-ass man who can make his own decisions on who I want to see or sleep with."

"Boy, I said take your hands off me. This whore has taken advantage of you. I know her better than anyone. She manipulates people. It's been that way since we were teenagers."

"Ain't that the kettle calling the skillet black? It takes a whore to know a whore!" Ko-Ko screamed.

"Don't call my mother a whore," Rayshawn said to Ko-Ko.

Lynn turned around and stared Rayshawn in the face. "I forbid you from seeing that trick. She's no good. She's fucked everybody!"

"Ma, you need to listen. I'm not a child anymore. I know what I'm doing. I was only coming here to see Felice. You saw my text. I don't know why Ko-Ko is here," Rayshawn responded. "What we had was over with awhile ago, but I don't think she wants to let go. She's crazy."

"No, you're not listening. I don't care who you were

coming here to see. All I know is if you plan on living in my house, you'll follow my fucking rules," Lynn said, jerking Rayshawn's hands off once again.

Rayshawn shook his head. "And that's why I haven't been living there lately."

"Whose room is this?" one of the security guards asked, breaking up their conversation.

"That would be her, Kourtney Jackson," Rayshawn answered. "I'm sure her name is on the reservation."

"I'm sorry but we're going to have to ask you to come with us," the guard said to Ko-Ko.

Ko-Ko gave Rayshawn an evil look. "Go with you for what? I ain't going anywhere."

"Look at all of this damage. Someone is going to pay for this," the manager chimed in.

"I'm not paying for shit. If any one is going to pay, it will be her." Ko-Ko pointed at Lynn. "She got a key to my room without my permission."

"Fuck you, bitch. Don't be mad because you got caught," Lynn said.

"I'm not going to be any more bitches. You need to go home and let Rayshawn be a man for once," Ko-Ko countered.

"Actually we're gonna remove both of y'all from the room, but we'll start with you first." One security guard stepped toward Lynn. As she began to back up, they both grabbed each of her arms. When Lynn started to resist, they became frustrated and grabbed her tighter.

"Get your fucking hands off me. You're hurting me!" Lynn screamed.

"This won't be necessary if you just come with us," one guard replied.

Rayshawn had seen enough. He quickly rushed to get the men's hands off his mother. Rayshawn locked up with the larger of the two. When the other guard went to help his partner, Lynn jumped on his back then Ko-Ko ran over and began helping Rayshawn. The manager didn't do anything but call 911.

The five of them were still going at it when the police arrived. It took three police officers using their batons and exces-
sive force to handcuff Rayshawn, Lynn and Ko-Ko, who
resisted all the way down to the lobby. The police weren't really
sure who started the brawl, and didn't really care. All three of
them were going to jail. Destruction of property, assault, resist-
ing arrest…they were all possible charges. Things turned from
bad to worse, when one of the officers made the mistake of putting Lynn in the back of the same car as Ko-Ko. Even in handcuffs the two managed to start a kicking war, which ended up
with Ko-Ko getting badly bruised.

"Oh shit!" an officer shouted once he saw the car shaking and Ko-Ko's body banging violently against the door.

When he ran and yanked open the door, Lynn tried to get
a last kick in as he pulled her from the car. "And you call yourself a friend!" she yelled.

Lynn continued to shout as the police officer escorted her
in the opposite direction. With only two squad cars outside, they
had to wait for a third one to arrive. Before being placed in the
second car, Rayshawn stood outside with his head sunk on his
chest wondering what had just transpired and if Felice was alright.

Lynn tried to get Rayshawn's attention. However, the
anger he felt about his mother embarrassing him wouldn't allow
him to look at her.

"Rayshawn, I forbid you from seeing any of those
women. Can't you see they're no good cradle-robbing whores!"
Lynn belted.

All the officers turned and gave Lynn's remarks their full
attention. Rayshawn on the other hand stared straight ahead. He
still wouldn't look over at her. Rayshawn's silence made Lynn's
anger build even faster.

"You're choosing that bitch over your own flesh and blood? I've given you every thing you ever wanted and I've never lied to you. How dare you turn your back on me?"

Rayshawn cut his eyes toward Lynn. "How dare I? No, how dare you go through my phone, burst into a hotel room and treat me like a child?"

Lynn laughed. "You are a child. You're my child."

"I'm not a child; I haven't been one for a long time. I know exactly what I'm doing with Felice. As for Ko-Ko, I don't even know how or why that crazy bitch was even there. I told you that before, and I'm getting tired of repeating myself."

Lynn laughed again. "If that's the case, then why were the two of you sneaking around for so long?"

"I don't know," Rayshawn answered as the third squad car finally arrived.

Minutes later, Rayshawn was on his way to the DC jail where they housed the men, while Lynn and Ko-Ko were headed to the Correctional Treatment Facility, which was a block over. After arriving, all three were taken to the central cells downstairs to await their bail hearing. Not taking anymore chances, Lynn and Ko-Ko were placed in separate holding cells which officers thought would help cool the two hot heads down. However, with the cells being right next to one another, their logic didn't really work for one of them.

"This shit ain't over. When we get out of here, we're going to settle this!" Lynn yelled out to her friend.

Ko-Ko held the side of her hip and slowly walked over to the metal bench and sat down.

"I know you hear me talking to you!" Lynn yelled again. For a Thursday afternoon, the cells weren't crowded at all, so with a low noise level, Ko-Ko could hear her just fine.

"You have every right to be mad at me, Lynn. If things were reversed, I'd be pissed off too. I didn't plan for this to happen. It started off with a night of too much to drink and we crossed the line. I knew it was wrong, but I couldn't stop thinking of Rayshawn."

"I took up for you when no one else would. I never judged how you lived your life, and you pay me back by sleeping with my son."

Ko-Ko stared at the dark grey bars. "I tried so hard not to see him any more, but my feelings continued to grow until he was all that I could think of. I've never wanted to hurt you, but I fell in love with him. From that point, I didn't think it was wrong."

"You didn't think it was wrong? Fucking a guy who's young enough to be your own son isn't wrong? I truly believe you're crazy," Lynn replied.

"I got jealous when he started ignoring me and spending time with Felice. I didn't know why it hurt me so bad but it did. I've changed since me and Rayshawn hooked up. I just wanted to do things to please and make him happy, which is how the men in my life normally treat me, " Ko-Ko advised. "I could've really seen us together…you know as a couple. I would've given him the world."

"So, that's what this is all about. You got jealous that my son wanted another woman and not you. So, everything has to be about Kourtney Denise Jackson at all times or can't exist at all. You know Melyssa and Tootie were right about you. You don't care about any one except yourself."

"That's not true. I love Rayshawn and I care about you. That's why I couldn't let him be with Felice!" Ko-Ko shouted.

"How did you figure that keeping my son away from Felice was helping me, too? I mean what do you hate about this woman? What, is she a little more freakier than you? Is that it?" Lynn question.

Ko-Ko grunted. "A woman? That's funny that you keep saying that." She stood up and walked toward the bars then placed her hand around the cold steel. "Do you remember Raymond Wilson?"

Lynn paused for a few seconds. "Of course I remember Raymond. But what does he have to do with anything?"

"Because Felice is Raymond," Ko-Ko blurted out.

Chapter Twenty-One

Luckily, Lynn was sitting down once Ko-Ko stopped talking, otherwise her knees would've buckled immediately. Knowing Ko-Ko had lied to her all this time, Lynn wasn't exactly sure if she was telling the truth, but something in her friend's voice said that it wasn't a lie. "What…what do you mean Felice is Raymond? Felice can't be Raymond."

"It's true. It's pretty sick, but it's true. I told y'all he was gay back in the day anyway, and none of y'all wanted to believe me. Hell, the only manly thing about his ass is that he was good in baseball. All y'all thought he just didn't want to date any of the round the way girls. The real reason he didn't want to go out with girls in the neighborhood was because he preferred dick to pussy. Hell, I should know because he never tried to fuck me, which was odd, so I knew something was wrong."

Lynn was stunned. "I can't believe this."

"Well, believe it. Raymond Felippe Wilson is Ms. Felice Contour. I don't know where the fuck he got that last name from. Remember me and him used to boost together all the time, so that's how he even got the money to go out to Colorado to have his sex reassignment surgery. As you can see that he-she bitch has one hell of a plastic surgeon. Besides, her being so damn tall you can't even tell. I can barely see her Adam's Apple."

"Why didn't you tell me? How could you keep something like that away from me?" Lynn asked. Even though Ko-Ko couldn't see her, she knew Lynn was upset.

"I know this news only makes things worse, but I've been blackmailing Felice for years once I found out. She's been giving me hush money to keep quiet, so I couldn't say anything. See back in the day, Felice had a call girl service, where I'll admit, I once used to work. At the time, I didn't know anything about Felice, and I use to wonder why this tall amazon bitch came to recruit me for her business in the first place. I just thought at the time, she'd heard about my impressive resume. Anyway, she had this one customer who she fell in love with, but what her ass didn't know was that he was fucking me at the same time." Ko-Ko stopped. "You listening, Lynn?"

"Yeah," Lynn and another female answered at the same time. Lynn turned around and looked at the crack-head looking woman, but didn't say anything.

"Okay, so Felice's dumb-ass ends up telling the guy everything once he got a little suspicious. Of course, he gets mad and then turns around and tells me. In return, I confronted her ass and asked for some money to keep quiet. It went well for a while, but when she acted like the money was running low and wouldn't give me anymore, I ended up calling the police to get the call girl service shut down. When Felice got out of jail, she was broke, so that's when she came to me with the idea about the magazine. I ended up using her money to start the shit. It was foul what I did, but brilliant at the same time."

Lynn began sobbing uncontrollably. She began banging her fist into the wall and screaming, "This can't be happening. That bitch can't be Raymond."

"Lynn, what's the matter? Why are you tripping?" Ko-Ko inquired.

Lynn stood up and began to pace around the holding cell while Ko-Ko stood at the bars wondering what was going on. Lynn then began mumbling something before running to the metal bars and trying to grab Ko-Ko. When Ko-Ko jumped back, Lynn was only able to get a hold of her shirt. Lynn yanked the sleeve off, trying to pull Ko-Ko closer.

"What the hell is wrong with you? I told you that I was sorry for everything!" Ko-Ko pleaded.

"You don't know what you've done. It's all your fault for getting him that stupid job at the magazine in the first place. Rayshawn would've never come into contact with her!"

"Lynn, you need to calm down. Your son isn't gay. He has no idea that Felice was born a man. In fact, I think that the two of us are the only people who do."

"You still don't get it," Lynn stated.

"You're right, I don't. The way you're acting is confusing."

Lynn closed her eyes and began to reflect back to her younger days. It all began with the silly things she and Raymond did in gym class at Anacostia High School. Even though Lynn was much better than him in dodgeball, she would always allow him to hit her with the ball. The moments of patting her butt when no one was looking eventually turned into long kissing sessions under the bleachers. Lynn had always found Raymond to be very attractive with his curly hair, and muscular build. The fact that the other girls thought he was kind of feminine and even called him sissy at times seemed to make him more desirable. Another fact that increased her feelings for Raymond was that he was the first cute boy who Lynn liked that Ko-Ko didn't try to steal.

Lynn and Raymond were in the house all alone watching Night Rider on television one night when Lynn felt his arm slide down over her shoulder. She looked over and lost her control in his soft smile. They began kissing then Raymond removed her shirt and bra with ease. She quickly turned off the light as he stood to remove his shell toe Adidas and Sergio Tacchini sweat suit. Raymond softly rubbed her arms trying to make her feel more comfortable before taking off her jeans and panties. Moments later, he climbed on top of her and inserted his dick into her dry pussy. It was her very first time, so it took him several tries just to get the tip inside. Lynn cried, but didn't want to stop. She wanted Raymond to be the one who took her virginity for some strange reason.

"Lynn, you didn't tell me what you meant by that," Ko-Ko said, interrupting Lynn's trip down memory lane.

"I slept with Raymond in high school…lost my virginity to him. We did it everyday for a week. We did it so much that he's the one who got me pregnant. Do you get it now? Raymond is Rayshawn's father." Tears began to stroll down Lynn's face like a river. "I wasn't raped by my Aunt's boyfriend like I told everyone. I was just embarrassed. Embarrassed that I'd had sex with a guy who was obviously gay. After the last day we had sex, he told me that I was just an experiment. That he wanted to see how it felt to have sex with a girl, and that he really liked guys. I felt so fucking stupid because I had a feeling he was gay before we even did anything. I couldn't believe my self-esteem was that low. That I was so insecure about my body, I slept with someone who wasn't even interested in me. And now because of you and that trashy fucking magazine, Raymond is in love with my son, his son, but in the wrong way!" Lynn screamed.

"Oh my God, that's some sick day time drama shit," the crack head lady added.

Ko-Ko was completely stunned. "Damn. I could use a cigarette right now."

"I could use something a little more," Lynn advised.

"I'm sorry, Lynn. I honestly didn't know. Is that why you named him, Rayshawn?"

"Yeah. I wanted something similar, which was also dumb," Lynn admitted.

"I had no idea that you and Raymond were fucking back then. Ugh, the vision of the two of you doing it has my stomach turning," Ko-Ko said.

"Well, just think what my heart is doing knowing that my son is fucking his father. How am I going to tell Rayshawn? I don't think he'll be able to handle it." Lynn shook her head. "That bitch came up to me at the wedding and played me for a fool. She said that I'd gained weight and that I was still pretty, but it never occurred to me who she was."

"So, what are you going to do?" Ko-Ko asked.

"I'm going to kill her!" Lynn cried.

"I think you mean him not her," the crack head said. "Plus, this the wrong place to be talking like that."

"Do you mind? I have a real fucking dilemma going on here. You're not helping at all," Lynn replied to the woman.

"Well, whatever you got planned, if it has something to do with getting *his* bitch-ass back, then count me in," Ko-Ko included.

After getting his bond hearing early the next morning, Rayshawn made his one allowed phone call to Felice, then sat in his holding cell waiting for her to come and bail him out. Thinking back to the events, he couldn't believe that Ko-Ko had pretended to be Felice in the first place, but then again, she'd done so much crazy shit over the past few weeks, he shouldn't have been surprised. Even his mother was on a rampage now, which added even more stress. He wondered how his mother and Ko-Ko were going to get out, but he also knew that he didn't want to be around either one of them. Rayshawn began to flirt with a female guard who'd been eyeing him since he first arrived in order to get a piece of paper and a pen. After slipping him the two items a few minutes later, Rayshawn sat on an uncomfortable bench and began to write.

Once the same female guard called his name and told him he'd made bail, two hours later, Rayshawn stood up and waited for the bars to open. "Can you get this note to a female who just got locked up? Her name is Lynn McMillan?" Rayshawn asked in a low tone.

"I don't work at CTF," the guard responded.

"Yeah, I know, but it's important. Please. Not only that, I need you to give me your phone number." Rayshawn flashed a sexy smile.

The guard smiled in return. "Alright." She looked around, grabbed the note then quickly called out her number. "I get off in a few hours so hit me up."

"Will do, beautiful."

While Rayshawn walked out of DC Jail, holding Felice's hand, a guard in the women's facility walked to the holding cells and called out Lynn's name. "Lynn McMillan!" he shouted.

Lynn lifted her head. "Yeah."

The guard held out the note for her. "This is for you."

Lynn got up from the bench and walked over to the bars. She slowly took the paper from his hand. Lynn wondered who would be sending her a note but realized it was from Rayshawn once she saw his hand writing. She opened the piece of paper.

Ma,

I'm not sure why you still think of me as a little boy, but I'm not. I'm a man. I can make the important decisions that affect my life. You need to respect and trust me. You did a great job raising me, but it's my life and I'm going to live it the way that I want. With that said, I'm not going back to school, so please just accept my decision. Felice just bailed me out. I'm going to ask her to go away with me so everyone can calm down. I need you to search your heart and find that trust so when we get back you will be more open minded to the fact of me and her dating. I love you.

Rayshawn

Lynn walked over and began banging her fist against the bench as the tears streamed down her face at full speed

Chapter Twenty-Two

"Thank you for getting me out of there. I don't think I could have lasted another night in that nasty-ass place. Now, I know why I've never committed a crime," Rayshawn said to Felice as they drove down the street.

"It was my pleasure. But would you like to tell me what the hell happened?" Felice questioned.

"Ko-Ko is a crazy bitch, that's what. She texted me from your phone to meet her at a hotel, and I thought it was you. So, I went to my mom's house to get some toys and my mom obviously found my phone and read the message."

"I was wondering where my damn phone went. She must've stolen in out of my purse when I was in her office," Felice informed him.

"It sounds like some shit she would do," Rayshawn continued. "When I got to the hotel, the two of them were fighting like cats and dogs until the security came. Then we all started fighting the guards until the police arrived and locked us up."

"Kourtney is one crazy bitch. I can't believe she did all that. I wish I could fire her ass."

"Why can't you? I don't understand why you allow her to talk to you the way she does or get away with the blatant disrespect," Rayshawn said. "That's your company, so she's out of line."

Felice gave Rayshawn a quick glance. "It's a long story and I really don't want to get into it. Why don't you tell me what toys you went to get?" Felice wanted to change the subject quick.

"Listen, I was thinking of taking a little break away from all this and heading to some little hide away. Why don't we just drive until we find a nice spot and then I can show you what I had in store?"

Felice reached over and rubbed the back of Rayshawn's head. "I know the perfect place where we can go and relax." She took out her newly replaced cell phone and called a friend.

While Felice was on the phone, Rayshawn closed his eyes and listened to Maxwell singing, *Bad Habits* through the car's speakers. Taking in Maxwell's smooth silky voice, he began to visualize what he was going to do to Felice once they arrived at their destination. However, the kinky thoughts didn't last long. Before he knew it, Rayshawn had fallen asleep due to his lack of rest from being locked up. It wasn't until Felice shook his leg an hour later, that he finally woke up.

Rayshawn opened his eyes to find a huge mansion sitting in front of him. "Where are we?" he asked looking around.

"We're in Stevensville, MD. It's right outside Annapolis. I come here to get away sometimes."

"Who's house is this?"

"It belongs to a friend. Now, get out the car and follow me," Felice ordered.

Rayshawn did as he was told and followed his girl through the huge, glass door entry and into the marble foyer. They then made their way to the first floor master suite which had beautiful floor to ceiling windows with panoramic views of the Potomac River. Felice went over to the gas fireplace and started it up. Rayshawn was extremely impressed.

"Damn, this place is nice."

Felice pointed to the bathroom. "Why don't you go and take a dip in the Jacuzzi tub, and I'll be in to join you in a minute. I need to make a few calls to the magazine to make sure some things get done while we're here," she said, removing her clothes. It wasn't long before she was only in a pair of red thongs.

Rayshawn threw his jacket on the bed. "Damn, baby. Don't take too long." He opened the bathroom door to find several peach colored candles burning on the toilet, the sink and around the tub. A tub that consisted of bubbles and peach rose petals. "Wow, how the hell did she pull this off," he said to himself.

"Why don't you get into the water and I'll wash every inch of you," Felice said through the door.

"Alright."

Rayshawn didn't waste time taking off his clothes and slipping into the hot water. The water was so hot, he took a couple of deep breaths before lowering his balls into the tub. Rayshawn could hear Felice moving around, but had no idea what she was up to. He leaned backed and closed his eyes then heard the door opening. Felice stepped inside wearing nothing but her birthday suit. The closer she got, it was the first time Rayshawn had ever noticed two long scars under her breasts. He knew the scars were obviously from breast implants, but it still didn't matter. Natural body or not, Rayshawn really liked Felice, and planned on showing it through his sex drive.

She kneeled down next to the tub and pulled out a blue sponge, dipped it into the water and poured the hot water down his chest. Rayshawn's erect penis peeked out from the bubbles, acknowledging his excitement. They spent the next twenty minutes joking and softly splashing each other with water. When the erection disappeared back under the bubbles, Felice took it as a sign that Rayshawn was ready to get out.

"Let me dry you off, baby," Felice whispered.

When Rayshawn stood up, his dick jumped at attention as she used a plush white hotel towel to dry off his body. Felice gave his manhood a little extra attention before bending down on her knees. His eyes bulged when he saw Felice remove the towel then slide her tongue around the tip of his dick. She moved her mouth over his shaft repeatedly before inserting him into her mouth. Once Rayshawn glanced downward to see her head bobbing up and down, his toes began to curl.

Felice stopped and looked up. "Oh no, don't cum yet. You're going to need your strength," she said, standing to her feet. "You go ahead, I'll be right out after I let the water out and clean up the petals."

Even though Rayshawn was a little disappointed that she'd stopped so quickly, he decided not to put up a fight. He walked out of the bathroom to find more candles burning on the nightstand and a few along the floor. However, when Rayshawn turned the corner he immediately became amazed.

Lying on the king size bed was a beautiful naked woman inserting a nine inch dildo into her pussy. Rayshawn's feet felt like he was stuck in a bucket of cement. His mouth wanted to say something, but the words just wouldn't come out.

"This is my girlfriend, Michelle. She wanted to join us. I hope that's okay." Felice said, exiting the bathroom.

Rayshawn was still speechless. He stood there like a kid in a candy store. "Umm…yeah of course.

Felice grabbed Rayshawn's hand and he followed her over to the bed where there was a bowl of grapes, a can of whip cream, honey and chocolate syrup sitting on the nightstand. Rayshawn was getting ready to put a grape into his mouth when Michelle's loud moans got his attention. He looked over and watched as she pulled out the dildo and squirted thick cum all over the comforter.

"Don't stop, Michelle," Felice ordered. She then turned to Rayshawn. "You sit here and relax. I want you to watch me be with a woman."

Rayshawn couldn't believe what was happening and had to pinch himself when he sat on the edge of the bed and watched as Felice got on all fours and crawled between Michelle's legs like a hungry lion. She wiggled her ass and licked Michelle's pussy lips, swallowing the remaining cum. When Felice opened her friend's pink pussy lips and made circular motions with her tongue, Rayshawn's dick throbbed repeatedly. Felice looked over to see him rubbing his penis with his free hand a few seconds later.

"Michelle, let me lay on my back. I want my man to see what I look like when I'm getting my pussy ate out."

Michelle rolled over and immediately took position between Felice's legs like a certified gynecologist. Before long, Rayshawn could see Felice beginning to jerk from delight and damn near drooled as Felice's eyes rolled in the back of her head. She arched her back to allow Michelle's tongue to reach her ass hole and eat her faster.

"Babe, I want you to fuck Michelle in her ass," Felice moaned in pleasure.

Rayshawn truly believed that he was dreaming. *Was she really asking me to have sex with her girlfriend?* Rayshawn wondered. However, he wasn't going to give her the chance to think about her plea and change her mind. Rayshawn jumped to his feet and walked around to the end of the bed then rubbed the tip of his dick against Michelle's ass. *Damn, even her ass is wet,* he thought.

Rayshawn slowly eased his tool between Michelle's butt cheeks. He smiled as her head rose, acknowledging that she felt every inch of him entering her. Seconds later, he grabbed her hips and began to find a nice steady groove.

"Don't stop eating this pussy. I'm about to cum," Felice demanded.

Michelle lowered her head and went back to work on Felice as Rayshawn squeezed her small hips and gently moved his dick in and out. Michelle and Felice both started to make little sound effects of enjoyment.

"Come on baby, I said fuck her in the ass. You only make love to me and no one else. You better pound that ass like Michelle owes you some money," Felice commanded like an Army General.

Rayshawn glanced around Michelle's tiny frame and locked eyes with Felice, who gave him this wild look. It sent a feeling of rage through his body. Rayshawn didn't know what came over him. He felt a rush build up in his head and it ran straight down to his dick. He reached up and snatched a handful of Michelle's long, black hair then began to bang against her inner walls with tremendous force. Michelle began to moan louder. When Felice raised her head to see Rayshawn diving deep into Michelle's ass, her pussy began to tingle again. The mere sight of him fucking Michelle was causing her pussy to experience another orgasm.

"That's my baby. Fuck the shit out of her. You better give her everything you have," Felice said with a little laugh.

This gave Rayshawn another burst of energy. He rotated his hips to allow him to venture deeper inside Michelle. He began to speed up his movements until Michelle cried even louder. Rayshawn pushed her head back down into Felice's pussy and pounded forcefully.

"Stop and lay on your back, babe," Felice said.

Not knowing what was going on, Rayshawn wanted to keep beating Michelle's ass, but curiosity of what Felice had in plan made him stop. He rolled off and fell onto his back. As Rayshawn's dick dripped with juices, Felice quickly scurried to the sink and wet a wash cloth. She returned and wiped Rayshawn's tool clean. Michelle quickly straddled Rayshawn when Felice got out the way.

Her pussy was warm and slippery. She leaned back and began to ride his dick like a rodeo star from Texas. Rayshawn's toes began to curl as he banged his fist against the head board. Seconds later, he was surprised to see Felice's leg flying over his face and her pussy lips coming down on top of his mouth. Rayshawn grabbed her ass and stuck his tongue inside her wet cave. Both women began to grind their pussy's faster in unison. Rayshawn tried to move his tongue to keep up the pace with Felice's increasing movements, but her big ass was making it hard for him to breathe. Rayshawn pinched her thighs to make her legs open so air could flow, but she did just the opposite and squeezed them tighter.

The anxiety of not being able to breathe forced Rayshawn's body to bounce and jerk harder, causing his dick to tap the right spot deep inside Michelle. She moaned in pure delight. Still needing some air, Rayshawn did the one and only thing that he could think of. He sunk his teeth into her lips and gave a slight nibble.

"Ouch muthafucka!" Felice barked. She quickly jumped off Rayshawn and slapped his chest.

Once Rayshawn was free to change positions, he slid to the edge of the bed and lifted Michelle into the air and bounced her up and down like a yo-yo. He then turned her body to get a better angle and saw Felice rubbing her lips with ice cubes. Felice then squirted chocolate syrup and whip cream all around her manicured vagina.

"Hey babe, I made you a sundae. Make that hoe cum so you can hurry up and taste this. You owe me," Felice announced.

At that very moment, Michelle's screams of pleasure acknowledged that another orgasm was getting ready to make its debut. After watching her body squirm, Rayshawn quickly went to get his desert from Felice. He wasn't even downtown five minutes before Felice wanted something else.

She pulled Rayshawn's head up and whispered, "I'm ready to feel my dick."

Damn, I wish she would let me finish at least one task. Rayshawn crawled up and inserted his penis into her pool of juices. Their bodies were made for one another. Rayshawn loved the way her tight pussy always surrounded his dick like a glove. He reached under her and lifted her butt to open her pussy a little more. Once he did, within seconds, his penis began to unload a large amount of cum inside of Felice.

Rayshawn fell back onto the bed and his back landed on all the wet spots from Michelle squirting from the dildo earlier. He was too exhausted to even move. Rayshawn heard another moan and lifted his head just a little to find Michelle using the dildo on Felice. Rayshawn knew that he only had minutes to get his soldier ready for another battle because the war wasn't over.

Chapter Twenty-Three

The day seemed extremely long as the sun finally began to set. Even though Ko-Ko had called Kiara after their bond hearing, Lynn's fear was that they would have to stay another night, so she paced the cell like a mental patient. She felt claustrophobic...like the walls were closing in on her...like she was in a concrete womb. As if she wasn't stressed before, Lynn was starting to feel a high level of anxiety just as a guard made his way to the cells.

"Kourtney Jackson and Lynn McMillan, lets go. You've made bail."

"Oh, my God. Thank you," Lynn said as she quickly made her way to the door.

"Hope you find that she/he bitch and fuck it up," the crack head woman stated.

Lynn looked back and gave her cell mate a slight smile before making her way out. It wasn't long before Ko-Ko exited her cell and joined her friend. Lynn never said a word as they made their way to the processing area of the facility. It wasn't long before they spotted Kiara waiting for them at the information desk. The guard walked both ladies over to the cage so they could get their personal items.

Lynn snatched her phone out of the plastic bag and frantically dialed Rayshawn's cell number, but it went straight to voice mail.

"If you calling Rayshawn, he got out already," Kiara informed. "After my mother called me, when I got down here, I was gonna bail him out, too, but I found out that he was gone already."

"Yeah, I know. He wrote me a note," Lynn stated.

Kiara walked over to her mother. "Are you okay?"

"I've had better fucking days," Ko-Ko mentioned. She used her fingers to comb through her unruly hair. "Did you bring me a fresh pack of cigarettes?"

Kiara nodded.

"I need you to take me to my house right away," Lynn urged in a strong tone.

Kiara didn't sense the urgency, but would've been a fool not to cooperate. "Sure, Aunt Lynn."

As Lynn hurried out the door, Kiara and Ko-Ko strutted behind her quickly trying to keep up with her pace. After jumping in the car, both Kiara and Ko-Ko tried to make small talk with Lynn about anything from food to shoes, but it just wouldn't work. Lynn decided to make the trip to Maryland in complete silence except for her heavy breathing. When Kiara pulled up a few uncomfortable minutes later, Lynn's passenger door was already open before the car came to a complete stop.

"What's going on?" Kiara asked as she watched Lynn run up the steps to the front door.

"Come on, I'll tell you later," Ko-Ko said headed behind her friend.

Lynn opened the door and began shouting Rayshawn's name like he was a lost child. As they entered the house, Lynn was already walking upstairs from the basement. They walked over and went to take a seat on the sofa.

"Take me to the Doubletree so I can get my car. I have to find Rayshawn," Lynn demanded.

"Dag Aunt Lynn we just got here. I need to catch my breath," Kiara responded.

"I don't want to hear that shit. I need to find my son. So, either you take me to get my fucking car or I'm taking your car and driving myself!" Lynn screamed. She grabbed her purse off the couch.

Kiara looked over at her mother. Lynn kept staring at Kiara until she sucked her teeth and walked over to the door like she was about to leave.

"Not unless you parked in the garage across the street like I did, they probably towed it already," Ko-Ko assumed.

"I doubt that shit because I valet parked when I got there," Lynn advised then looked at Kiara again. "Are you going to take me or what?"

Kiara knew she didn't have much of a choice in the matter, so after following behind Lynn once again, they all jumped back into the car and headed downtown. Twenty minutes later, Kiara pulled up in front of the hotel and watched Lynn jump out, and head straight toward the valet.

"Girl, you gonna be okay?" Ko-Ko called out.

Lynn didn't respond.

"Can you tell me what's going on?" Kiara asked.

"Let's just go," Ko-Ko answered.

"Why is she freaking out?"

Ko-Ko leaned back into the seat. She closed her eyes and wondered where Rayshawn could be. *I know he's probably with that freak, but I wonder where they are.*

"Ma, for the last time. What's going on?" Kiara asked.

Ko-Ko sat up. "Well, first of all, we got locked up because me and Lynn were fighting at the hotel you just dropped her off at. I was up to some shady shit regarding Rayshawn, and she caught me in the room waiting on him."

"What?"

"Yeah, but you know what, that ain't even the bad part." Ko-Ko paused for a brief moment. "I can't believe what I'm about to tell you, but fuck it. It's not a secret anymore. Felice is a woman now, but wasn't born a woman. She used to be a man. She actually grew up in Berry Farm with us."

Kiara's mouth flew open. "Oh, my God! You're joking right? Does Rayshawn know that she used to be a man?"

"No, he has no idea" Ko-Ko replied.

"So, that means that Rayshawn had sex with a man. Oh, shit. I love it," Kiara replied with a huge grin.

"If you're going to interrupt me, then you won't get the whole story," Ko-Ko continued. "Felice grew up with us as a boy…as my neighbor actually and apparently he and Lynn had sex," Ko-Ko paused and looked at Kiara's stunned look. "I had no idea about the two of them until now."

"Okay," Kiara didn't felt like there was something else.

"So, now Felice is running around having sex with her biological son. Shit, I meant *his* biological son."

"Ugh…Oh my God. That's some real sick shit. Some real Jerry Springer shit." Kiara looked over at their mother as a devilish little smirk appeared on her face.

"Yeah, it's sick, but that's what his ass gets. I told him to leave Felice alone, but he wouldn't listen so now look at 'em," Ko-Ko bragged. "Oh, by the way. I never got a chance to thank you for switching out the video at Melyssa's wedding. Thanks for also keeping the DJ away for a while, too. I'm not even gonna ask you what your ass had to do to make that happen."

Kiara smiled. "Thanks. I guess I learned from the best. I can't wait to see the look on that nigga's face when he realizes that he's been fucking a man all this time. Not only that, he's fucking his father. They better have room at the mental hospital for his ass."

"It sounds like you're enjoying knowing this about Rayshawn." Before Kiara could respond, Ko-Ko's cell phone went off. It was Lynn. "Hello"

"Have you gotten in contact with Rayshawn, yet? Please tell me that you've talked with him," Lynn begged.

"No, I haven't."

"Can you think of any place that the two of them could be? I know I don't have to remind you of the importance of us finding him. It's already going to be so difficult to explain how this happened," Lynn replied.

"I know. I just can't think of where the two of them

could've gone," Ko-Ko answered.

"I hope you didn't tell Kiara about what's going on with Rayshawn. You know she can't keep a fucking secret. I would hate for Rayshawn to find out from somebody else."

Ko-Ko looked over at her daughter. "Don't worry Lynn, I didn't say anything to anyone. Shit, who's gonna believe me anyway."

"Ko-Ko, I'm still mad at you, but I also want to thank you for being here for me. You could've just left me in jail, but you didn't so I appreciate that. Besides, the shit you did doesn't even compare to what I just learned."

"No problem." After hanging up, she wanted to say, that's what friends are for, but thought that might've been pushing the envelope.

"Who was that?" Kiara inquired.

"It was Lynn. Look, I know I don't need to remind you that what I said regarding Rayshawn is not to be repeated to anyone. We have to figure this thing out first."

Kiara sighed. "Please, ain't nobody thinking about him. Me and my friends are going to Atlantic City next weekend, so all I'm worried about are my outfits. I got better things to do with my time."

"I'm serious, Kiara. I already got Lynn mad at me, so I don't need anything else to spark the fire."

"Sure, whatever you say," Kiara replied with a snicker, but in the back of her mind all she could do was laugh and hope to find Rayshawn first.

Chapter Twenty-Four

Rayshawn woke up the next morning still exhausted from his night of amazing sex with Felice and her girlfriend Michelle. After rolling over to see both of them still asleep, he eased out of the bed and walked toward the bathroom. However, he stopped and looked back at the two ladies one last time. A puzzled look came over his face as he realized that they were all snuggled up against each other like a real couple. Rayshawn wondered how often the two of them got together as he went into the bathroom and turned on the shower. He stepped inside and stood in the middle of the tub allowing the warm water to run down his naked body. Rayshawn placed his hands on the cream colored tile and began thinking of how he would work things out with his mother.

Once Rayshawn lathered up his body and sang a few Trey Songz tunes, he pulled back the shower curtain and found Michelle sitting on the toilet. He stood frozen as she smiled up at him. Surprisingly, Rayshawn's first reaction was to reach for the curtain to cover himself up.

"You didn't seem so shy last night, honey. No need to cover up. I do believe I've seen everything you've been blessed with," Michelle said.

"It's not that, you just startled me. I guess it was a reflex for me to cover up," Rayshawn answered as he finally stepped out of the shower.

Michelle continued urinating as Rayshawn wrapped a towel around his waist and walked out into the room. Felice had rolled over but was still sleeping. Rayshawn walked over to the nightstand and picked up his cell phone. After turning on the power button, the vibration started and never seemed to stop. When it was all said and done there were fifteen voice mails and twenty-six text messages from his mother and Ko-Ko combined. *They must've got out*, he said to himself. Knowing exactly what they wanted, he ignored the two, and called his boy, Gary instead.

"Hey slim, what's up," Rayshawn said when he answered.

"Where the hell you been? Your mother called me like a thousand times last night askin' me over and over if I'd seen you, talked to you or knew where you were," Gary replied.

"That's not surprising. We all got locked up the other night and I left her in jail when my baby came to bail me out."

"You bullshitin'. You left your mother in jail. Are you crazy? She's gonna fuck you up real bad when she gets her hands on you," Gary teased. "Ms. Lynn ain't to be fucked wit'."

"Look, I need to holla at you about something important. Why don't you meet me at Annapolis Mall?"

"Annapolis Mall? Man, do you know how far that shit is?"

"Nigga, not far at all. Shit, you live in Bowie, muthafucka. Damn, can a brotha get some love?"

"Yeah, I guess nigga. Why the fuck you out that way, anyway? You hidin' from your moms or some shit?" Gary's question had himself laughing hysterically.

"Wrong, my shorty brought me out here to some mansion in Stevensville, so I could calm down and clear my head. I wanna run an errand while she's still sleep. Plus, I wanna get out the house. Her girlfriend is trying to get shit started again, but I'm not feeling it right now," Rayshawn explained.

"Hold up, you're in a damn mansion with two women and you're not in the mood to fuck? How many times did you drop the soap in the pen last night, fool? Look, tell old girl that reinforcements are on the way. I'll be there in no more than forty-five minutes. Gotta get fresh," Gary said hanging up.

"Hey sexy, would you like me to give you an early morning blow job to get your day started?" Michelle asked, walking out the bathroom.

"Naw, I'm good," Rayshawn answered, reaching for his underwear and socks.

"Okay baby, I'll just wake up Felice with a little tongue action."

Rayshawn sat on the dresser and watched as Michelle eased into the bed and crawled underneath the covers. Before long, she'd made her way down between Felice's legs. Even though he wanted to stay and watch the show, Rayshawn knew that their sex session would take all day, so he decided to slide on his pants then his shoes. He slowly walked over to the door as he heard Felice began to moan.

Felice rose up to see Rayshawn opening the door. "Where are you going? I know you're not intimidated by Michelle." Felice pushed Michelle from between her legs and jumped up. She walked over to Rayshawn. "I only asked her to join us because I wanted to show you that there is nothing that I won't do to satisfy you."

"There's nothing wrong. I'm definitely not intimidated by her. I just have to make a run real quick. You stay here and have a little fun with her and when I get back I'll have a surprise for you that I know you're going to love. Do you mind if I take your car?"

"Of course not. Take your time."

Felice went to kiss Rayshawn. He held her tight as his hands rubbed up and down her naked back. When she tried to pull him back over toward the bed, he resisted. He looked over at Michelle using a dildo to get her juices flowing and realized that he needed to leave right away or he would never make it out.

"You just don't wear yourself out with her and save some

of your energy for me. I'll be back in a little while," Rayshawn said, opening the door.

He gave one last glance back at Felice as she got back into bed with Michelle. He then closed the bedroom door and slowly walked to the front door. He imagined all the wild things that the two of them were about to do as he walked out to Felice's Benz.

"You got to give me every little nasty detail about what you did with the two freaks you had last night," Gary said, as the two men entered the food court section of Annapolis Mall. After receiving just a few details, Gary's dick was hard by the time they made it to Chick Fil A. "Is this the same freak from the gym."

"Man, my girl ain't no freak. You better watch how you refer to her. Just because she likes to please me doesn't make her a freak," Rayshawn said defensively.

"Damn, fix your tampon, dog. I just can't remember if I've ever seen you raise your chest over a comment made toward one of your other broads."

"That's because this one is different. I think she's the one. That's why I wanted you to meet me here. I want to get her a gift that will really show everyone I'm serious about this one. I've never met anyone like her. Felice is the kind of woman who's like a friend first and a lover second. I don't think I know the words to really express how she makes me feel inside whenever I'm with her, or thinking about her," Rayshawn admitted.

"Damn, nigga. You sound like you been watching Oprah. Can you at least tell me all the freaky shit the other broad did or is she special, too?" Gary asked.

Rayshawn was becoming frustrated. "Why do you always act like you ain't had no sex in years. Damn. I'm trying to tell you how I feel about my girl."

"I'm not tryin' to hear that mushy shit. If you like her that much, buy a damn teddy bear or something. Hell, I don't know. I don't buy bitches shit." Gary stopped when he saw a thick young lady walk past him. "Umph…umph…umph she phat as shit."

Rayshawn knew that it was going to take at least an hour for his friend to end his manhunt. "Look, I'm going to Kay Jewelers. Meet me there when you finish following ass."

Gary threw up his hand to show that he was at least listening.

When Rayshawn walked into the well-known jewelry store a few minutes later, he slowly leaned over the clear glass counter as a well-dressed man in a taupe-colored suit came over. He stood there for a moment and tried to size up his approach for Rayshawn.

"That sparkle in your eye suggests that must be one special lady you're shopping for. I think I have just what you're looking for in this other showcase," the salesman finally said. "Rings, right?"

"Yes, I need to look at some of those, but before we start I can tell you now, I don't have a lot of money so don't be pulling out no big shit."

Just as Rayshawn went to the other case, and started talking with the salesman, Kiara and her girlfriend walked past the open door being loud and ghetto as usual. "Hold up. I know that ain't who I think it is," Kiara said to her friend. When she took another look inside the store, her eyes lit up. "Oh, shit…it is." Without a seconds notice, she pulled her friend inside.

Kiara crept up behind Rayshawn and tapped his shoulder. "Well…well…well, while everybody is looking for your ass, you've been up in the mall shopping. Who would've ever thought? What you doing?"

Rayshawn knew her voice instantly. He turned around. "I'm minding my own business. What you and your girl doing…shoplifting?"

"Fuck you, nigga. Everybody is looking for you. I think

your mother would pay big bucks if I called her and turned you in. You're like number one on the America's Most Wanted List," Kiara said, laughing with her friend.

"Look Kiara, I don't have the time or patience to be playing your childish little games. What do you want?"

Kiara looked over at the burgundy tray on the counter that had several engagement rings, causing her smile to quickly disappear. Her eyes began to tighten as all the conversations she and Rayshawn had in the past of him never wanting to commit to one girl flooded her head.

"I know you're not looking at damn engagement rings. Who you thinking of giving a ring to?" Kiara asked loudly. *It better not be who I think it is,* Kiara thought waiting for his reply.

"Well if your nosy-ass must know, I'm in love with Felice. I'm ready to slow my life down and become one with her. She's the missing void I've been looking for," he responded with a huge smile.

Kiara burst out laughing. She began slapping her hand against her leg almost falling over to the floor. "Oh my God, this shit is crazy." She looked back at the rings. "You gonna give her that small shit anyway? Are those rings even a half of a carat?" she asked the salesmen. "You might as well go to the bubble gum machine."

Rayshawn was pissed. "Can you leave?"

"No. Besides, you might wanna give me that ring, especially since I'm carrying your child." She rubbed her stomach in a circular motion.

Rayshawn's eyes widened. With Kiara and her crazy mother playing so many games, he didn't know if she was lying or not. "I don't believe you."

"Well, believe it. Remember…the last time you made love to me and my mother at the same time, you didn't put a condom on."

Rayshawn got hyped. "I didn't have a fucking choice!"

At that moment, Gary walked up and wondered what was going on. Rayshawn looked over at Gary and twirled his index finger in a circle next to his temple to acknowledge that Kiara was truly crazy.

"What did I miss?" Gary asked. He looked at Kiara's petite frame up and down. "Damn Kiara, you fillin' out them jeans, baby."

"Don't start, Gary," Kiara warned.

"I just told Kiara that I was going to ask Felice to marry me and she lost it," Rayshawn said. He didn't even comment on the pregnancy issue.

Gary started laughing uncontrollably himself. "I know you didn't say you're going to ask that old lady to marry you. No wonder Kiara cracked up. You need to stop playing, Rayshawn. You got my stomach hurting."

"I do believe it's illegal to do what you're planning," Kiara said between laughs.

"What's illegal? You're making absolutely no sense," Rayshawn replied.

"You'll find out soon enough, dumb-ass," Kiara replied before walking out.

Felice reached down and turned off the shower then slowly stepped onto the white towel and began drying off her body. Michelle had left hours prior to her getting up so the room was very quiet. Felice walked out and retrieved her cell phone and adaptor from her purse. She then turned it on. Moments later, it began to buzz repeatedly.

The same message was on each text: **This is Lynn. My number is 202-555-6309. I need to talk to you now. This is an EMERGENCY!! Please call ASAP.**

Felice sat on the bed and contemplated on dialing the

number. Even though she didn't want to, Felice knew that Lynn had no plans on giving up. Not to mention, it was time for her to be a women about the situation. She couldn't keep hiding like a little girl. After drumming up the confidence, she slowly pushed Lynn's number into her phone and pressed call. Even though she was fucking someone near and dear to her heart, Felice wondered what Lynn wanted to talk to her about that would was considered an emergency.

"Hello."

"May I speak to Lynn, this is Felice."

"Felice? Don't you mean Raymond?"

"Excuse me," Felice replied. Her heart began to speed up rapidly.

"This is not a time for games. Ko-Ko told me who you really are."

That no good bitch, Felice thought. She was quiet for what seemed like eternity.

"You still there bitch or would you like to be called nigga," Lynn taunted. Felice still didn't respond. "So, you gonna say something?"

Felice sighed…deeply. "Okay, you're right Lynn. I just haven't been Raymond for a really long time."

"How dare you not tell me that you changed everything about yourself? Did you ever think this could possibly affect the people who knew you?" Lynn asked. "The people who fucked you!"

"What are you talking about? I didn't owe you anything, Lynn. We had sex a few times when we were young, so what? Why would I announce my personal business to the damn world? I wasn't obligated to tell you anything. I wanted to leave all aspects of my early years of being Raymond in the past. The distant past."

"I can't believe you were all in my face at the wedding talking about you used to date Raymond Wilson, knowing you were Raymond the entire fucking time. You're a manipulator just like Ko-Ko. You manipulated Rayshawn. That decision you made has caused you to hurt the most precious thing in this world to me and you," Lynn said.

"I had no idea that Rayshawn was your son. Besides, I didn't influence him to do anything. He made his own decision. I didn't plan on falling in love with him or having him fall in love with me. Some things are just left up to fate."

"You don't understand, you shouldn't love Rayshawn in that way. It's not normal for a parent to love their child in that way," Lynn informed.

"What are you talking about?" Felice asked. She was beyond confused.

"Rayshawn is your son."

Felice paused. "What?"

"You got me pregnant, but I never told you. I blamed it on my Aunt's boyfriend, told everyone he raped me because I didn't know what else to do. You told me that you liked men, that I was just an experiment, so I was embarrassed."

Felice dropped the phone. While she stopped and had a moment, Lynn sat patiently and waited for her to return.

"You're lying. How far are you going to take this Lynn? You're making this up just to get me to break up with him, right?" Felice questioned.

"Honestly, I wish I was making this up. If Rayshawn ever finds out that he slept with his biological father, it's no telling how he'll take it. Something like this will push him over the breaking point, and I wouldn't risk that just to tell you a lie."

"I can't believe this shit. Why didn't you tell me?" Felice yelled.

"I didn't tell anyone! How the fuck was I supposed to know that you would end up having a sex change and fuck my son? Do you know how sick that shit is? I haven't worried about you for the last twenty-one years. My weirdest dream couldn't have prepared me for my first sex partner getting me pregnant, going to Colorado to have a sex change then returning to start a relationship with our off-spring," Lynn stated.

She knows damn near every detail, Felice thought. "I…I

just can't believe this," Felice repeated over and over again.

"Where's Rayshawn now?" Lynn asked.

"He took my car. He said he had some errands to run. I'm not sure where he is. How am I going to ever face him again?"

"I don't think you should say anything. It'll kill 'em. You need to find a way to end it with him and in a way that will hurt him, so that he'll go back to school," Lynn suggested.

Felice paused again, then suddenly had a change of heart. "I'm just supposed to take you for your word. I need to know for a fact that Rayshawn's really my son. And if he is, then we'll have to find a way for him to find out. I was out his life for all those years because I didn't know."

"Are you fucking listening to yourself right now? You want me to tell my son that the woman he's been fucking is really his father? Are you serious? He thinks the man who raped me is dead, and that's the way it should stay. That operation must've fucked up your common sense, too," Lynn replied.

"It sounds crazy, but I want to be in Rayshawn's life one way or another."

"I'm tired of talking over the phone. You need to stop whatever you're doing and get over here to my house so we can really come up with a logical response to how we're going to move forward. It's important that we put Rayshawn's feelings at the top of the list."

"I'm getting ready to put on my clothes now. I'll be there once I get dressed and find a way over there," Felice responded.

"Please don't do anything stupid like telling Rayshawn before we meet to discuss this. We both have to be on the same page."

The phone clicked. "That's Rayshawn calling me now."

"Raymond, please don't tell him anything," Lynn begged. She couldn't find herself to call her Felice anymore.

Chapter Twenty-Five

"Hey, what's up?" Felice asked. Any other time she would've said something freaky, but all of that had instantly been suppressed.

"Hey, you. I was calling to see if the two of you had finally gotten out that bed or if y'all might be in need of some company," Rayshawn replied.

"Are you on your way back here?"

"That depends on what you have planned for the rest of the day."

"Umm, actually I have to go take care of this situation that just popped up. But I really might need to see you when I'm finished," Felice said.

"What about your car? How are you gonna get to wherever you're going? If you wait, I can bring your car back, and have Gary take me to get my own car."

"That's not really necessary. I can just call Michelle, and borrow her car." Felice's hands wouldn't stop shaking. Her nerves were beyond wrecked.

"Well, it's up to you. Either way, I might stop by and talk with my mother. She's left me about a hundred messages, so I think I need to go sort things out, especially since we're going to be together."

"No, you can't!" Felice yelled.

"Why? Do you think it's too soon for me to go over and talk to her?"

"I think you need to come back here and relax. Let me be the one to take care of you tonight. I would love to just have a romantic night with dinner. No sex…no Michelle…just me and you. It shouldn't take me that long to resolve this problem, so you won't have to be there by yourself that long," Felice answered.

"If you wait a minute, I'll come go with you and be your support," Rayshawn suggested. The more he talked with Felice, the more he felt a stronger connection with her. He'd never felt this way about a woman in his life. "Plus, I have a surprise for you, remember?"

"I appreciate the offer, but I need to handle this on my own. You just be here when I get back."

"You sounded like my mother when you said that. Barking out orders for me to be somewhere when you get back. That turned me on," Rayshawn said in a deeper tone.

Rayshawn's reply sent a nasty taste down Felice's throat and made her stomach tighten all at once. Rayshawn had no idea how ironic that statement truly was. Felice said her goodbye's then hung up the phone. She quickly got up, went to Michelle's closet where she kept some extra clothes and put on a pair of Juicy sweatpants, a hoodie, and some boots just to be ready if Lynn had some other ideas.

When Felice pulled up to Lynn's house two hours later, she didn't know what to expect from this meeting, but walked up the steps and knocked on the door. A surprised look overcame her face when it was Ko-Ko who answered the door instead of Lynn. There was a long moment of silence between the two.

"Come on in, *Raymond*. Don't just stand out there letting all of your baby mother's heat out," Ko-Ko joked.

"You're one evil bitch," Felice said.

"Don't get made at me. I told your ass to stay away from my man, but you wouldn't listen," Ko-Ko continued to taunt.

Felice didn't respond verbally. She just rolled her eyes and stepped past Ko-Ko into the house. However, she was in for even more of a surprise, when she saw Lynn, Tootie, Melyssa and Kiara all sitting around in the living room like an intervention. All of their eyes stared at her as if she was one of those side show freaks in the circus. Ko-Ko slammed the door to break the temporary frozen state that everyone was stuck in.

"Why don't you and I go talk in the kitchen?" Lynn said getting up.

"You don't have to go anywhere. The two of you can get that shit off both your chests right here," Ko-Ko chimed in. "Maybe when this is all over with, he'll let us see his pussy. I've been dying to see it for years."

Tootie laughed. "Girl, it don't matter anyway. We'll still be able to hear them."

"How does it feel to be committing incest," Melyssa added. She was obviously still mad about the video at her reception.

"Look, I need to talk with Raymond. Now, you all can stay in here and behave or I'll put all y'all asses out and we'll finish this plan another day," Lynn replied.

Felice watched as the women all leaned back into their seats. She then began to follow Lynn toward the kitchen. She kept moving her head back and forth pretending to be checking out the house, but actually she was eyeing Lynn's friends so that none of them could sneak up on her.

"Would you like me to make you a drink before we talk?" Lynn asked as she stopped at the bar next to the kitchen door. She studied Felice's body like an exam. "So, how much did all that stuff cost?"

"Listen, I didn't come here to talk about this. Also, if you don't mind, I would like to be called by my name," Felice said, with her hands on her hips. "Now, I would love to have a shot of

Grey Goose or Belvedere, if you have any."

"I'm not a top-shelf vodka type of person. How about some Ketel One? If not, I have a bunch of different wines."

"If that's all you have, beggars can't be choosers," Felice said giggling.

Lynn glanced over at her friends in the living room. All of them could read her mind. *Who the hell does this high-priced man-bitch think she is acting like my shit ain't good enough?* Lynn poured two glasses of Chardonnay then walked into the kitchen. They both sat down at the wooden stools around the island. Felice took a sip from her glass then quickly sat it back down. Lynn tipped her glass up until every drop was gone.

"I don't think I'm going to be able to let Rayshawn go one way or the other. I've realized that for the first time in my life I've found someone who makes me extremely happy. If he's really my son, there has to be a way that I can remain a part of his life," Felice said breaking the silence.

"You've lost your fucking mind, if you think I'm going to let that happen. How do you think Rayshawn is going to handle knowing who and what you are? Not only would that break his heart, but have you stopped to think about his future in all of this? He has the potential to be something great. Don't take that away because of your own selfish reasons. How could you live with yourself for doing that?" Lynn questioned.

"I'm not saying it would be difficult, but there has to be a way," Felice answered.

"You'll destroy our son. All you have to do is look into his eyes and you'll understand that the best thing for you to do is break this crazy thing off with him," Lynn said, reaching over and grabbing Felice's hand. It was the first time, she'd noticed how big it was.

They both sat staring at one another until a loud commotion disturbed them. Lynn wondered what was going on out in the living room. She quickly got out of her seat and went to see what was going on.

Lynn entered the living room to find Rayshawn standing

by the television. Her heart rate increased not knowing how Felice was going to handle the situation, and wasn't quite ready to find out.

"What are you doing here?" Lynn shouted.

"I came here to talk to you about a decision I've made," Rayshawn answered. "I just didn't know we would have an audience."

Kiara burst out with a great laughter. "This is going to be good."

"You need to stay out of this. You really need to get over it and realize what we did was a mistake," Rayshawn said to Kiara.

"You have it all wrong. What you're about to do right now is the mistake, and I can't wait until you do it," Kiara replied with a huge grin.

At that moment, Felice walked out of the kitchen. When she saw Rayshawn yelling back and forth with Kiara, she slowly walked over to join the group in the living room. Rayshawn had his back to her.

"Rayshawn, I thought I asked you to wait for me back at the house," Felice said.

Rayshawn turned to lock eyes with Felice. "What are you doing here? I thought you had a situation that you needed to handle."

"I'm taking care of it right now. You need to leave and let me finish what I came here to do," Felice responded. The palm of her hands began to sweat profusely.

"No, I'm glad that you're here. There's something that I want to ask you and this is the perfect place to do that," Rayshawn stated. He reached into his jacket pocket and pulled out a small black box. All the other women eye's got larger by the second as they watched Rayshawn carry it over to Felice and slowly drop to one knee.

"I know he's not about to do what I think he's doing," Ko-Ko said out loud.

"Felice, I've never met anyone like you in my life. I love

spending time with you, and even though it's only been a few weeks, I know that I'm in love with you. Would you…"

"Hell no! Get your ass up. It ain't no fucking way that I'm going to let this happen," Lynn shouted.

"Ma, enough!" Rayshawn belted. "This is my damn life and I'm going to decide how it goes and who I'm going to be wth. Don't you get it? Felice makes me happy in so many ways. Isn't that what you want for me? A woman who makes me feel amazing. That's what she does for me." He had no problem expressing his feelings about Felice in front of anyone.

Kiara couldn't stop laughing. Her chuckles and gasps for air made Tootie and Melyssa grab and cover her mouth. The tension in the room was getting to the boiling point and they knew her laughing was sure to take it over the edge.

"Felice, you need to end this shit right now!" Lynn screamed.

"Felice, will you marry me?" Rayshawn asked. He opened up the box and pulled out a small diamond ring. The total weight was only .25.

Felice looked down into his dark eyes. She felt goose bumps running like sprinters up and down her arms and legs. It felt like her chest was squeezing down on her lungs and she couldn't catch her breath. Felice slowly lifted her head and turned to stare at each pair of eyes in the room. When she stopped at Lynn's, she noticed that they were filling up with tears.

"I'm sorry Rayshawn, but I can't," Felice said, after the long pause.

"What do you mean? I love you so much. We can make this work. Don't let my mother scare you and destroy what we can have." Rayshawn got up off the floor.

"My decision has nothing to do with Lynn. I was just out to have some fun with you. The main reasons I'm saying no is because you're just too young. Besides, you work for me, and I just don't love you in that way," Felice responded.

Ko-Ko had a huge smile on her face, while Lynn let out a

sigh of relief. She also did all she could to fight back her tears. Lynn looked over at Felice and mouthed the words, Thank You.

"Don't do this to us, Felice. My love will make us work. You just have to trust in that. I know you love me. You're just afraid to express your feelings in front of all these people," Rayshawn begged.

Felice shook her head. "You need to grow up. I was out looking for a lot of fun with a young man who could satisfy me. Now, you're making this real easy for me. You seem real weak right now. Your behavior is showing me that we aren't going to be able to work together after all of this."

"I can't believe this." Rayshawn looked over at Ko-Ko, Kiara and Lynn. "Are y'all happy now? This is what y'all wanted from the very beginning. I'm never going to forgive none of you," Rayshawn added on with tears rolling down his face.

"You're acting like a real bitch right now. I guess the apple doesn't fall far from the tree after all!" Kiara yelled out.

"What the fuck did you say?" Rayshawn yelled, turning his focus toward Kiara.

"No, Kiara, don't you dare!" Ko-Ko belted.

"Fuck that, I can't believe I was interested in such a weak-ass nigga. Fucking faggot," Kiara said.

Everyone looked over at Kiara. The rage on her face was evident. She was about to take this gathering to a whole new level. Kiara stood with a cold blank stare on her face.

"Who the hell are you talking to, bitch?" Rayshawn barked.

"After all the fucking you been doing, I can either be talking to you or your father," Kiara shot back.

Lynn tried to get over to Kiara, but was too late.

"You're so stupid. Felice was born a damn man. If you weren't so pussy whipped, you probably would've noticed that shit by now. Not only is she a man, she's your fucking father!" Kiara yelled out.

Rayshawn looked over at Kiara then toward Felice.

"What the fuck is she talking about?"

Felice glanced at Lynn. Rayshawn then looked over at his mother. Her facial expression had his mind really wondering now. Tootie and Melyssa both seemed to be shocked about how the sequence of events were going. Rayshawn walked over to his mother who was crying hysterically by that point.

"Is that true? Is Felice my father? A father who was supposed to be dead?" Rayshawn asked. He stared at Felice trying to find some male features. *Is that why her pussy was always so tight and I couldn't go but so deep?*

"I…I didn't know. I just found out about this just the other day. I told you he was dead because to us he was. I never meant to lie to you, baby" Lynn said, through all her tears.

"I can't believe this. I've been sleeping with my fucking father!" He wanted to throw up. Rayshawn looked at Felice with confusion and anger. "Is it true?"

At that moment, Felice started crying and lowered her head. It wasn't quite the confirmation Rayshawn wanted, but it was enough.

"I don't see you laughing now. You tried to be cute and disrespect me and my mother, but look who got the last laugh," Kiara continued.

Rayshawn had heard enough. He was beyond his tolerance level. He lunged at Kiara, knocking Felice backward. Rayshawn wrapped his hands around Kiara's neck and began to squeeze with all his might. While he was choking Kiara, he had no idea that Felice had lost her balance and fell onto the glass coffee table.

Ko-Ko and Lynn rushed over to try and pry Rayshawn off Kiara, but it wasn't working. He began shaking her body, yelling all sorts of profanity. Kiara's eyes started to bulge out of their sockets as Rayshawn continued to cut off her air supply. Seconds later, Tootie's horrific screams made everyone turn and look down. Rayshawn couldn't believe what he had done.

Felice was lying on the floor with a large piece of glass sticking through her chest. The blood pouring from her body and onto the glossy wood floors wouldn't seem to stop. In that instance, Rayshawn didn't see a man or his father, he only saw Felice's pretty face gasping for air and coughing up blood. Rayshawn quickly released Kiara's neck and dropped to his knees. Kiara began coughing vigorously trying to refill her lungs with air as Rayshawn started to remove all the broken pieces of glass around Felice's body.

"Do something to try and stop the bleeding, Rayshawn!" Melyssa yelled.

Lynn ran over to the phone and quickly dialed 911. Rayshawn began trying to apply pressure around the sharp glass, but the blood continued to flow. When Felice began to fade in and out of consciousness, he made the crucial mistake of removing the glass from her body.

"Please Felice, just hold on. Help is on the way," Rayshawn whispered trying to comfort her.

"Somebody call an ambulance!" Rayshawn bawled.

"Your mother is on the phone with them now," Tootie answered.

"Are you in lover mode or family member mode?" Kiara said, once she was able to speak. "I need to take a picture of how soft your ass looked down there crying over your gay-ass father," Kiara added on, holding her throat.

Dropping the phone Lynn ran over, balled up her hand into a tight fist and swung with all her might. Her fist landed on the side of Kiara's face. Everyone was in shock, but knew Kiara deserved it. Moments later, several loud bangs against the front door caught everyone's attention. Tootie rushed to open the door and found the paramedics waiting outside. She stepped to the side and allowed them to come in. They scurried across the room and took positions next to Felice.

When they saw the sharp piece of glass on the floor next to her body, it was an immediate concern. "Who removed the object?" one of the paramedics asked.

"I did. Did I do something wrong?" Rayshawn replied.

"You should never remove the object. Pulling it out

could do more damage to the surrounding flesh, which can lead to more bleeding and risk of infection," the frail white man answered.

"What about that woman? Is she okay?" the other paramedic asked in reference to Kiara. She was still lying on the couch holding her face.

"She passed out when she saw the blood," Melyssa quickly answered. "She'll be okay."

Once the paramedics stabilized Felice, they put her on the infamous stretcher and whisked her out the door. All of Lynn's neighbors stood on their porches as they brought Felice out and quickly put her in the ambulance. Tears made their way down Rayshawn's face as he climbed into the back with her.

"Baby, I'll follow you in my car!" Lynn shouted.

"Girl, you shouldn't be driving. Give me your keys and we'll take you to the hospital," Melyssa suggested.

"I hate all of y'all bitches. Especially you, Ma. I can't believe you stood by and let Lynn hit me like that!" Kiara screamed as she walked out of the house. "How could you let her hit a pregnant woman?"

Everyone looked at Kiara in shock…even Ko-Ko. She wasn't sure if her daughter was lying.

"You needed that reality check. I can't believe you told Rayshawn when I told your ass not to say anything. Do you ever follow fucking directions?" Ko-Ko questioned.

"Fuck you. Don't act like you're innocent in all this." Kiara looked over at Melyssa. "She's the one who gave me that DVD to show at your wedding!"

When Melyssa's eyes widened, Ko-Ko began to shake her head. "Don't believe that. Can't you see, Kiara likes to start trouble? She's been in love with Rayshawn all along, and will do anything to keep him from being happy. She had the DVD. She even fucked the DJ to get him to put it in the projector. Didn't y'all notice that he was gone when you all were trying to cut the machine off?" Ko-Ko hated the fact that she had to sell her daughter out, but she wasn't about to go down…for anyone.

"I'm going to kill you!" Melyssa shouted, running over toward Kiara.

However, before another episode of drama could go down, Tootie was able to grab Melyssa around her arm. "Don't worry. Kiara is going to get hers soon enough. Right now, Lynn needs us. We can't let her drive in her condition," Tootie convinced.

"You better pray I never get my hands on you. This shit is far from over," Melyssa said as Tootie pulled over to Lynn's car.

"I can't believe you. You're as much to blame for this shit as me," Kiara yelled at her mother. She began throwing sticks and small rocks at the back of Lynn's car as Lynn, Tootie, Melyssa and Ko-Ko piled in and pulled off. When a police car suddenly pulled up and observed Kiara throwing objects at the car, they instructed her to stop and calm down as they jumped from their patrol car.

Kiara began hollering. "You shouldn't be harassing me. I just saw a woman get stabbed by a piece of glass and the criminal rode with her to the hospital. He even put his hands on me. You should be arresting Rayshawn McMillan for assault!"

"You need to slow down. Now, run that by me one more time," one officer requested.

"You heard me. I want to press assault charges against Rayshawn McMillan for choking me and stabbing his father!"

Chapter Twenty-Six

Felice's blood pressure began to drop rapidly as her heart rate began to increase, which sent the paramedic into a frenzy. "Her body is going into shock!" he yelled. Trying to maintain her body temperature, he grabbed at least three blankets and threw them over her body. He then tried to stabilize her vital signs, before telling the driver to radio ahead to the hospital. Felice was going to need major surgery to correct any damage the glass had caused.

"Don't worry sir, your mother is going to make it. You just keep thinking positive. You can't give up. She needs for you to be strong for her sake," the paramedic said, tapping Rayshawn on his shoulder.

Rayshawn looked at the white man then lowered his head. "She's not my mother."

The ambulance raced down Central Avenue and onto 295 until it arrived at Prince George's Hospital Center about ten minutes later. Rayshawn jumped out and followed along side the gurney and straight into the emergency room. However, a nurse stopped him from entering the double doors which lead to the area where trauma patients were treated.

"Sir, you'll have to wait out here. We'll do everything possible to help her," the nurse informed.

Suddenly, a young-looking Indian doctor ran up behind him. "Yes sir, I'm doctor Guppta, and I've just been paged. We'll do everything possible."

As Rayshawn looked through the two rectangular windows in the door, his heart pounded against his chest. He could see them wheeling Felice through another set of doors and before he could blink, everyone had disappeared. When Lynn finally came running into the emergency room lobby, she found Rayshawn banging his head against the two doors.

"It's going to be okay," Lynn said, putting her hand on his back.

Rayshawn quickly removed her hand. "Don't touch me. This is as much your fault as it was Felice's. At least she didn't lie to me on purpose."

"Don't be like that, son. I love you more than anything," Lynn pleaded.

As Rayshawn stomped off down the hallway, Lynn began to walk after him until Tootie and Melyssa stepped in front of her.

"You're not going to get through to him, right now. What you should do is let him calm down and try a little later," Melyssa suggested.

Lynn threw up her hands in the air. "You just don't understand. He's probably gonna hate me now."

"No, he's not. He just needs time to calm down," Melyssa responded.

"I have to make his pain go away. That is what a real mother does. I'll give him some breathing room, but he can't leave my sight," Lynn replied.

"That's him right there!" Kiara shouted a few seconds later.

Everyone in the emergency room looked in her direction as two officers approached Rayshawn. "Rayshawn McMillan!" an officer shouted.

"Yeah. What is it?" Rayshawn turned to see two white officers walking toward him.

"We need to ask you some questions," one officer said.

Kiara laughed as the two officers walked even closer to Rayshawn. Lynn heard Kiara's annoying voice and looked down the hall to see the two officers standing near Rayshawn. At that moment, Lynn power walked past Tootie and Melyssa.

Ko-Ko returned from smoking a cigarette to find Kiara laughing like a deranged lunatic. "What are you doing here?" Ko-Ko asked.

"I brought the police to arrest Rayshawn for trying to kill Felice. I told y'all not to mess with me. I won't be ignored any longer," Kiara warned.

Ko-Ko stared at her daughter. "Oh Lord! What have you done? You know it was an accident."

"Excuse me, that's my son you're talking to. How can I help you?" Lynn said walking up.

"We've had a complaint about a crime being committed by your son. We just want to ask him a few questions," the white officer stated.

"I don't think so. You're not talking to my son without a lawyer. You have the wrong one here. What crime are you fishing for anyway?"

"That young lady said that your son assaulted her and a woman by the name of Felice Contour. We just want to find out what happened. You might want to call that lawyer and have him or her meet us at our precinct," the white officer replied.

"I've watched enough Law and Order to know that unless you're arresting my son, he doesn't have to go anywhere with you. My son rode here with Felice in the ambulance and is worried sick about her health. Felice had an accident at my house and fell into my glass coffee table. Nothing more," Lynn stated.

Rayshawn turned to see the doctor and nurse who wheeled Felice into the emergency room. He took off down the hall toward them. "How is she? Tell me she's going to be alright," Rayshawn grabbed the doctor's shoulder and swung him around.

Sadly, the doctor eyes fell to the floor, which caused Rayshawn's heart to drop like a ton of bricks. Cold breezes seem to blow over his body. Rayshawn quickly scanned the face of the nurse. She didn't make eye contact with him either.

"No, it can't be," Rayshawn said.

"I'm so sorry, sir," Dr. Guppta said. "We were prepping her for surgery, but I'm afraid there was just too much blood loss. If the object she was injured with hadn't been removed, there would've been a greater chance of survival. It would've made the blood clot." He placed his hand on Rayshawn's shoulder. "I'm so sorry for your loss."

"So, what you're saying all this is my fault. I'm the one who removed the glass. I can't do anything right. I'm a total fuck up," Rayshawn said.

"No, you're not. I raised you to be so much more. But this should be your wake up call son. It's time for you to stop wasting your life and go finish school," Lynn interrupted.

Lynn walked over and hugged Rayshawn. She held him tight against her body and searched for the right words that would comfort his pain. No matter how hard she thought, nothing seemed appropriate for this moment. Lynn just remained silent and rubbed his back.

Rayshawn was devastated. "Can I at least see her?"

"Of course," Dr. Guppta agreed. "I've instructed them to remove her body from the operating room and into another room. The nurse will show you."

Rayshawn didn't say another word to anyone as he followed the nurse to the destined room and stood next to what appeared to be another gurney. He stared at the blood stained sheet covering the body as tears strolled down his face. He wanted to lift the sheet, but couldn't find the strength to do it. He didn't really know how to feel at the moment. The only women he'd ever had any emotional connection with other than his mother was now dead. A woman who was really his father; a father he thought was dead. The visions of the two of them holding hands, passionately kissing each other and making love for hours were now nightmares.

Suddenly, Rayshawn walked away. He needed be alone and get some fresh air. Rayshawn wiped the tears from his eyes then walked back toward the emergency room lobby. However, when he walked out the double doors and into the waiting room, the police grabbed him and slammed him up against the wall.

"Rayshawn McMillan, you're under arrest for the murder of Felice Contour," the white officer said, clamping the handcuffs on his wrist.

"What the hell are you doing? Get those fucking things off him! His father just died and you're going to arrest him for that. It was an accident. Rayshawn would've never done that!" Lynn wailed.

"You need to calm down, Miss. We're charging him with the murder of a woman by the name of Felice Contour," the officer stated. "You just said something about his father."

"I know, that's what I'm trying to explain to you. Felice Contour is really Rayshawn's father. He would never purposely hurt his father. He just found out that was his father only hours ago," Lynn added.

The confused look on the officer's faces showed they were extremely lost. "We're taking him in. This sounds like something the court is going to have to work out," one officer chimed in.

"Please, don't take my son. He's been through enough," Lynn pleaded.

Melyssa and Tootie both rushed over. All the hate Melyssa had for what Kiara had done to everyone, pushed her over the boiling point. "I saw the whole thing. It was her who really pushed Felice and made her fall over the table." Melyssa pointed toward Kiara. She only wished Ko-Ko could go down in flames with her daughter.

All of the spectators turned and followed her pointing finger. Kiara's eyes and mouth popped open. Kiara turned her head left to right to see who Melyssa was pointing at.

"That's right officer, I saw the whole thing, too. It was that girl right there who caused all this mess. I didn't want to get involved and say anything at first, but I can't stand here and let her try and get away with what's she's done," Tootie added.

"They're lying. I didn't do anything. It was Rayshawn!" Kiara roared.

Kiara couldn't believe what Melyssa had started. The look on the officer's face told her they were getting real suspicious of her story. The trouble she'd tried to place on Rayshawn was now staring her in the face.

Kiara looked toward Ko-Ko. "Are you just going to stand there and let them tell these lies on me? Tell these police officers who really pushed Felice. It wasn't an accident. Rayshawn pushed her!"

Ko-Ko stood there listening to Kiara's pleas for help, but when she turned to see Rayshawn with his head slumped over in his hands her focused changed quickly. *This might be my only way back into his heart*, Ko-Ko thought.

"I can't lie to the police baby girl." Ko-Ko turned to one of the officers. "It's true. I saw my daughter push Felice into the coffee table. Rayshawn wasn't anywhere near her."

Kiara felt as if she'd been punctured in her own chest. "You lying bitch. You know I didn't do it. How could you do this to me? You sold me out for a man who can't and will never love you. I should've left your ass in jail!"

One police officer walked over to Kiara while his partner took the handcuffs off Rayshawn. "We're going to need for you to come with us young lady. Your mother wouldn't lie on you. Why don't we go down to the station and talk about this."

"They're all lying including my good for nothing mother. It wasn't me!" Kiara continued to shout as the officers escorted her out the door.

Lynn looked over at Ko-Ko. She was stunned that Ko-Ko had gone against her own daughter just to save Rayshawn. *I guess she really does love my son*, Lynn thought.

Rayshawn sat down on one of the chairs in the waiting room and buried his head in his hands. Lynn quickly followed, then stood next to him then rubbed his head. She knew that this was a very critical moment. And it was because of that reason why she took several deep breaths trying to figure out the right words to begin the healing process.

"All I can say to you is that all this was a big mistake and you'll make it through this. I love you. I've always loved you. I'm here for you and always will be," Lynn whispered.

"If I would've stayed in school, none of this would have ever happened," Rayshawn replied.

"You may be right, but if this incident has taught me anything, it's taught me that anything is possible. This is one of those stories that make a good late night movie on Lifetime. Maybe we can sell our rights to a story and get some money," Lynn tried to lighten the mood.

"I can't stay here. I have to get away. Everything about this area is going to remind me of Felice. I mean…" Rayshawn stopped. He finally wanted to know his father's name. "What was his name?"

"Raymond," Lynn replied.

Rayshawn paused. "This was my awakening moment, so I'm going back to school. I'm gonna go to medical school like you always wanted."

"What does that mean for me and you?" Ko-Ko asked walking up.

Lynn glanced over at her. *Just when I think Ko-Ko is a human being, she shows her true side. I truly believe that this bitch is crazy like her fucking child. How could she dare walk her ass over here when I finally get him thinking sensibly and stir up some more shit?* Lynn thought.

Rayshawn looked up. He stood to his feet, hugged his mother then grabbed Ko-Ko's hand. "I'm so confused about everything. I know you love me, but this is a lot to swallow right now. Thank you for what you just did for me." Rayshawn released her hand. "I've experienced love in so many ways that have made me grow as a man. I know that this is a feeling I want to have again. But right now, I just have to be alone. Can you understand that?"

"I love you, Rayshawn. And yes I do understand. I'll be right here waiting on you if you decide to come back to me,"

Ko-Ko said with tears in her eyes.

"I'll meet you back at home Ma, then we can discuss going back to New Orleans," Rayshawn said to Lynn.

As Rayshawn walked down the hallway, Ko-Ko yelled out, "I love you!" He slowly turned around and smiled. Lynn stared over at Ko-Ko and realized that this was not a ploy. Ko-Ko really was in love with her son.

SOME WOMEN WILL STEAL MORE THAN JUST YOUR HEART...

COMING SOON

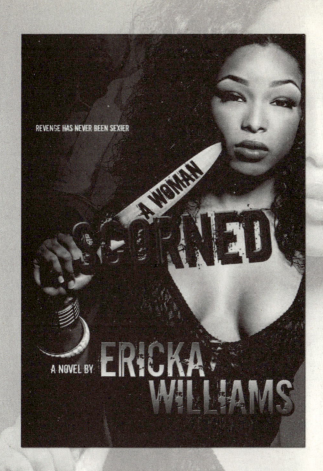

IN STORES NOW   COMING SOON

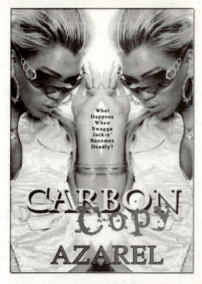
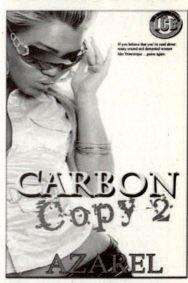

Meet Dominique Lewis, a foul, hard-boiled, go-getter who spends most of her days yearning to be just like her sister, and plotting on taking her man. For her, it's all about money, sex, and power. Although she possesses the perfect physique and sexy features, her life-long dream is to become wealthy and a house-hold name. By any means necessary, she vows to get what she wants.

As Dominique's mission unfolds, she manages to get connected to Yuri, a violent replacement for the man she really sought. After realizing she's partnered with a beast, her world turns upside down. And soon, after the tragic murder of her sister, all hell breaks loose when Dominique's cover is blown.

Armed with revenge on the brain, and a status goal in mind, Dominique soon appoints herself as Rapheal's woman, the most sought after millionaire in Atlanta. Raphael's lavish status in town would put her on a new level, right where she always dreamed...the only problem ...he never said he wanted her. In an effort to hold on to Rapheal, and all the elaborate material possessions, Dominique sets out on a deadly mission to remove anything that stands in her way.

ORDER FORM

MAIL TO:
PO Box 423
Brandywine, MD 20613
301-362-6508

FAX TO:
301-856-4116

Ship to: _____

Address: _____

Date: _____ Phone: _____

Email: _____

City & State: _____ Zip: _____

Make all money orders and cashiers checks payable to: **Life Changing Books**

Qty.	ISBN	Title	Release Date	Price
	0-9741394-5-9	Nothin Personal by Tyrone Wallace	Jul-06	$ 15.00
	0-9741394-2-4	Bruised by Azarel	Jul-05	$ 15.00
	0-9741394-7-5	Bruised 2: The Ultimate Revenge by Azarel	Oct-06	$ 15.00
	0-9741394-3-2	Secrets of a Housewife by J. Tremble	Feb-06	$ 15.00
	0-9724003-5-4	I Shoulda Seen It Comin by Danette Majette	Jan-06	$ 15.00
	0-9741394-4-0	The Take Over by Tonya Ridley	Apr-06	$ 15.00
	0-9741394-6-7	The Millionaire Mistress by Tiphani	Nov-06	$ 15.00
	1-934230-99-5	More Secrets More Lies by J. Tremble	Feb-07	$ 15.00
	1-934230-98-7	Young Assassin by Mike G.	Mar-07	$ 15.00
	1-934230-95-2	A Private Affair by Mike Warren	May-07	$ 15.00
	1-934230-94-4	All That Glitters by Ericka M. Williams	Jul-07	$ 15.00
	1-934230-93-6	Deep by Danette Majette	Jul-07	$ 15.00
	1-934230-96-0	Flexin & Sexin by K'wan, Anna J. & Others	Jun-07	$ 15.00
	1-934230-92-8	Talk of the Town by Tonya Ridley	Jul-07	$ 15.00
	1-934230-89-8	Still a Mistress by Tiphani	Nov-07	$ 15.00
	1-934230-91-X	Daddy's House by Azarel	Nov-07	$ 15.00
	1-934230-87-1-	Reign of a Hustler by Nissa A. Showell	Jan-08	$ 15.00
	1-934230-86-3	Something He Can Feel by Marissa Montelih	Feb-08	$ 15.00
	1-934230-88-X	Naughty Little Angel by J. Tremble	Feb-08	$ 15.00
	1-934230847	In Those Jeans by Chantel Jolie	Jun-08	$ 15.00
	1-934230855	Marked by Capone	Jul-08	$ 15.00
	1-934230820	Rich Girls by Kendall Banks	Oct-08	$ 15.00
	1-934230839	Expensive Taste by Tiphani	Nov-08	$ 15.00
	1-934230782	Brooklyn Brothel by C. Stecko	Jan-09	$ 15.00
	1-934230669	Good Girl Gone bad by Danette Majette	Mar-09	$ 15.00
	1-934230804	From Hood to Hollywood by Sasha Raye	Mar-09	$ 15.00
	1-934230707	Sweet Swagger by Mike Warren	Jun-09	$ 15.00
	1-934230677	Carbon Copy by Azarel	Jul-09	$ 15.00
	1-934230723	Millionaire Mistress 3 by Tiphani	Nov-09	$ 15.00
	1-934230715	A Woman Scorned by Ericka Williams	Nov-09	$ 15.00
			Total for Books	$
			Shipping Charges (add $4.25 for 1-4 books*)	$
			Total Enclosed (add lines)	$

* Prison Orders- Please allow up to three (3) weeks for delivery.

For credit card orders and orders over 30 books, please contact us at orders@lifechaningbooks.net

*Shipping and Handling of 5-10 books is $6.25, please contact us if your order is more than 10 books.